## "There is no way..."

Suddenly, Jun felt the hopelessness of the debt she owed Kai. Her son's life might have cost him his surfing career.

"I'm sorry, Kai." It wouldn't make things right, but it was the only thing she could think of to say. "It's...my fault. Ours. It's..."

"No, it's not. Don't ever say that." Anger still simmered in his voice.

Kai took three steps toward her, and suddenly his mouth was on hers. He wrapped her up in his arms and pressed her into his body. She opened her mouth to receive him and felt the rage and the passion all at once in his lips.

He tasted like the ocean, salty and wild.

She was kissing him back, powerless to do anything more.

Dear Reader,

I became obsessed with big wave surfing after reading Susan Casey's *The Wave: In Pursuit of the Rogues, Freaks and Giants of the Ocean*, which details how a group of fearless surfers decided to do the impossible: surf waves taller than ten- or even twenty-story buildings. One of the most dangerous breaks in the world exists in Hawaii. Called *Jaws*, the surfers regularly drown here as they search for the next, most extreme wave.

*The Big Break* focuses on Kai Brady, one of these extreme surfers, who's trying to overcome a serious leg injury in order to make it back into his favorite sport. He's haunted by the tsunami that injured him and struggles to get back into shape. It's only when a strong-willed trainer named Jun and her adorable little boy, Po, come into his life that he starts to see that maybe surfing *isn't* all there is to life. Maybe having a family, or *ohana*, as they say in Hawaiian, means even more than riding the perfect wave.

I love this story because Jun helps Kai see that healing can't be forced, and the growing bond between them proves that the only thing more powerful than the ocean is the power of love.

I hope you enjoy this little trip to the Big Island of Hawaii, my absolute favorite place on earth.

*Mahalo!*

*Cara*

USA TODAY Bestselling Author

# CARA LOCKWOOD

---

## The Big Break

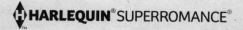
HARLEQUIN®SUPERROMANCE®

Recycling programs
for this product may
not exist in your area.

ISBN-13: 978-0-373-60951-2

The Big Break

Copyright © 2016 by by Cara Lockwood

**Printed in U.S.A.**

www.Harlequin.com

**Cara Lockwood** is a *USA TODAY* bestselling author of eleven novels, including *I Do (But I Don't)*, which was made into a Lifetime Original Movie, and *Dixieland Sushi*, which was loosely based on her experience growing up half-Japanese in a multiracial family in Texas. She's also the author of the Bard Academy series for young adults. Her work has been translated into several languages. She's currently divorced and lives with her two daughters near Chicago, where she is hard at work on her next novel.

### Books by Cara Lockwood

**HARLEQUIN SUPERROMANCE**

*Her Hawaiian Homecoming*

**COSMOPOLITAN RED-HOT READS FROM HARLEQUIN**

*Boys and Toys*
*Texting Under the Influence*

# CHAPTER ONE

Jun Lee tried to steady her nerves as she walked up to the front door of Kai Brady's luxury beachside villa on the west coast of the Big Island. Bright Hawaiian sunshine warmed her bare shoulders as she breathed in the scent of hibiscus, which grew in bunches along his pristinely manicured yard. Every local on the island knew Kai Brady—millionaire, entrepreneur, world extreme-surfing champ. Even his massive koa door was intimidating, not to mention the mansion itself: an impressive two-story glass-and-concrete structure that loomed above her, looking expensive and enormous.

Jun tried not to feel a pang of envy. She couldn't afford to rent a single room in a house like this, much less own one. Not so for Kai Brady, gorgeous and wealthy, who ranked three years running as Hawaii's most eligible bachelor in the local magazine, beating out even legendary rock stars who had taken up residence on Kauai. It was no wonder she was nervous. But she wasn't a groupie, she reminded herself. She was here on a mission.

She rang the bell and waited. Her sweaty hands squeezed the handle of the bag holding the thank-you gifts she'd brought: two of her homemade aromatherapy candles, which she hand-dipped, and some crayon drawings her four-year-old son, Po, had made for him. Then there was the gift certificate for a free session of Tai Chi, not that she thought he'd use it, but she didn't have much money, and lessons she taught fell into the category of the meager things she could offer.

She considered, for a minute, leaving the package on his doorstep, but she thought the candles would melt in the afternoon sun. Besides, she had it in her mind that she wanted to thank him personally. He deserved at least that. That was why she hadn't just sent the gifts in the mail.

She glanced at her reflection in the glass door. Jun kept her pale skin flawless by applying excessive sunscreen and avoiding the sun like the plague. Her mother, born in Beijing, had been insistent on that long before anyone really knew about the benefits of SPF. She'd come before her shift as a personal trainer at the big local gym, so she wore her fitness-instructor outfit of yoga capris, flip-flops and an athletic tank top, her dark hair up in a high ponytail. In the shadow of Kai's villa, she felt suddenly underdressed. Then again, what *was* the proper attire to wear when thanking the man who had saved your son's life?

This week marked the year anniversary of the tsunami that had nearly drowned Po. If it hadn't been for Kai Brady, her precious boy would've died.

She'd never forget that morning. Jun had dropped Po off at day care as usual, but then, when she was already at work, on the tenth-floor gym of a high-rise, the earthquake hit, the tsunami came ashore, wrecking much of the western shoreline, and she got the worst news a parent could receive: her boy had never made it to the evacuation center. He was missing.

Then, after a horrible day of waiting, she got a message on her Facebook account: friends of Kai Brady were trying to reach her. Kai had broken his leg saving her son, and they were both in the hospital. Po, thankfully, had only scratches. Thanks to Kai.

Jun's heart constricted anytime she thought of that miserable day: the horror and bone-chilling fear when the day-care center told her Po was missing. Jun lived for her boy. He was her whole world. She'd had him at age nineteen, barely older than a child herself. It didn't matter to her that he had been an accident, the result of a brief relationship with a football player on the island for the Pro Bowl, a father who wanted nothing to do with Po.

Jun never fought Dante Henley, Po's father, for support. She wasn't going to beg anyone for anything. She didn't like the idea of being indebted—to anyone, for any reason.

Which was why, as grateful as she was to Kai, she hated the feeling that she owed him. One way or another, she was going to find a way to pay that debt. Right now the only thing she could think to do was honor him on every anniversary of that tsunami.

She told herself her preoccupation with the famous surfer had nothing at all to do with the fact that he had the kind of sculpted body and bright white smile expected of a Calvin Klein underwear model. Or that he had enough cash from endorsements to live in a place like *this*.

She rang the bell once more and peeked in through the wall of glass windows along the front of the house. All she could see was tasteful granite, smooth-finished wood and gleaming floors. Was that a lanai out back? The wall-less living room was bigger than her whole condo! It overlooked a glistening mirrored pool that looked as though it cascaded *into the ocean*.

Jun blinked rapidly and tried not to press her nose against the glass. This might be the most beautiful house she'd ever seen.

She saw movement inside and held her breath. Was he going to answer the door? Or was he too rich for that? Did he have a butler? Her stomach lurched. She fought the urge to smooth down her ponytail, to double-check her tinted lip balm in the glass. She didn't know why she cared. As a single mom, she didn't have time to date. She barely had time to sleep.

She heard the door lock click and the knob turn and Kai stood there, shirtless, clad only in swim trunks.

For a second, all rational thought fled her head. The words she'd been about to utter simply dried up on her tongue. All she could think was…tall… broad…*chest*. Miles of smooth tanned skin, a wall of rippled, strongly defined muscles and not a single ounce of fat anywhere. She tried to swallow, but she couldn't. Her mouth was parched. He was so…tall. So…big.

*Big muscles. Big, big muscles.*

She felt as if she'd devolved instantly into a cavewoman. *Big muscles. Me like.*

The last time she'd seen Kai, he'd been recovering in a hospital bed, fully clothed, his hurt leg in traction. He'd been tanned and attractive, sure, but he'd been *clothed*. That fierce six-pack had been safely tucked away under a white hospital gown.

She realized she was staring at his perfectly formed abs, her fingers itching to touch them. How did he get such…definition? She worked at a *gym* and she was stumped just looking at them.

Also, she noted, he was a lot taller than she remembered. A *lot* taller. Her eyes were level with his chest. And, wow, what a chest.

His full lips curled up in an amused smile. "May I...help you?"

*Oh, yes. Yes, you can.* She immediately felt her face grow bright tomato red. She normally wasn't this forward, even in her own head. She didn't go around panting after men like a teenager. What was wrong with her? As if she'd never seen a man without a shirt on before. *Get a grip, Jun.* All those meatheads at the gym should've long since inoculated her against the power of the male form. And yet...clearly they hadn't.

"I...uh..." Why couldn't her mind form words any longer? She felt as though she'd been hit on the head. Could a person get a concussion from close proximity to Hawaii's hottest and richest bachelor? He probably got this all the time: women who lost the ability to speak in his presence.

"Yes?" Kai asked politely. With great effort, Jun pulled her attention away from his physique and tried to focus on his face.

She found that was a mistake. His chest might be distracting, but his face was worse. He was all chiseled perfection up there: dark, intelligent eyes, expressive yet playful eyebrows, sensual mouth and the kind of just-there stubble on his square jaw. He slumped his broad, muscled shoulders against the doorframe and crossed his arms, patiently waiting her out. She had to *say* something. Why wasn't her mouth working?

"Hi…" *Say your name. Your name.* "Jun."

"June? Like the month?"

This was going even worse than she'd feared.

"No. *I'm* Jun." Heat flared up the back of her neck. "Uh… Jun Lee. I…"

Kai's face showed zero recognition. She felt a little pinch in her chest. It had been a year since she'd seen him and she didn't have Po with her, and yet, somehow, she'd been hoping he'd remember her.

"Maybe you'd like to come in? Get out of the sun?" he offered, looking concerned.

Yes, because clearly she was acting like a sunstroke victim.

She just bobbed her head and stepped inside the cool interior, into the masterful space of a living room leading out to a huge terrace, the massive lanai she'd seen from the window. Cushioned couches filled out the open space, and what appeared to be a small wooden footbridge led out over a koi pond and to the patio surrounding a glassy square pool. Beyond that, there lay miles and miles of pristine blue Pacific.

This didn't help. She felt like hyperventilating. She didn't know what was sexier: his house or his body.

"So, Jun, how can I help you?"

"We met last year?" Jun said, now distracted by his expensive furniture and what had to be an $18 million view. At least. Eighteen, maybe even twenty.

"Last *year*?" He scoffed a little, staring at her blankly. Then he studied her, his dark eyes giving her body a slow, appreciative sweep. "Uh… did we…?" He trailed off.

Jun realized with a start he thought they might have hooked up.

"Oh, no. I mean, no, we didn't." Now her neck felt as if it were on fire. Even her ears burned. *Not that I wouldn't go for that. Right here on this gleaming wood floor.* "We met at the hospital."

Kai's face darkened, the playfulness instantly disappearing. "The hospital," he repeated.

The tsunami had been life changing for her and Po, but for Kai, clearly it hadn't made much of an impression at all. And, she understood with sharp disappointment, neither had she.

"I'm…uh…Po's mom."

Kai furrowed his brow as if trying to remember. "Po?"

"Kai?" A woman's voice called from one of the hallways.

"Oh, uh…one minute." Kai turned toward the voice, moving away from the rich koa-wood table in his living room.

"Kai? Everything okay?" The woman's voice drifted in from a back room, and as Jun turned, she saw a tall blonde, wearing nothing but a man's white button-down oxford with the bottom three buttons done up, long tanned legs on display and her ample, gravity-defying cleavage showing. Her mascara had seeped into dark rings around her eyes, but given her half-naked state, Jun doubted anybody else noticed. The woman clearly didn't care about anyone seeing her either, as she moved closer to Kai and the door. Of course a mansion like this would have an accessory like that: a gorgeous model type ready to serve the owner's every whim.

"Sorry, sweetheart, just give me a minute," Kai said as the blonde wiggled her way in for a kiss, putting her hands on the man's amazing chest, *exactly* where Jun would have, too, right in the sternum, her other hand trailing the ridges of his abs. Jun felt a hot flash of envy.

"But today's our last day on the island!" the woman said, jutting her lower lip out in a pout. *Great, a tourist, too! Figures.*

"Babe?" *Another* woman emerged from somewhere in the house. Jun moved a little and saw a glimpse of stainless steel, granite and an ornate minitiled backsplash, all slate gray and white. This woman wore a bikini and held a fruity drink in her hand. "We're out of ice."

Jun nearly barked out a harsh laugh. Now it had gone from uncomfortable to downright ludicrous. She'd assumed someone as gorgeous and rich as Kai wouldn't be single, but *two* women at once? Was it the Playboy Mansion in here?

It was the cold, brisk wake-up call she needed. She'd been in some kind of daze, drawn in by the power of Kai's charisma, but now she snapped to attention. Every fiber in her all-organic, holistic-yoga-loving body rebelled against the scene. There was such a thing as too much sex. She'd done a whole paper on it for her graduate class last year on Qigong, the study of meditation and healing. You gave away too much of your Chi during sex, and then you didn't have enough energy left over for anything else. Kai looked as if he barely had enough energy to hold open his front door. Obviously these women had spent all night draining the man of his…Chi.

She didn't need any ancient Chinese alternative-medicine theories to tell her that Kai was on the wrong path. And that if she got involved with him, she'd be, too. The realization made her feel a little bit better somehow. *You couldn't get with him anyway, but even if you did, would you want to be one more woman through a revolving door?*

The two women, apparently sensing competition, closed ranks around Kai. The other came up and slid her hand through the crook of his free arm. Both women eyed her with interest, trying to surmise if they needed to defend their territory. Jun felt like telling them not to bother.

"I'm going to go," she said, wanting to get out of there, fast.

*What did you expect? A red-carpet welcome? Why would Kai remember you, when he's got beautiful women falling at his feet?*

*And why do you even care?*

It hit her that for the past year she'd been idolizing the man a little bit, making him out to be the kind of selfless hero who only existed in novels and movies and comic books. Kai was just a man. The woman wearing only the shirt lazily grinned at her. Okay, a very flawed man.

Belatedly, she remembered she was still holding the thank-you gift. It seemed so childish now, so inconsequential. What had she been thinking? The man had everything he could possibly want.

"It's been a year, but I just wanted to...uh, thank you. For Po." She thrust the bag at him as if it were a hot potato and bolted for his front door. She'd been planning a whole speech, but at this point, she didn't care about it at all. Kai stared at the bag, puzzled, as she nearly tripped over the two steps leading to the door. But she swung open the door and was outside, then hurried toward her old used hatchback, an ancient car that ran only by her sheer will and her mechanic cousin's generosity. It looked like such an eyesore there at the edge of his beautiful lawn.

"Jun!" She turned at the sound of his voice to see him running after her, barefoot in his swim trunks. She tried not to notice his muscled calves work. "Wait."

She hesitated, car keys in hand.

"How's Po?" Now she could tell that he remembered. Po's small scrapes and scratches from the tsunami had long since healed, but he still woke up screaming at night sometimes, haunted by nightmares. Then there was the fact that he hated water. He'd refused to swim ever since that day, not that she blamed him. But Jun looked at Kai, at his kind eyes, and then back at the frowning women waiting on his porch. She couldn't tell him all that. Why would he care? He was having the time of his life apparently.

"He's good," she said, which was 80 percent truth. "He talks about you all the time. He really wanted to come see you…"

Kai glanced back and for a split second looked embarrassed. That was something.

"Oh, right. But I'm…well, not G-rated." He grinned sheepishly, as if half-naked women were just the price he paid for being…*him*. Maybe that was true. "I'll straighten out my act sometime. I just don't know how."

"You could change that," Jun said sharply,

more sharply than she'd intended. Kai looked surprised for a moment. She guessed he wasn't used to people talking to him like that, but Jun had zero patience for self-pity, even the hint of it. Self-pity was just a selfish, useless waste of time. She thought about all the days she could've wallowed after Po's dad left or later, when her mother died. But she hadn't. She had things to do, a son to raise. Kai needed a good shake. Her tiger mom would've agreed if she'd still been alive.

"Well, I've got to go." Jun turned the keys in her hand.

"Uh...wait. Maybe you could bring Po around sometime? I'd love to see him."

"No," she said before she could even think about it, imagining an orgy of alcohol and sex and half-naked tourists.

"No?" Kai looked taken aback by her flat refusal. She got the impression women didn't tell him no very often. Which was why two of them were standing near his front door. "Just no? Come on, at least pretend to consider it!"

Usually, men were put off by her bluntness. She'd rarely had one take rejection so lightheartedly before.

Kai flashed his bright white smile, radiating warmth from his brown eyes, the ones she'd thought about often in the past year. He reached out and touched her arm, and the electricity nearly bowled her straight over. For the briefest of seconds, she found herself leaning into him. She glanced down at his hand and wondered what it would feel like on the small of her back, pulling her in for a kiss. She glanced up and found him looking at her, longer than he ought to, and all she wanted to do was sink into those eyes.

That was before Jun's brain kicked in again. What was she doing? Pining over a man who plainly had more women in his life than he could handle? She wasn't going to throw herself on top of the pile. She wasn't a maiden who planned to sacrifice herself to the volcano.

"I mean, it's not a good idea." Po already hero-worshipped Kai. He didn't need to learn the fine art of being a heavily partying bachelor at age four.

Kai looked at her intently. It was as if he could sense her inner conflict, as if he knew she was struggling to keep control, as if by grasping her arm, he could feel her pulse tick up.

"Kai!" called one of the women from his front stoop. "Kai, we're hungry!"

"You'd better go," Jun managed.

"Jun, wait…" But Jun ducked into her car and turned over the ignition. She drove off, not looking back.

# CHAPTER TWO

KAI SAT IN his manager's office waiting room in Kona, nursing the headache that only seemed to get worse the longer the day went. He'd had a hell of a time extricating himself from the two tourists who seemed to have wanted to move in with him overnight. Thank God they'd had a flight to catch, or they might still have been lounging around his pool, drinking his booze and eating his food. He was a man who appreciated women, but he vowed, *once more*, to stop. He couldn't keep falling into bed with strangers. Well, technically, he *could*. It was a fine way to spend a Saturday. Or hell, a Tuesday. But even he knew they were just a quick fix, a way of distracting himself from his real problems. Chasing women meant he didn't have to chase waves. He didn't need a psychologist to tell him he was deep into avoidance.

He frowned, thinking about his damn knee. He flexed it, wondering whether it would ever be 100 percent again. The World Big Wave Surf Championship was coming up soon. He was nowhere near ready, and he knew it, and that thought scared the hell out of him.

The damn tsunami.

Everything had been fine before the wave tore through half the island and broke his leg in three places and completely dislocated his knee. Doctors told him he was healed, but he didn't *feel* healed. His knee felt as if it was going to slip out of place. The ligaments like loose rubber bands. It could've been worse. He knew that. And he was glad he'd gotten the broken leg and not Po.

Jun and Po.

He had almost forgotten about them. He'd been so fixated on the tsunami and his own leg that his thoughts had crowded out little Po. In some ways, the boy was impossible to forget. Kai couldn't look at his battered knee and the long ugly scar that ran the length of his thigh without thinking about the dreadful day, about being washed out with Po, about barely surviving. But Kai didn't look at the day the same way Jun did. He didn't know why Jun was trying to thank him. She kept sending him food all through that first month and then the second, too. Kai had thought maybe she'd forgotten him at last, but then she showed up on the *anniversary* of the damn thing. He really wished she'd stop *thanking* him.

He hadn't done anything. He'd simply stayed with the boy. In the end, it had been just dumb luck they'd not both been killed. He'd thought countless times, what might have happened if he hadn't gone to the day care that day to check on his cousin? If he'd simply headed straight to higher ground?

He remembered Po, the small dark-haired boy, recalled that the two of them had huddled in the second story of the day care before the first wave hit. He'd obviously been scared, but he'd worked so hard to be brave. Just three then, barely older than a toddler, he'd swum for his life and made it. After the wave had wrecked half of the building and torn them from it, he'd lain crippled in the flood with Po, who was magically unharmed. He'd done nothing special then but pray.

But he couldn't convince Jun of that. Jun, with those serious dark eyes and that delicate heart-shaped face. He'd forgotten how striking she was, how pretty. His thoughts wandered where they shouldn't, and he felt sleazy for even wondering what her petite, toned body might look like naked in his bed. She was a mother, for goodness' sake.

*There you go again, avoiding the real problem.* It was easy to avoid problems, he thought, when he had a pretty face to think about.

Kai reached into his pocket and pulled out the small business card Jun had slipped into his gift bag. It read "Jun Lee, personal trainer, life coach. Live life organically."

She must be one of those New Age nuts, the kind that ate only granola and rabbit-pellet food. Kai had never been in that camp. He had always been a barbecue-rib kind of guy. He flipped the card over and saw the "Good for One Free Tai Chi Class" scrawled on the back. He thought that was something only old people did, but Jun wasn't old. At least it wasn't yoga. Kai couldn't see himself doing yoga. But Tai Chi, maybe he'd try it.

Or maybe he'd just call her and ask her out for a drink.

Then he remembered the look of complete horror when he'd asked her if he could see Po, how quickly she'd squealed out of his driveway. Maybe she had a boyfriend. Po's dad, maybe?

*Or maybe she's just not interested.*

Somehow, the thought electrified him just a little. It had been weeks since he'd found any girl a real challenge. He couldn't remember the last time a woman flat out told him no.

He held the card between his two fingers, thinking about her lean, athletic body. She was sexy, no doubt, but there was something else that intrigued him about Jun Lee.

*You could change that.* She'd seemed so sure he could turn around the disaster his life had become, as if she had some magic bullet to solve all his problems. He knew she couldn't, that it was probably just talk, and yet the way she'd said it, with unwavering conviction, got him wondering. Could he?

He glanced at her card again and then nearly laughed out loud. What was he thinking? The Tai Chi instructor didn't have the answers. It was just his little head doing all the thinking again. It was just about him being attracted to the woman, nothing more.

Besides, she was far too serious for him, he reasoned. *A grown-up.* That was what came to mind when he thought of Jun Lee. The exact opposite of the tourists he'd been having fun with lately. They never took anything too seriously, which was fine by Kai. Right now taking anything seriously just seemed like a waste of effort. After all, in the end, what was the point? You get all serious and the next thing you know, a freak national disaster and a freight train of water takes away everything you cared about.

The office door swung open and Kirk Cody, Kai's manager—tall, blond and excessively tanned from spending too much time on the beach—leaned out. He wore his trademark Tommy Bahama gear from head to toe. "Sorry about that, Kai! You ready?" Kai walked in and was quickly surrounded by pictures of himself: him endorsing all kinds of products; him on a Wheaties box; him launching his clothing company nearly two years ago.

Kai had made Kirk rich, but Kirk had done the same for Kai. Kai never thought in marketing terms. He just liked to surf. When Kai was at the top of his surfing game, the relationship worked perfectly. These days, however, Kai felt as though it was only a matter of time before Kirk found out his knee hadn't healed right. Then the endorsement deals would disappear overnight.

Hanging above Kirk's desk was a giant photo of Kai surfing a stomach-churning nearly forty-five-foot wave at Mavericks, California, the break so heinous even some pro surfers steered clear of it. Kai thought about his performance earlier that week on a wave not even a fifth that size. He'd made his fortune risking it all on big waves, and now he couldn't even stand upright on five measly feet.

"How are you, man?" Kirk asked Kai, who simply shrugged.

"Fine, I guess," he said, studying the old picture on the wall.

A quarter Hawaiian, a quarter Japanese and half Irish, Kai had always felt as if he had the pulse of the water. All of his ancestors came from one island or another, and that brought with it a healthy respect for the sea. But lately, it felt as though he'd simply lost his gift.

A knock at Kirk's office door drew Kai's attention. He realized with a start that Bret Jon stood there. Bret was Kai's tow partner, or had been, before the tsunami. Bret was the one who'd driven the Jet Ski that took him out to the big waves, the seventy-footers that no one could physically paddle to. Bret was also the one who had risked his life to go in and get him whenever Kai wiped out.

Bret glanced at Kai and frowned.

"You didn't tell me he would be here," Bret said. "You asked me to come here to talk about a new job. Now I see why you didn't want to do it on the phone."

He had good reason to be angry. Kai couldn't look his once-good friend in the eye. He lived on Maui, so what was he doing here?

"Maybe I ought to go," Kai said, standing.

"Both of you—sit. You used to be the best team in big-wave surfing, but now you're not speaking." Kirk looked back and forth between the two men, who weren't saying anything. "You guys have been doing this for more than fifteen years. Come on, you and Laird Hamilton, Buzzy Kerbox, Sandra Chevally...you *invented* this sport. You guys found a way to surf waves that everyone else said were impossible to surf. Tell me why you girls are fighting so we can put this behind us." Kirk leaned back in his chair.

Bret, who was built like a linebacker, all broad, hefty muscle across his back, stared a hole through Kai. "He knows why."

"Bret, I said I'm sorry." Kai moved toward his old partner, but Bret backed away, hands up.

"I don't want your apology, man." Bret's eyes had gone cold and flat. "You can keep that, along with your endorsements and your clothing line. Just...stay away from Jaws. I *told* you once."

"Bret, come on, man," Kirk pleaded. "Let's sit down and talk about this. The Big Wave Championship is coming up. You and Kai, you're like gold."

"Keep your gold," Bret muttered, shaking his head. Kai wished he could say the right thing, but no matter how often he apologized, he could never make it right. He knew it and Bret did, too.

He felt a pang. He remembered, years ago, back when only a few crazy souls would even attempt a ninety-foot break, and yet there the two of them had been, taking turns towing each other into waves that should've killed them. They'd learned as they went, instincts and grit the only things keeping him upright and alive, out of the mouth of the beast. Together they'd been brave or crazy or both. They'd been pioneers. And now here they were, barely speaking.

"Look, Kirk, nothing personal, but I'm done talking." In seconds, Bret had stalked out of the office. Kai watched him go, feeling as if a chapter in his life was closing, yet he wasn't done reading it yet.

Kirk let out a long sigh. "You going to tell me what's going on there?"

Kai shook his head. "Not my story to tell." If Bret hadn't told him the details, then Kai wouldn't.

"You've got a new tower? Someone you can trust?"

"I'm working on it," Kai lied. He wasn't. Why recruit a tow partner when his knee was 50 percent at best?

"You'd better work fast."

"I know." Kai shrugged, thinking about his wipeout earlier in the week. He hadn't been on his board since. In fact, the very thought of getting out there again made his stomach buzz with nerves, as if he'd drunk too much of the Kona coffee served at his sister's café.

Kirk studied him a minute. "Knee okay?"

"Still stiff," Kai admitted, avoiding all eye contact, as if the truth would be evident on his face. Kirk nodded, looking somber, and then leaned forward, clasping his hands together on his desk.

"Gretchen says you're blowing off training."

Gretchen was Kai's personal trainer, but even he had to admit he hadn't been very trainable lately. Gretchen had told him to cut back on the bar life, but there wasn't anything scarier than not being able to surf again except dealing with that sober.

"You gonna be ready?"

Kai met Kirk's gaze and for a split second considered spilling his guts and admitting everything. *I'm not going to be ready. I might never be ready again.*

"I'm gonna try," Kai said. He thought it was safely the truth, but as soon as the words were out of his mouth, he wasn't sure. *Was* he trying?

"The new surfboards are ready to go, but we need some promo shots," Kirk said, leaning back in his chair. Pure Kona sunshine filtered in from the big bay window behind his desk. "Maybe you on a big practice wave? Maybe on Jaws? You know, after you find a new tow guy."

"Yeah, sure. Sometime." *No way. Never.*

"How about next week? Photographer has openings a week from Sunday."

"Can't do it." Kai nearly clipped off the end of Kirk's sentence in his haste to decline. The idea of a photographer or anyone else recording one of his recent surfing disasters filled him with white-hot embarrassment. He glanced at his fine form in the oversize photo above Kirk's desk. He was a lifetime away from the Kai Brady of two years ago.

"Kai, this has to be done."

"I know." Kai eyed Kirk, who didn't blink as he crossed his arms across his chest.

"Fine." Kirk sighed, frustrated. "You're going to have to talk to me sometime about what's going on with you."

"Nothing's going on with me." *Nothing that can be fixed by talking about it.* Kai stood, and even in that brief motion, he felt the loosening creak of his right knee. He didn't care what the orthopedic surgeon said—those tendons and bone just hadn't healed right. He nearly stumbled a little but righted himself in time. "Is that all, Kirk?"

"Need your signature on this," Kirk said, sliding contracts his way. "Just a renewal for the Mountain Dew endorsement. Oh, and Todd Kolkot wants to talk to you. Says he needs to get your approval on the new fall line."

Kai bent down and signed his name with a flourish, all the while wondering how fast Mountain Dew would have dropped him if they'd seen him surf this week. Kai turned to go.

"One more thing, Kai. Somebody from *Time* magazine keeps calling. They're doing an anniversary piece on the tsunami, you know, 'The Big Island a Year Later,' and wanted to interview you for it."

"No," Kai said. He'd woken up in a cold sweat from nightmares about reporters asking him questions about how well he was surfing, how his knee was, all of which would be part of any interview, no matter how it started. Besides, he didn't like talking about the tsunami. Not just because of his knee, but because of a whole host of other reasons, namely that people he knew had lost their lives that day.

"But it would be good for your brand. You know no publicity is…"

"I *said* no."

"Okay, okay!" Kirk's hands went up in a gesture of surrender. "I know you don't like to do interviews about the tsunami, but at some point, you're going to have to talk about it."

"People died that day. I just got my leg broken. So what?" *Might as well have died, though.* Self-pity began to creep in again and he tried to shoo the thoughts out of his head, but they had sticky, gooey edges. No matter how hard he pushed them out, some gunky residue always remained behind.

"You're famous. You're a hero. You can inspire people."

At this, Kai barked a caustic laugh. "I'm no hero." Last night he'd been so drunk he barely remembered what had happened between him and the two tourists. He woke up in bed with a new girl nearly every weekend. He hardly knew if he was coming or going. He was the farthest thing from a hero.

"Course you are. There's that little boy you saved."

"I didn't save him. We were both just lucky."

Kirk rolled his eyes. "Fine. Then what about all those amateur surfers at Jaws? How many did you pull out of the rocks?" Kirk stared at him. Kai shrugged. "Two? Four? More than that?"

"They had no business being out there in the first place," Kai said. "I only saved them so I could chew them out and tell them to find another hobby. Doesn't make me heroic."

"It doesn't matter. It only matters if people *think* you are." There was the Kirk Kai remembered, the one always looking for the angle and hardly caring about the truth. It was this side of the business, the marketing whatever sells, that just rubbed Kai the wrong way.

"Why not make that the next shirt slogan?" Kai said, a bit of bitterness creeping into his voice.

Kirk laughed. "We should, bro. We totally should." He leaned forward, his antique wooden desk chair creaking. "By the way, that gossip columnist called again for a quote or confirmation. Said something about you and some wild escapade with two tourists. They have a picture. Looks like you."

Kai's stomach lurched. He didn't want to know what picture they could've gotten ahold of.

Kirk tapped his tablet and then handed it to Kai. There he was, sitting in his hot tub with the two women he'd just dropped off at the airport. They were both topless, but the picture was pixelated. One of the women was kissing his face and the other was taking a selfie. Kai groaned. If his aunt Kaimana saw this, he'd be in for another lecture.

"Yeah, that's me, but it's not as bad as it looks."

Kirk threw his head back and laughed. "Bad? Man, I'd kill to be you for *one* weekend." The wedding ring flashed on Kirk's hand as he took the signed contracts from his desk and tucked them into a file.

"It's not as fun as you think it would be," Kai said, remembering the awkward goodbyes that afternoon after he dropped the tourists at the airport. They hadn't even gotten out of sight before they'd started posting to Instagram, clearly.

"As long as you can train *and* do this. You sure you can?"

"Yeah, of course." *Such a lie.*

SEEING BRET AGAIN had made Kai itch to get out on the surf. He had something to prove. In the surf just beyond his beach house the next day, he started paddling. The wind was low, the waves gentle. It would be an ideal time to try to test his knee.

Kai paddled hard against the sparkling Pacific surf as he spied the perfect wave rolling in. He redoubled his efforts, sea spray hitting his face as the early-morning light glinted off the tip of his prototype surfboard. Kirk would be happy to see him on it, at least. Kahaluu Beach stretched out behind him, and the crystal-blue water was clear and relatively calm, the waves easy for even a beginner to handle. A few tourists were out, trying out their rental boards for the first time.

Kai still thought his board looked too new and flashy. If he'd been on one of the serious breaks, the locals would've ribbed him for it, and they'd have been right. Neon colors and cool graphics didn't make you a skilled surfer. Sweat and blood did.

Maybe he'd forgotten that. He admitted loving the spotlight, the interviews on ESPN, the legions of followers online. Who wouldn't enjoy dating the models and actresses who gravitated toward his rising star? He hadn't turned them away. He'd passed the millions mark before he turned thirty. Since then, it had just been about building his empire of shirts, boards and even waterproof video cameras small enough to fit in your palm.

Of course, that was all before the tsunami.

Ocean spray hit his forehead and he shook his head to clear his eyes so he could focus on the wave. He couldn't dwell on the past. Surfing was all about living in the moment.

He flexed his knee. It felt strong. Stronger than it had in weeks. Good. He was going to crush it today.

*Is that why you're hiding out on a tourist beach? Is that why you're riding these beginner waves, barely six feet? You used to say anything below twenty wasn't worth your time.*

A tingle of nerves pricked his stomach as he tried to shake off the uncertainty.

He was the three-time reigning big-wave champion. He'd survived some of the most dangerous breaks in the world. He'd surfed waves taller than an eight-story building.

*That was before the ocean shredded your leg and left you for dead.*

Kai shut his eyes against the memory.

Now was not the time for doubt. He knew it, and yet he couldn't shake the ghosts of uncertainty. He might never be good again, and he damn well knew it.

But now he was out of time. The wave was here. He'd have to attempt it or wait for the next one. He tried to blank out his mind, rely on muscle memory as the wave rolled toward him and he popped up on his board, the warm sun on his back, cool air whipping across his chest. For a shining split second, he believed he was going to do it. He felt the rush of the adrenaline as he struggled for a toe hold and a quick glance around told him nothing in the world could be as beautiful in life as this: glittering ocean beneath his board, shoreline in the distance dotted with gorgeous palm trees, like a line of hula dancers swaying in the tropical breeze.

Surfing was his first, and only, passion: he craved the rush of wind through his hair and the ocean spray on his face like a junkie needing a hit.

He was going to do it. He was upright, arms out for balance, both feet on the board.

And then something about the wave, the merciless engine of it, challenged him a bit too hard, bucked him ruthlessly, as if the water wanted him to fail. As if the ocean already knew what he was afraid to admit: he wasn't a world-class surfer; he was just the empty shell of an imposter, nothing more than a has-been.

He adjusted, trying to find his balance, but out of the blue, a sharp pain shot up his knee.

*No.*

He struggled to keep upright, but his knee buckled like a rusty hinge collapsing under the strain, and he fell backward into the surf, and suddenly, the moment of bliss was replaced by a moment of panic. The wave held him down, punishing him, as his leg flailed, ankle still attached to his board. The shiny neon board slid onward, dragging him beneath it under a dangerous weight of water.

And once more, the fear suffocated him: he was back in the tsunami wave, powerless against the angry force of nature. He again felt the paralyzing terror: *I'm going to die.*

Panic, cold and hard, drove down his spine.

He struggled wildly to breach the surface, but

tangled in the force of the wave, he felt helpless, as the expensive, shining new fiberglass board broke free of his ankle tether and shot across the wave.

*The water is going to kill me. The thing I love most in the world is going to kill me.*

He floundered, and then the wave released him, breaking across the reef, and he came up, gasping, sucking in big gulps of air.

*Alive, I'm alive.* And then he realized he wasn't back in the tsunami. The huge wave that had killed so many people and destroyed so many homes was long gone. Yet the wave, being under, had brought him right back to the worst day of his life.

He coughed as salt water stung the inside of his nose and ran down his throat, the brine threatening to choke him.

He saw his board floating out to sea and let it go, too shaken to fish it out of the surf. He needed to get to land, and he swam, heart thudding as he made it to the sand. He rolled up on shore out of breath, feeling as if he'd just run a marathon with a gorilla on his back.

His knee had failed him—again.

The disappointment welled up in him. *Months* of rehab, and his knee wasn't anywhere close to where it needed to be if he was ever going to surf seriously again. Hot tears of frustration burned the backs of his eyelids but he refused to let them fall. He was on all fours in the hot, wet sand and he felt like punching the ground but didn't.

It wasn't just his body that had disappointed him but his mind. He was *afraid* in a way he'd never been before. His whole life he'd been fearless, and now a simple dump off the board and he felt as though the ocean would kill him. He didn't want to go back out there. *Wouldn't.* Not today. Maybe not ever.

At the heart of it, he was a coward, plain and simple.

The wave knew it, too. That was why it had bucked him. It was the ocean schooling him for being a fool. He managed to drag himself back to his house, not proud of himself for leaving his broken board to the surf but too shaken to do much of anything else. He vowed to go look for it later, once he'd gotten his breathing under control. He felt as if he was going to have a heart attack, the panic pressing against his chest like a two-ton weight.

Was he really done with surfing at age thirty-three? Was it really *all* over?

When he got to his porch, he saw Gretchen waiting for him there, sitting on one of his patio chairs, clipboard in her lap, looking pissed.

*Training!* He'd forgotten entirely that it was a training day, that Gretchen would be working him on weights today. Everything about the tightness in her shoulders told him she was furious. He almost turned around and left, but she'd seen him, and he knew that would just make her angrier. Sooner or later, he'd have to take his medicine, and later would just be worse.

He trudged to the open patio, still dripping wet, his hands still shaking from nerves.

"You're late," she said, and he could feel her glare even through her mirrored sunglasses.

"Gretchen, I am so sorry. I was surfing and lost track of time…"

"What did I say about being late?" She cut him off, standing. Her short dark hair hung nicely around her face, but it was her muscled body that everyone noticed first. It was no wonder she was the most sought-after personal trainer on the island and had a library of exercise videos and apps under her belt. She got results. She knew how to push him in all the right ways.

Except recently.

In the past year, her go-for-broke, hit-the-weights-harder approach just hadn't been working for him. The more she yelled, the less he wanted to do anything.

But the fact that Gretchen wasn't yelling at him now only made him nervous. That she was suddenly so calm made him realize the situation was far worse than he'd thought. She gestured with her hand and her diamond wedding band caught the light and sparkled like fire. Happily married to one of the best tour-boat captains on the island, she was off-limits. Kai liked that their relationship had been strictly professional. Gretchen was one of the few women in his life who didn't feel complicated.

"You said I couldn't be late anymore or skip sessions."

"Or?"

Kai swallowed. "Or you'd quit." Panic rose in his throat. First Bret had quit on him. Now Gretchen, too? *Everyone's abandoning me because they know I'm finished.*

"Exactly." She ripped off the page on the top of the clipboard. "My official letter of resignation, effective now."

He glanced at the handwritten note, stunned.

"Gretch, you *can't* quit! I need you. I…" She'd been with him for almost all of his surfing career. As his star had risen, so had hers. They made a nearly unstoppable team. He'd never worked with anyone else before and hadn't even considered the possibility.

Gretchen raised her chin, determined. He knew that look, and it was the one where she usually told him he needed to run five more miles and do an extra round of strength training.

"I can quit and I am. I told you to cut out the partying and staying out late. You didn't. I told you to eat right. You didn't. I told you *to show up* at training sessions, and you haven't. It's not *me* who's quitting. It's *you*."

Kai knew she was right.

"But I pay you anyway," Kai pointed out. "And I can pay you more. Name your price."

"It's not about the money." Gretchen shook her head, a look of pity washing over her face. "I've got my professional pride, Kai. You're in some kind of really dark place, and you need to find a way out of it. Maybe me quitting will be the inspiration you need to figure out what's wrong and do something about it. I don't know, but what I do know is that I can't help you. Not until you get your head right."

"Gretchen, give me one more chance. I promise, I—"

"You promised last week. No, it's done. I'm done. I'm sorry, Kai."

"But the surfing competition is in a matter of months! Who am I going to find on this kind of short notice?"

"Maybe some of your *friends* can help you?" Gretchen held up her smartphone and showed him the picture of him drinking in the hot tub. That damn picture was going to be the death of him. He suddenly wished for a massive internet malfunction, or at least just some strange outage that affected only social media sites.

"That's not as bad as it looks." That was the second time in as many days that he'd said that, but it didn't make it true. "Look, I know I'm a mess, but…"

"I can't do anything for you, Kai. *You've* got to change that."

Now she sounded like Jun.

"Gretchen, please…"

"Uh-uh. Kai. That's strike three, and I told you, after strike three, you're out. I don't mess around."

There'd be no changing her mind. Kai was officially screwed, and not in the way that involved tourists and hot tubs.

*What am I going to do now?*

On his patio, he saw Jun's gift bag and next to it, on the tabletop, her card: "Good for One Free Tai Chi Class." He saw a list of scheduled classes on the back, one of which was being held this afternoon.

*It's not like I have anything else going on.* He went inside to dry off and get dressed.

# CHAPTER THREE

JUN WAS PACKING up her gym bag, trying very hard not to think about Kai Brady. She'd been trying for nearly an hour, but it wasn't any use. She'd made the mistake of searching for him online and found a photo of him making out with at least one of the women she'd seen at his house. That wasn't the only photo, either. It seemed that Kai made a point of posing with attractive women whenever he could. She didn't know why she was surprised. He was handsome, rich and a bona fide celebrity.

All she could think about were the women at his place, clearly in the mood for whatever three-some party he was throwing. She shouldn't care, but for some reason it bothered her. She'd spent a year thinking Kai was brave and selfless.

She didn't like the conflicting images of Kai she now held in her mind. It was much easier when she just thought of him as a nice-guy hero. *Or maybe that's just because you're jealous. Wish you were in the hot tub with him, Jun?*

"Earth to Jun. Come in, Jun." This was Tim Reese, the owner of Island Fit and her boss. He used to be an Olympic athlete and had won a silver medal in some track-and-field event. Now he was the charismatic bodybuilder who inspired people to come in his gym just by standing near the window up front.

"Sorry, Tim. I wasn't listening."

"I gathered that. I was asking if you could pull a double shift Friday. Jenna bailed on me and Rich's still on vacation, so that means just *me*, unless you save me."

Jun hesitated. It would mean paying extra for day care or calling in a babysitting favor from her sister, which would cost her in a different way. Then again, the overtime pay could always come in handy. Po had outgrown his clothes, again.

Tim put his hand on her shoulder and let it linger there. Jun stepped out of the touch automatically, putting space between her and her boss. Sometimes Jun wondered if Tim had a crush on her or if he was just the touchy-feely type. Either way, she felt a smidgen uncomfortable when he closed in on her personal space. But Tim offered her a decent job, a steady one, and she spent a good deal of time convincing herself it was all in her head.

"Hey, if it's a big deal, I mean, don't worry about it…" Tim worked hard to backpedal. He put his hands up and backed away, and it was times like these she thought, *I'm just imagining that he's coming on to me.*

"Let me see if I can get someone to watch Po," she said. "If I can, I'll do it."

"Great." Tim's eyes lit up in a way that was a little bit *too* excited. *Nope. Definitely not imagining it.* Jun definitely did *not* feel the same way about Tim. Not that he wasn't a nice guy, but Jun wasn't interested in dating or adding complications in her life right now. She'd never yet met a man who was okay with Po being her first priority.

"I've, uh, got to head out." Jun finished stuffing her bag and zipped it closed, itching to get some distance from Tim. She had only two hours of day care left and thirty minutes until her Tai Chi class on the beach.

"See you Friday," Tim called as she walked out the door. Jun waved, but thankfully, her phone rang, so she could ignore Tim's intense blue stare.

She glanced down at the screen and saw the number of Po's day care. Instantly, her heart slid into her throat. What had happened now? Every time she saw Day Care on her caller ID, she felt as if she were right back in that moment a year ago when she had been told by a crying teacher that somehow they'd lost Po.

She took a deep breath, shoring herself up for bad news, and answered.

"Hello?"

"Ms. Lee," said a crisp voice on the other end of the line. The director of the day care, Penelope Anne.

"Mrs. Anne, what's wrong?"

"I'm afraid you're going to have to pick up your son."

"Is he sick?" Jun's heart thudded. Sick, or worse, hurt? He always played rough on the playground, swinging his little body dangerously off the monkey bars. Jun fumbled in her bag for her car keys. They jangled in her hand as she searched for the right one. Her car was so ancient it didn't have automatic locks.

"No, no. He's fine. I'm afraid he's…" Mrs. Anne swallowed "…bitten his teacher."

Jun froze, her key in her door.

"Oh, no." Jun's stomach lurched. "Not again." White-hot embarrassment flared up her neck. She'd talked with Po often about biting, but nothing seemed to get through. Last week he'd bitten a boy who'd taken his crayon, and the week before, he'd bitten a girl who'd spilled water on him, and now this. She'd thought it was just a phase, something he'd grow out of, but now she was starting to wonder if it was related to the nightmares and the stress and everything else left over from the tsunami. "I am so very sorry. Is the teacher okay?"

"Just bruised, but I'm afraid you'll have to come get Po. And we'll need to talk."

Jun didn't like the sound of that. She'd already been warned twice before: third bite and he's out. She swung herself into the front seat and flew to the day care, nearly running a red light, she felt so flustered.

Minutes later, she was sitting in Mrs. Anne's tidy office, with the single computer on her desk and the row of children's artwork pinned to a clothesline running the length of the window behind her. Po was still in his day-care room, playing with big foam blocks, building some kind of castle. She'd sneaked a look through the slit of a window in the door on her way by.

"Ms. Lee, we've been very understanding about all the trauma Po has suffered in the last year, and we understand it's a process. Many of our children have been affected by that horrible day, but I'm afraid we haven't seen much progress with Po. And, as I don't need to remind you, this is the *third* incident in the month, and we have certain policies at Pacific Day Care."

Jun's throat went dry. "I've been working with him, Mrs. Anne. We've been reading the book you lent us, *Teeth Are Not for Biting.*"

"I'm sorry. I'm afraid, beginning tomorrow, you're going to have to find new care for Po."

It was one of the worst things a working single mom could hear. "But the other day-care centers are all full. Before we settled here, we were even on a wait list!" It was true. The tsunami had wiped out so many businesses on the west side of the island, and while some were still rebuilding, like their old day care, others had decided not to rebuild at all.

"I'm sorry, Ms. Lee. We've done what we can, but we have to think of the other children." A soft knock came at the door.

"Come in," the director called, and the door creaked open as Po's teacher led him in. Just four, yet he seemed to know he was in trouble and he came sheepishly to his mother's side, dark-haired head hung in shame.

Jun's heart thumped as she looked at him. For that second, she thought the expression on his face was exactly hers. Of course, strangers in the supermarket felt differently. Po's cocoa-colored skin was several shades darker than her own, a trait from his father, but he had her eyes and heart-shaped face. She saw the similarities clear as day, but others didn't. She supposed it was a mother's eye.

"I'm sorry, Ms. Lee," Mrs. Anne said in a tone that didn't sound very much as if she were sorry.

Jun stood, realizing it was pointless to stay. "Thank you, Mrs. Anne." She took her son firmly by the hand and led him out. Once outside the school, she turned and kneeled by Po on the sidewalk.

"How many times have we talked about biting? Teeth are *not* for biting." Jun grabbed her boy's arms and squeezed. Anger bubbled up in her, as it did anytime he acted out.

Po shrugged, eyes down, kicking his small Spider-Man tennis shoe into the ground. He was wearing his favorite Spider-Man T-shirt, faded from too many washings and already beginning to be too short at the waist. But Po wouldn't hear of parting with it. He'd wear it every day if she'd let him.

"Why did you bite the *teacher*?"

"She's mean," Po said, crossing his arms.

"Po, I'm sure she's not mean."

"She was going to throw me in the pool. I told her, I don't want to!" Po shrugged again.

Jun sighed and dropped her head in defeat. The day care had a small pool in the back where they taught kids how to swim. Po hadn't wanted to go near any water since the tsunami, not that Jun blamed him. It wasn't surprising he'd lashed out at a teacher trying to push him in.

"Why didn't the teacher let you sit on the edge?

Just put your feet in?" Anger boiled in Jun's chest. What were those teachers doing to her son?

"She said I'd done that enough." Po shrugged. "She said I needed to join the class. So she picked me up and took me to the diving board and was gonna throw me. So I…" Po hung his head, not finishing. Jun could fill in the rest.

"They should *not* have done that. They were wrong." Of course, Mrs. Anne hadn't mentioned *that* in the exit interview.

She wanted to march back into the day care and ask them what they were doing trying to force a boy petrified of the water into the deep end of a pool. Po wouldn't even take a bath. And they were trying to get him to swim in nine feet of water?

At the same time, she knew it wouldn't make any difference, and besides, Po shouldn't have bitten anyone.

Not that she couldn't understand why he had.

She felt frustration well up in her as she stared into the face of her beautiful baby boy. She wished she could fix him. Before the tsunami, he'd been the first kid in the water and the last out. Now she wondered if he'd ever swim again.

"Am I in trouble now? Big trouble?" Po asked, his dark eyes sad.

"We don't bite, Po," she said sternly. *"Ever."*

Po nodded, his eyes growing wide, his bottom lip quivering just a little bit. She hated to see him like that, especially when she knew it wasn't all his fault. But she couldn't *not* punish him, either. So while she wanted to hug him and tell him it would all be okay, the ghost of her tiger mom in her head told her, *Two wrongs don't make a right*.

"No TV today," she added.

"Mom!" he protested.

"I mean it." Even if her son wasn't completely in the wrong, she still had to lay down the law. Yet as she watched his little shoulders slump over in resignation, she wondered if she was doing the right thing. Should she have caved and told him it was fine to bite some crazy woman who tried to throw you in the deep end of the pool? She couldn't help but second-guess herself, something she'd been doing quite a lot in the past year.

Po may have gotten kicked out of day care, but why did she feel like the one who was failing?

Jun glanced at her watch.

"My Tai Chi class!" she exclaimed, realizing that she had just a few minutes to get there and no time to find a sitter. "You're coming to Mommy's class."

After a hectic drive, Jun managed to pull into a spot not too far from the beach. She grabbed her bag and took Po's hand, guiding him down the sand-strewn path next to the parking lot, which led to the swaying palm trees and sparkling blue ocean. Already, most of her class had gathered and she hated that she was late. It was unprofessional and unlike her.

"Come on, Po. We've got to hurry." She wondered why Po was always so fast when he was running from her, usually bolting straight toward a busy street, but when *she* wanted to get somewhere, it was as if his feet had grown lead soles.

This day just felt as if it had taken on a life of its own and was quickly spiraling out of her grasp.

"Hey, do you need a hand?" The deep rumble of a voice behind her made her whirl. Following her across the asphalt parking lot was Kai Brady. He grinned, showing his beautiful white smile in his smooth tanned face. *This* time he was wearing a shirt, but it didn't change the power of his magnetic pull.

Her heart lurched, and she was acutely aware of her windblown hair and the fact she was late, harried and completely disheveled.

What on earth was *he* doing here?

## CHAPTER FOUR

KAI OFFERED TO take Jun's bag, but it was clear by her expression that she wasn't going to let it go. She stood there looking uncertain, clutching her boy's hand, and he wondered for a minute if she was actually *not* glad to see him. He wasn't used to cool welcomes. Po, however, didn't disappoint.

"Kai!" the little boy cried, his voice pure joy as he whipped his tiny hand free of his mother's grasp and ran to him. Surprised that the boy even remembered him after all these months, he grinned. The boy charged straight to Kai, arms wide. Po's enthusiasm was infectious as Kai instinctively picked him up and swung him in the air, causing him to squeal in delight.

"Good to see you, Po!" Kai said, and meant it. Seeing him happy and healthy meant something. It reminded him how precious life was. In this moment of pure joy, Kai didn't think surfing even mattered. He wondered why he had stayed away from Po for so long. The elation on his innocent face warmed Kai's heart. He felt better than he had in months.

Kai caught the disapproving look on Jun's face and put Po down, suddenly noticing how much the boy had grown in a year. He'd lost some of the baby fat he'd carried then. His dark hair was shorter, but the devious smile on his lips as his mother whispered something in his ear was exactly the same. In his hand, he clutched a plastic Spider-Man figure, and he was dressed nearly head to toe in clothes depicting the web slinger.

Thinking back to the tsunami, Kai remembered Elmo tennis shoes as the boy scrambled up the stairs to the second floor of the day-care building just seconds before the first wave hit. Kai could hear the loud chest-thumping roar of the wave even now, could feel it reverberating in his bones.

"I have a poster of you in my room!" Po exclaimed, breathless. "You're like this!" Po mimicked a surfing pose.

"A poster, huh?" Kai glanced over at Jun.

"He saw it at the store and wouldn't let us leave until I promised to get it for his birthday," Jun admitted as she juggled the beach bag, a bottle of water and a clipboard.

"Can I take that?" Kai again offered to take the bag, but she resisted, moving her shoulder away from him.

"I'm fine," she said, tightly, like a woman who didn't want help. She probably didn't like men who opened doors, either. Stubborn and independent, he could tell. Yet the obstinate set of her chin just made her look even prettier, a fact she'd probably hate to know. "Can I...uh, we...help you? I've got a class here..." She nodded anxiously down at the modest crowd milling about in the shade of palm trees on the beach.

"That's why I'm here."

Jun looked at Kai as if he'd grown horns. He wanted to check to make sure his hair wasn't doing something strange. She cocked her head to one side, her dark ponytail flowing down one pale shoulder as her brown eyes studied him, confused.

"Your free class?" He held up her business card between two fingers and then her face lit up in recognition.

It had been on a whim he'd even come, but after Gretchen had quit, he'd been at loose ends. The card she'd given him had felt like serendipity.

Gretchen's words still ricocheted around his head. *It's not me who's quitting. It's you.*

He knew she was right, and yet he didn't know how to snap out of it, or he would. He glanced at the beach, at the people there in loose-fitting shorts, waiting on class to start. Part of him hoped Tai Chi would help him. But deep down, he knew Tai Chi wouldn't replace Gretchen's grueling training sessions. Tai Chi wasn't the answer, but it was a way to spend the afternoon that didn't involve heading to a tourist bar and seducing another hotel guest, which he thought *had* to be an improvement.

Unless it involved seducing a beautiful Tai Chi instructor instead.

He glanced at her fitted leggings and her bare toned calves. Yes, he wouldn't mind that at all.

"Oh...yes, of course." Her demeanor changed. "I didn't expect you today, but you're welcome to stay. Although today might not be the best class. Po, uh...is usually at day care, but..."

"I bit my teacher!" Po exclaimed, in the blunt honesty of a four-year-old.

"You bit your teacher!" Kai echoed, surprised. "Why?"

Kai saw Jun wince.

"She wanted to throw me in the pool!"

"But I thought you liked to swim," Kai said, remembering how amazed he had been at the then-three-year-old's advanced dog-paddling skills in the flood after the tsunami. They'd saved him. The boy's eyes grew wide and he shook his head slowly side to side. Kai got a feeling then that there was more going on with Po than his mother had let on when she'd dropped by his house. The look on his face when he'd mentioned swimming was plain old fear, and Kai recognized it clearly enough. It was the same way he felt about surfing.

"Po, come along now. We've got to start class. If you'd like to join, you're welcome, Mr. Brady."

Jun infused a formalness into her speech and Kai could almost hear a wall coming up, a protective mom's instincts. The day-care discussion or one about swimming was not one she wanted to have.

"Call me Kai," he said, flashing his best smile.

"Yeah, Mom. Call him Kai!" Po exclaimed, jumping up and down and clapping.

"All right," Jun acquiesced, but Kai noticed she didn't actually say his name. She looked away from him, a blush creeping up her cheek. "Come on, Po. Let's set you up so you can build sand castles while Mommy does her class. I need a good helper."

Po nodded solemnly in a way that showed he was taking this as seriously as a little kid could. He trailed after his mom as the three of them joined the rest of the class on the beach under the shade of some large palm trees. Jun waved to some of the people waiting as she bustled Po over to an outcropping of lava rocks at the edge of the shade, plopping him down on a towel with a bucket and shovel about thirty feet from the ocean. Kai tried to imagine this sweet boy as a wild child who would bite his teacher at day care. He just couldn't see it.

A man waiting for the lesson to begin sighed loudly near him.

"She brought her kid?" the fiftysomething man groaned, disapproving. "I didn't pay for a toddler class." Kai eyed the man with the silver hair in the black T-shirt and frowned. The judgment rolling off him was palpable, and Kai wanted to tell him to give Jun a break. What was she supposed to do? Leave Po in the car to die of heatstroke?

Kai felt defensive of single moms. After all, he'd been raised by one, and then, after she died, he'd been raised by his aunt, who'd done it all by herself. He knew how hard a job it was, and he also knew that this man had no idea at all the sacrifices Jun likely made.

Jun was too far away to hear and Kai was grateful. He hoped the guy kept the rest of his complaints to himself. Jun *and* Po didn't need his grousing. Kai took up a position beside him on the far side of the class as the dozen or so people fell into a loose grid in front of Jun. Kai had always thought that Tai Chi was only for older people, but the class included a wide variety of ages, and surprisingly, most of them were men. Jun unzipped her Windbreaker and was now in a sleeveless coral-colored tank and yoga pants. Kai couldn't help but notice the tight fit of black Lycra down her muscled legs, and instantly, his thoughts went to what it might feel like to run his hand up them. He realized he wasn't the only man who was thinking that way, either, as most of them stared openly at Jun, some eyes lingering on the hint of cleavage in her scoop-neck tank. Then he understood why there were so many men taking a Tai Chi class. He had no doubt she was good at what she did, but he also knew some of the men in this class probably didn't care about Tai Chi as much as ogling a hot teacher for forty-five minutes.

If Jun knew that was why she had so many men in her class, she didn't let on. Her smile was warm but not flirty as she, and everyone else in class, kicked off flip-flops. He did the same and sank his toes into the cool sand.

"I am so sorry we're getting a little bit of a late start," Jun said. "I had…uh…babysitting trouble today, so I really appreciate your patience."

Most of the class seemed fine, but the grumpy man in the black T-shirt let out a disgruntled sigh. Kai glared at him. "Kids," the man said to Kai with an eye roll as if Kai were in on the complaint.

Kai was about to say something, but Jun started the class and he didn't want to be caught talking. Jun led them in a warm-up. She was delicate and graceful. Kai noticed that the disgruntled man kept staring at Jun's body. That observation made Kai like him even less. After completing a series of stretches, she began the Tai Chi.

"We'll start with the motion called Hands on the Table," she said, putting her hands palm-down in the air in front of her. "And then we'll Calm the Water." She stepped out on her front foot, shifting her weight and pushing her hands, still palm-down, outward. Kai and the other students did the same. They went through the same motion on the other side. None of the moves were strenuous, and yet, doing them, Kai did feel a bit of a calm seep into the slow rhythm. Kai tried to keep his eye on Jun as they went through several more movements, including Moving the Water and Over the Drum. About fifteen minutes into the class, he saw that Po had abandoned his bucket and shovel and was mimicking every move his mother made, almost as if he wanted to do the class himself. The end result was an adorable, awkward preschooler's version of Tai Chi. In his little Spider-Man shirt, he was pretty darn cute.

A snicker or two went up from the class. The three women in the class, in particular, smiled warmly at the boy. Jun glanced anxiously over at Po, but seeing that he was really doing no harm trying the moves, she let it go. The grumbling man next to Kai, however, didn't like it.

"Can't concentrate with that *kid* interrupting," he groused. Kai was pretty sure what he meant was he couldn't concentrate on her ass with the kid nearby. He was willing to guess that the idea of her as a mom didn't factor into whatever perverted fantasy the jerk liked to concoct during class.

Kai shushed him, annoyed.

The man frowned in return but fell silent.

"We'll now move on to Ball in the Mountain.

Move those arms," Jun said. "Feel it building your Chi. This is a great exercise for making a stronger mind."

Po mimicked the same move, stretching his hands in a circular motion forward, but he over-exaggerated it and toppled over, like a puppy with oversize paws. Po, fine, bounced back up grinning, ready to start again.

"Honestly, if you can't control your kid…" the grumpy man said, very loudly this time as he shook his head in disapproval. He seemed to miss the fact that no one else in the class appeared to agree with him. A few shot him dirty looks. "I can't focus on these moves with him bouncing around like an idiot. Someone needs to teach that kid to be still!"

Kai wanted to teach the man how to be still and quiet. Jun heard his remarks, and her face turned beet red. She sent a worried glance at Po, but honestly, the boy wasn't doing any harm. The man was overreacting.

Jun transitioned the class into another pose, and this time Po decided to do his own headstand and rolled over in the sand.

Next to Kai, the irritated man bellowed, "If nobody is going to tell that kid to sit down, I'll do it."

Jun's head popped up in alarm. She was already on the move to intercept the angry man from getting to Po, but Kai was there first. He put a hand on the man's chest.

"Hey, the kid's not hurting anybody," Kai said, stopping the man's progress cold. Jun, who'd hurried to Po's side, stood still, a protective arm around her son.

"He's a distraction," the man growled, dark eyes flashing.

"*You're* a distraction," Kai corrected. "Why don't *you* quiet down?"

Murmurs and agreeing nods swept the class.

They were the focus of attention now, and Kai could feel everyone's gaze on them, even as some tried to continue the motions. Jun just stared, speechless.

The man, clearly not used to being called on his grumbling, glared at Kai. "I'm not going to be quiet. I'm going to get the goddamn class I paid for, a class *without* kids."

A few gasps went up from the class at the language.

Jun rushed, too late, to cover Po's little ears.

"Either quiet down or leave." Kai wasn't going to back down. He wasn't the kind of man who went looking for a fight, but he'd been pushed into plenty of corners by surfers defending turf on various beaches all over the world. Bullies were the same, no matter their age or nationality: you either stood up to them, or you let them walk over you.

And Kai had never backed down from a bully, not once in his life.

"I'm not going to have my afternoon ruined by some stupid fuckin' kid!" he roared, pointing at the little boy, whose bottom lip quivered as his eyes filled with tears threatening to spill.

"Hey!" Jun's voice was like steel, her eyes glinting fiercely. "You do *not* talk about *my* son that way." Despite her small frame, she'd stalked right up to the angry man, fearless. She was an angry mama bear, protecting her cub. "And *watch* your language!"

Instantly, the man seemed cowed. There was something in her voice that said she wasn't messing around. Kai admired her in that moment. *What a little firecracker.* Here he'd thought she'd needed rescuing, but he had a sneaking suspicion she could've handled this man all on her own.

"You have *two* choices, Mr. Hiram. You can stay in this class *and behave.* Or you can leave."

"I—I…" Mr. Hiram sputtered, temporarily taken aback by Jun. "But that stupid kid!"

"You've made your choice. Time for you to go," Jun said, and Kai tightened his grip on the man.

"You can't kick me out. I *paid* for this class!" the man sputtered.

Kai dug his wallet out of his back pocket and pulled out a hundred-dollar bill. He tucked the money in the man's shirt pocket.

"Consider it refunded."

"But..." If he was hoping for a reprieve from Jun, he wouldn't get one.

Jun just pointed her finger to the parking lot and gave Mr. Hiram a look that would melt a weaker man. "Let's go." Kai swept his hands forward.

Mr. Hiram looked as though he was going to dig in his heels.

"Stupid bitch," he muttered under his breath.

"*What* did you say?" Jun was livid now. So was Kai. She stepped over, as if she planned to do something about it, but Kai wasn't going to let that happen. He was filled with a protective kind of fury. "That's it." Kai grabbed the man's arm and with one quick move twisted it up behind his back.

"Ow," he cried. Kai steadily marched the man, arm still behind his back, up the beach and to the parking lot.

Once near the asphalt, Kai stopped. "You can go home either with *or without* a broken arm." He twisted the man's arm harder and Hiram squealed. "Which one is it going to be?"

"Without," he ground out.

Kai released him with a shove, and the man stumbled into the parking lot, holding his arm. Eyes full of fear, he glanced back at Kai. He scampered to his car, a rental, and got in. Kai watched while he backed up and drove away.

The class broke out in spontaneous applause as Kai made his way back to them. Apparently, he wasn't the only one who felt that the man needed to be shown out. Jun, her arm around a now-grinning Po, nodded once at him. Kai just shrugged—no big deal. And anyway, she'd had it covered even without his help. He had to admire her grit, especially for a woman so…seemingly delicate. But, he realized, there wasn't anything delicate about her.

"Thank you," she whispered to him as she squeezed his arm.

"It's nothing," he said. Po threw his tiny arms around Kai's legs, his silent hug saying more than Jun ever could.

"Come on, now, sweetie," she said, pulling Po back. "Time we finish the class." Po went back to his bucket and shovel, happily digging in the sand, and Jun moved to the front of the class.

"Well, I'm sorry for that, everyone," she said, addressing the others. "I guess Mr. Hiram kind of missed the point of using Tai Chi to calm his Chi."

A murmur of laughter rippled through the class.

"Okay, let's start again with Moving the Water," Jun said as she swept her arms forward as if pushing air.

FORTY MINUTES LATER, after a cooldown session, as the class dispersed, gathering their towels and bags and heading back to their cars, Jun saw that Kai had stuck around. He was kneeling next to Po, helping him add another turret to his sand castle. They had their heads together. Kai talked softly to the boy, the conversation not carrying over the wind. For a second, she just stood by, watching them. Kai showed him the trick to getting the wet sand out of the bucket without crumbling the top: three hard taps to the flat side of the bucket before gently lifting. Po listened and watched carefully and then repeated everything he'd just learned. Jun marveled at her son's attention. He rarely sat still long enough to learn tips from her, and yet here he was, soaking up Kai's every word.

Maybe Po could use another adult in his life, someone else to help him learn about the world. Someone other than his mother or aunt. Yet as soon as the thought entered her mind, defensively, she pushed it out.

No, they were just fine on their own. Her and Po against the world. Always had been. Always would be.

Kai wasn't someone you could depend on, she reasoned. Jun remembered the two tourists at his house and the empty beer bottles on his floor. *He might have done us a favor today, but he's not the fathering type.*

"Hey, Po, time to pack up, buddy," she said, interrupting the scene.

"Aw, Mom." Po looked up, disappointed. "Do I have to?"

"Yes, young man. You know the rule." She prayed he wouldn't test her on it. Not today. Not in front of Kai.

"When you say it's time to go, it's time to go." Po hung his head in defeat and shuffled his feet in the sand.

"Sandals on. Go on." Po reluctantly went to fetch his sandals, which he'd flung off earlier near a palm tree.

"He's a good kid," Kai said as the two watched him sit in the sand and put his shoes on.

"Yeah, he is." Jun knew that in her heart to be true. The biting just wasn't him at all. He really was a sweet kid, and he minded her so well, most of the time. "Listen, thanks for what you did. With Mr. Hiram. I don't know what made him go off like that…"

"Who knows? But it wasn't anything. Bullies are the same wherever they are." Kai smiled, and the air between them got suddenly heavy. Jun was aware of how close Kai was standing, his dark hair ruffled by the sea breeze, his deep eyes like a warm, familiar place that she'd visited before.

He flashed a dazzling smile and Jun felt her

heart shift just a little bit. She liked it when he smiled. She liked it a little too much.

Kai cleared his throat. "Your class was…really good." He sounded surprised, but Jun tried not to take that personally. A lot of people had misconceptions about Tai Chi, and few realized how relaxing it could be when you really put yourself into it. It could have the same centering effects of yoga, she thought, but without all the contortion.

"Listen, this may sound crazy, but I recently lost my personal trainer. I looked you up. You've got all kinds of classes at Island Fit. I know you know your way around weights and training, because I called the gym and checked up on you. How much would it take for you to come work for me…full-time?"

## CHAPTER FIVE

JUN STOOD FROZEN to the spot. Work for Kai Brady, *full-time*? She stared at his warm brown puppy-dog eyes and right at that moment she almost blurted out "Yes!" before her brain suddenly caught up to her mouth. She pressed her lips together. *Careful*, her brain said. *There's got to be a catch.*

Did she want to work for him for the job, or to be closer to that smooth, unlined face, those strong, kissable lips?

She needed to figure this out. She wasn't used to being recruited. Every job she'd ever had, every class she'd ever started, was her own doing, brought to life with blood, sweat and tears. Nobody ever handed her opportunity, ever. She was stunned, her mind trying to work through all the implications, even as her whole body reacted to the possibility. Working full-time for Kai Brady? All the hours they'd spend in close proximity… Her heart sped up a little.

"I used to pay my last trainer six figures to

clear her calendar for me. I'll offer the same thing for you."

Jun's knees felt weak. Six figures! She'd never made that kind of money in her life. It would double her salary. "But I..." With that, she could afford a nanny, she thought, and much more. Her head spun.

"I don't know..." Jun couldn't think. It was the promise of money, but it was also Kai, standing so close to her, the hem of his thin T-shirt fluttering in the beach breeze, giving a tantalizing glimpse of his flat tanned stomach and the muscled V just below his abs. She blinked, trying to regain her senses once more. But work for Kai Brady? She'd have to quit all her jobs, Island Fit and her private classes. That would mean counting entirely on the surfer, who might hire and fire at will. Jun remembered the scene at his house. *Could* she even train someone like that? And what if he got mad? He'd fire her, and she'd be completely out of work and completely out of luck. She didn't like relying on anyone, and if she took the job, she'd have to rely on Kai for...everything.

"Po doesn't have day care. And I wouldn't have time to find a nanny..." This would be the deal breaker, she thought. Then she wouldn't even have to think about accepting the job. Po would be her out.

"I know." Kai shrugged, indifferent.

"You *know*?"

"When we were building sand castles, Po told me that he can't go back. Because of the biting. But I've got someone who could watch him while we train. My aunt is really great with kids. She raised me, like a mom, and I know she'd be happy to stay with Po. I'd need to ask her, but I bet she'll say yes. He could be at the house while we train. You wouldn't be far from him."

Jun felt dizzy with possibilities. It seemed like a dream job in so many ways, except one: she really didn't know if she could do it. Could she whip Kai into shape?

"I don't know…"

Kai grabbed her hand. Electricity shot up her wrist. She glanced at his strong hand on hers.

"Don't say no. Just think about it, okay? Take two days."

Jun wanted to say no. So much about it seemed perfect, which was why a small part of her screamed, *It's too good to be true!*

And yet Jun found herself nodding.

"Okay, I'll think about it."

"What's to think about?" Jun's sister, Kiki, said, as she picked up her toddler daughter and held her on one hip. "He's offering day care and more money than you've ever made. *And* you've had a crush on him for a year."

"I have not." Jun crossed her arms and leaned back against her older sister's kitchen counter in her small house near Hilo, about an hour away from Jun's apartment. Her heart beat a little faster in her chest, making her wonder if she was telling the truth. "He saved Po's life. I've just been trying to figure out how to pay him back."

"Take the job, then," her sister said, shrugging as she stirred chicken stir-fry in an oversize wok on the stove. She took a sip of her iced tea. "What? Afraid you'll fall into bed with him before the first week is up?"

"Kiki!" Jun instinctively glanced at Po, worried he'd overheard, but he was out of earshot, busy playing awful music on his cousin's baby electronic keyboard, shaped like a smiling Cheshire cat, with the ivories as teeth. He was singing "Twinkle, Twinkle, Little Star" and pounding ruthlessly on the keys. His cousin, two-year-old Rose, squirmed to be let down, and so Kiki put her on the ground. She tottered around "helping" by dancing and shrieking in delight.

"Oh, come on. He can't hear us, and even if he did, he'd have no idea what we're talking about." Kiki tossed an oven mitt on her countertop. "Your problem is you've been in mommy mode *far* too long. You need to think about your whole self. You're a woman, too, not just a mommy."

"I'll have plenty of time to think of that later." Jun shook her head. "Like when Po is eighteen."

Kiki sputtered a derisive laugh. "You'll be shriveled up and dried out by then."

"Kiki!" Jun slapped her sister's arm.

"You know I'm right." Kiki bustled over to the refrigerator and pulled out ingredients for a salad. She handed the lettuce, tomatoes and carrots over to Jun, and immediately she knew it would be her turn to wash them, Kiki's to cut. She ran the lettuce under the sink and briskly shook it out.

It was no surprise Kiki worried about how much Jun was getting laid. Kiki had always been more into going out and having fun when they were younger. She'd been the rebel who butted heads with their tiger mom for years: getting a tattoo, coming home drunk, showing up with a new boyfriend every month. Jun had been the picture-perfect daughter with the impeccable grades and dreams of going to med school, and yet, irony of ironies, Jun's one drunken mistake ended with her pregnant at nineteen. And now Kiki was the one who'd gone to college, come out the other side a nurse and had a doting husband, the cozy house, the nice green lawn, while Jun had had to drop out of college and work odd jobs to support Po.

Jun still remembered her mother's face when she told her she was unmarried and pregnant at nineteen. Her mother had reared back and slapped her hard across the face. If she thought about it, the blow still stung. Her tiger mom, so angry, so completely rigid about her rules, hadn't even come to the hospital when Po was born. Jun felt her mother had abandoned her then, and when a sudden heart attack took her six months later, it was more like a formality.

"You need to stop living like a nun," Kiki said as Jun handed her freshly washed pieces of lettuce that she broke off by hand and tossed into a waiting teak bowl. "Po needs a father. All the research says that boys with single moms are at a disadvantage. You don't want Po to be a statistic, do you?"

The more Kiki had settled down into her white-picket-fence life, the more judgmental she'd gotten, a quality Jun liked less and less the older they both got.

"Po and I are doing just fine."

"Is that why he got kicked out of day care?"

"Kiki." Jun hated when her sister brought up her shortcomings, especially now, since she had so many and Kiki had so few.

Jun still couldn't believe Kiki used to listen to punk rock, wear black lipstick and stay out all night. Now she was the spitting image of their mother, down to the way she wore her hair in a short bob. One of these days, if Kiki pushed her too far, Jun might just point that out. "Come on. That's not fair."

"Po needs a father. He wouldn't be biting if he had a father."

"You don't know that." Jun exhaled a long, frustrated sigh. Her sister meant well, she knew that, but she just didn't understand. She wasn't a single mom, and she probably would never be one. It was easy for her to backseat-drive when she had a loving husband with a good job who spoiled her at every turn. Kiki didn't know what it felt like to be on her own, worrying about paying her bills or frantically finding last-minute child care. How could Jun realistically date when she had no one to watch Po? And even if she did, somehow she thought it was selfish to take time away from her boy chasing after a man who probably would only disappoint them later.

"Jun, I'm sorry. I just... I just hate to see you unhappy." Kiki paused, wiping her hands on a tea towel. "Kai Brady is rich, he's handsome and he sounds like he's into you."

"No." Jun shook her head furiously, thinking of yesterday when she had rung his bell and he didn't even remember her. Not to mention, she couldn't compete with the leggy blondes he seemed to prefer. "That's not why he wants to hire me."

"It's not?"

"I think it's for Po." Jun had it all figured out.

Kai seemed to like Po for some reason, like maybe he was one of those rich celebrities who every now and again decided to adopt a stray.

"Great! He's dad material, then."

Jun felt panic in her throat. A party-happy millionaire was *not* good dad material.

"No. You don't get it. I don't think he's got it in him to commit to Po...or anything. Surfing is his life, *extreme* surfing at that, and even that's something he puts aside to party. Besides, if I take this job, I'll have to quit my others, and what if he fires me after one month? *Then* what?"

"Then you and Po come live with us. We just finished the guest room."

"Kiki..."

"I mean it. Opportunities like this don't come along any old time, Jun. You've got to take them when you can."

Jun sighed as she washed the tomatoes beneath the tap. "Even if I take the job, I'm not sure I can train him. He doesn't want to be trained."

"Is *that* what the hesitation is about? You know what Mom always said about training people." Kiki began slicing the tomatoes Jun had placed on her cutting board.

Jun smiled at the memory of their no-nonsense, sugar-coat-nothing mother. "'In a contest of wills, the laziest one loses.'"

"See? All you have to do is work harder than

he does, which doesn't sound like it would be too difficult. Why don't you channel Mom and see if you can't whip that surfer into shape?"

Jun imagined what her mother might do to Kai if she'd been assigned the job of getting him in shape for a surf competition. She'd crush him in one week flat.

"You did it before when you worked at CrossFit two years ago. Didn't they have a name for you there?" Kiki asked.

"The Terminator," Jun said, and laughed a little. She had been a tough trainer then. It had been one of her first classes, and she'd maybe overcompensated for nerves by being extra tough on everyone. But the nickname had stuck until she'd transferred over to Island Fit and discovered Tai Chi, yoga and a more Zen approach to fitness.

"See? You've already got this in the bag. Plus, *I* know you have a thing for surfers. What was his name? John?"

"James." Jun thought about the year in high school she'd spent following around James McAlister, the towheaded surfer whom she'd had a crush on. Nothing had ever happened. James never even knew she existed, really, but she *had* learned how to surf. Still, she wasn't anywhere near Kai's caliber.

"I don't have a thing for surfers." Jun saw Kai's

inviting dark eyes once more in her mind's eye. Or did she?

"Okay, then, well, you owe Kai a debt. You know how Mom felt about debt."

The woman had paid cash for everything and had never owned a single credit card. If a neighbor brought her a basket of fruit, she'd somehow turn it into a full meal, which she'd return the following day. Jun knew herself well enough to know that her staunch independence came directly from her mother. She knew she couldn't turn Kai down. She owed him.

So why did working for him fill her with dread? Why did repaying a debt feel as though somehow she would just be asking for more? Because she had a sinking feeling that Kai was so far into self-destruct mode that she might not be able to help him. What if she tried and failed?

"It's not how I wanted to repay the debt," Jun said. "Besides, how is it being repaid if he's paying me to do it?"

"You want to take the job for free, that's your business, but he's asking you for help. You know you can't turn him down."

Jun knew her sister spoke the truth. Yet, as she thought about his devilishly charming smile and the way his dark eyes suggested he knew just how much he got under her skin, she really wished she could.

"He told me to think about it for two days."

"So?"

"So I'm going to take two days to think about it."

# CHAPTER SIX

KAI SAT OUTSIDE Island Fit in his open-top Jeep, the warm tropical sun beaming down on his wavy dark hair. His golden-brown skin didn't need more of a tan, but it was a crime to put the fabric top up and shut out the beautiful Hawaiian weather.

It had been two days and change since the Tai Chi lesson on the beach, when he'd offered Jun a job. He'd not heard a word from her. He had to admit, he'd expected a call that same day. The fact that she hadn't jumped on the opportunity made him wonder if he was losing his charm. Women rarely told him no. Hell, he hadn't even found a woman who'd told him *maybe* in a very long time. He'd been the recipient of so many enthusiastic yeses, so many women who threw themselves at him, that he'd forgotten what it was like to actually chase someone.

Personally or professionally.

Not many people on the Big Island had the kind of money he did, and those who didn't succumb to his smile usually rolled over when he opened up his checkbook.

Jun, clearly, was different. But why? He wanted to find out.

It had been a while since he'd cared enough about a woman to get out of bed before noon. Here it was, eight in the morning, and he was sitting outside the gym, watching Jun move about inside. He didn't know what it was about her. Maybe the grounded confidence she wore easily, like a second skin?

He might have saved her from a rude client on the beach, but part of him thought she would've handled it just fine on her own. He'd never met someone so completely independent, someone who had herself together the way she did. He used to be like her, before the tsunami. He remembered feeling as if he could tackle any challenge, surf any wave, no matter how big. But now he wasn't sure he could even get out of the bed in the morning. He wanted a little bit of Jun's certainty, a little of her glue to hold himself together.

That was why she had to work for him.

It had nothing to do with the fact that she was 100 percent alluring: athletic and gorgeous yet delicate all at the same time. She was like a hormone cocktail that made his head buzz.

Even now he shifted in the front seat of his car, his groin growing taut as he watched her march across the gym in black spandex capris that hugged her fit curves, her gleaming black ponytail bouncing as she went. His body's response surprised him. It wasn't as if he lacked for sex, but to be so struck by a single mom? He believed in the power of family, of *'ohana*, as his aunt called it. But when it came to having one of his own, he always thought he would someday, but that always seemed *far away*, years down the road, when his surfing career was long done. He'd never been one to seriously consider dating a single mom, and he'd never once found one as sexy as he found Jun.

*But this is professional, not personal*, he reminded himself. He needed a trainer. She needed to earn more than what *this* place could no doubt provide. Island Fit might be a nice gym, but it was small and probably relied heavily on tourists streaming in from the big hotel resort next door.

He swung open his Jeep door and stepped out into the temperate tropical breeze rolling in off the ocean, ready to go see why Jun hadn't already accepted his offer, and he wasn't going to leave until he got the answer he wanted. He flipped his expensive shades to the top of his head as he pulled open the glass door.

He saw Jun first, standing near the front desk, and then noticed she was being crowded by a stout, muscled man who seemed to be trying to find a reason to keep his hand on her lower back. Instantly, jealousy blazed up in his chest. Surprised by the possessiveness he felt, he pushed the territorial feelings down. He had no hold on her. Yet.

"Kai," Jun blurted, surprise flickering across her face. The man next to her, he noticed, didn't pull away but moved closer to her side, eyes narrowing as he looked warily in Kai's direction. Jun tried to delicately untangle herself from the man's iron grip on her as she made introductions. "Um, Tim, this is Kai Brady. Kai, this is *my boss*, Tim Reese."

Tim released her, but not fast enough for Kai's taste. *This* guy was her boss? He had sexual-harassment lawsuit written all over him.

"Kai, I've heard of you, man. You've got that baggy line of board shorts everyone's wearing." Tim sent him a guarded smile, showing that the compliment was intended to be anything but. He held out a hand and Kai shook it. He noticed Tim's grip was harder than it should be, and Kai realized the man saw him as competition. If it was a pissing contest he wanted, Kai already knew he'd win.

"Yeah, we just hit the three-million mark for numbers sold but projections are to double that by next year. Even mainland kids are wearing them." That figure shut up Tim in a hurry, and Kai had known it would. He hated talking money, but some guys wouldn't back down until it was in their face.

"Kai, what are you doing here?" Jun looked stricken, almost panicky.

"You forgot already? You promised me a work-out session." The lie came easily.

"I did?" Jun's face went blank.

"You did." Kai nodded back to the half-empty gym.

Tim still stood a little too close to Jun, but Kai could see the wheels moving in his head. A three-time surf champion at Island Fit would bring in more customers. He could see Tim struggling with what he wanted more: Jun or the business. If Kai had had to make the same call, he wouldn't have hesitated.

"I double booked, then. I've got another client in ten minutes." Jun glanced down at the computer monitor in front of her.

"I'll take it, Jun," Tim said, and rubbed her arm for good measure. Kai wanted to slap the meat-head's hand away, especially when he saw Jun smile at him in relief.

"Thanks, Tim."

"No problem. You go help Kai." He rubbed her back again and it took all of Kai's energy not to leap over the small counter and grab the dude by his muscle shirt. Jun moved away from him and Kai followed her to the far corner of the gym.

"You didn't ask for a session," Jun said when they were far enough away from Tim not to be overheard.

"I asked for *all* your sessions," Kai corrected, and Jun nearly lost her footing on the rubber-matted floor near the weights. Kai's arm shot out to steady her. "You okay?"

"Fine." Jun held his arm for a second and then let it go as though it were a white-hot poker. Kai could feel Tim glaring at them from the desk.

"It's been two days. I was expecting your call."

"I…" Jun looked fully flustered now. "I was just taking the time to think about it."

"What's to think about?" Kai really wanted to know. He was offering her free child care and six figures. Did she want stock options in his clothing company?

"Let's start out with some free weights and some squats," Jun said, trying to direct his attention to the weight stand. "Good for building those surfing muscles."

"I'm serious, Jun. What will it take to convince you to say yes? I want to make this happen." He needed her confidence, her no-nonsense "you can fix that" attitude. Plus, he'd like to have Po around. The kid made him smile. Made him think about something other than his knee. That was a good thing. "Where's Po?"

"My sister is watching him today."

"Can your sister watch him every day?"

"No," Jun admitted. Kai grabbed thirty-pound weights for each hand. "You can do more than that!" She made him switch for fifty-pound weights. "Now, we're going to do lunges first. Like this." She took one huge step forward, showing him the form. He'd done free-weight lunges often and knew what she wanted. He started in on the first rep, using his good knee to take the weight first.

"Come work for me."

"But...Tim has been good to me," Jun said. Kai flinched as he heard the affection in her voice. Did she have a thing for that guy? He certainly had one for her, based on the way he stared at them, as if he was prepared to run on over if Kai so much as breathed on her.

Sweat popped up on his forehead. It had been a while since he'd worked so hard.

"Tim has a thing for you, you know." Kai watched Jun carefully to gauge her reaction. She winced a little, an uncomfortable squirm, much to his relief.

"Is it that obvious?" Jun glanced back at Tim.

"You see how he's staring daggers at me right now? He's pissed off I interrupted his back-rubbing session."

"His what?" Jun looked bewildered.

"He touches you. A lot. Borderline sexual harassment if he's your boss." *Not that I haven't fantasized about doing the same thing.* Of course, the difference was he'd wait until she wanted him to do it. That was what separated him from Tim.

"He's not that bad." Jun tried to shrug it off. Maybe she liked that Tim put his hands on her at every available opportunity. That thought irked him.

"Come work for me. Get away from Handsy McHands." Kai grunted a little as he worked to finish one set of lunges on his good knee.

Jun laughed. "Time to switch legs," she said.

Kai strained slightly as he switched over to his weaker knee. Surprisingly, the knee held.

"What guarantee do I have that you won't hire me one week and fire me the next?" she asked him as she watched his form. "Remember, don't extend the knee over your foot. Keep it aligned." She kneeled down to touch his knee to show him what she meant. Her touch was cool and electric all at the same time. He wasn't going to be able to balance at all if she kept touching him like that.

"We can sign a contract. It'll say you're entitled to six months' severance, even if I fire you after day one." His breath came quicker. Working the weak knee took more concentration and a lot more effort.

Jun froze, staring at him, her mouth slightly open. "Are you serious?"

"Look in my shirt pocket."

Jun reached into his open pocket and pulled out a folded piece of paper. She unfolded it and saw it was a contract just like the one he'd described.

"I told you I'd do what it takes for you to come work for me."

Jun considered this, biting her lower lip. "I don't know."

What was it going to take to get this girl to say yes? Kai grunted as he did three more lunges, the weights growing heavier in his hands, the strain on his bad knee building.

Sweat trickled down Kai's temple. The muscles in his legs burned. His weak knee felt as if it could buckle at any moment. He badly wanted a break.

"We can stop now, right?" Kai was only partly joking.

"Three more." Jun nodded at him to keep going. He wasn't sure he could. Then, after the very next lunge, his knee gave out, wobbling unsteadily beneath him.

"Watch out..." he grumbled, and in a panic, he dropped the fifty-pound weight, nearly sending it crashing into the free-weight stand as it bounced to the ground. Thankfully, Jun was nowhere near it, nor was anyone else, and Kai managed to regain his balance by steadying himself against Jun, who was suddenly right beside him, holding him up with an arm around his waist.

"You okay?" Jun breathed, eyes wide with fear as she looked down at his bum knee. The muscles on that leg looked fine to the naked eye, but Kai was convinced they were still smaller than those of his other leg. Nobody saw it—not Gretchen or his doctors—but when Kai looked at his knee, he still saw the pale shriveled leg they'd pulled out of the cast ten months back.

"The knee isn't...healed?" The fact that Jun seemed to be able to see right through him, right to the heart of his whole problem, made him feel naked suddenly, and vulnerable. Too vulnerable.

"I'm fine," he said, shaking it off. Shaking *her* off, and stepping away from her touch. "It's no big deal."

But he suspected Jun knew he was lying. He could tell from the way she stared at him, the skepticism evident in her dark eyes, her lids blinking away the judgment. He wouldn't be able to bluff his way through training with her. Yet the thought of admitting the depth of his problem, of the ways his body was failing him, made him panic. Saying his body was weak out loud just made it more real than he wanted it to be.

"I'm fine," he said again, this time not looking her in the eye. He didn't want to see the flash of pity there.

"Everything all right over here?" Tim appeared then between them, an unwanted intrusion.

"Just slipped out of my hand," Kai lied. "Not her fault."

Tim glanced at Jun and then back at Kai. "Maybe that's enough for today?" Tim didn't bother to disguise his animosity toward Kai, which didn't bother him a bit. They both wanted the same woman. No sense in trying to dance around it.

"Kai, need some water?" Jun asked, nodding toward a dispenser in the corner.

"I'll get it," Tim offered, eager to do what he could to speed Kai's exit from his gym, no doubt.

Once he was out of earshot, Kai looked at Jun. "I guess you can tell training me won't be easy." Kai couldn't help sounding defeated. His knee had failed him again, and this time in front of Jun. He was a lost cause and he knew it. But he wasn't ready to throw in the towel. Not yet. Not when Jun could help him.

"But...tell me, which way are you leaning?"

Jun studied him a second, and Kai felt for sure she'd tell him a flat no. Her face told him that was *exactly* where she was leaning. He couldn't let that happen. He felt suddenly seized with panic. If she didn't help him, who would?

Kai had an idea in that moment, one that he might regret, but she was going to turn him down, so what did it matter anyway?

"Wait," he interrupted, hoping his Hail Mary

would work. "Before you turn me down, come to dinner."

Her eyes widened in surprise and then narrowed in suspicion. "Excuse me?" Clearly, she thought he was asking her out on a date.

"Not just with me. With my sister, my aunt. My friends Dallas and Allie. You remember them?"

Jun slowly nodded. Dallas and Allie had pulled Po and Kai out of the floodwaters and to safety on their kayak. Without them, Kai knew he could've died out there. They were also the ones who'd found Jun and reunited her with Po.

"They're having a dinner tonight at the Kona Estate. Why don't you come? Bring Po."

"I wasn't invited," Jun began, unsure. Kai noticed she was still a little distrustful, as if she suspected it was some kind of trap. And, really, it was. Kai knew she might be able to tell him no, but Aunt Kaimana would be another story. She loved kids, and he knew that once she saw Po, it would be love at first sight. She'd practically insist on taking on the babysitting.

"They always cook more than we can eat. Dallas is barbecuing, which means he can't stop unless he's seared the whole cow. I'm serious. Besides, Aunt Kaimana knows me better than anyone. If after you talk to her, you still want to tell me no, then I'll leave you alone."

"One dinner tonight with them and then if I say no, you won't show up at my work? Stalk me?"

"I wasn't stalking you," Kai said.

Jun stared at him, dubious.

"Okay, so I was. I admit it. But come tonight and if you don't want the job after that, then I'll leave you alone. I promise."

Jun mulled this over. "Okay," she said. "I'll come."

"I can pick you both up at six."

"No," Jun said quickly. "I'll meet you there."

Kai decided not to press the issue. She'd agreed to come. He'd have to be satisfied with that.

## CHAPTER SEVEN

THAT EVENING AS Jun made her way to the Kona Estate, she griped her steering wheel and thought, once again, about turning around and going home. She glanced in the rearview and saw Po happily kicking his feet out from his booster seat, staring out the window and clutching his favorite Spider-Man figure in his tiny fist. She felt nervous about meeting Kai's family—his aunt and sister. She already felt an unnatural pull to the man. Maybe meeting his sister and aunt would show just how hopeless he was. If they were in any way rude, she vowed to leave. Plus, he'd offered his aunt as a babysitter while they worked. If she found fault with the aunt—say, if the woman was mean to Po—then it would be easy to tell Kai no and walk away. Maybe the dinner would give her the excuse she needed to bow out of the job offer.

Dallas and Allie, of course, were another story. She remembered them from the emergency room last year, when they'd looked after Po and helped find her. Jun had liked them immediately, but then, she would've loved anyone who delivered her son safely to her. She still remembered how Po's hands had been sticky from mango candy that Allie had fed him. Under different circumstances, she would've been disapproving of the sugar, but right then she was just so happy Allie had shown her boy kindness in a difficult time that she didn't care. She knew Dallas and Allie were good people: they'd risked their lives going out in the flooding to find Kai. And by doing so, they'd found Po, too. She'd seen the couple around the island since and always said hello, but this would be the first time she'd been to their house.

She glanced at the seat next to her and the bag with her hostess gift tucked inside: another home-made candle and some macadamia-nut cookies she'd baked herself. At least she'd get a chance to tell Dallas and Allie thank-you once more.

She saw a sign for the Kona Coffee Estate and drove up the long gravel drive, lined on each side by lush coffee trees bursting with brightly colored cherries. It was hard work running a coffee plantation but Dallas and Allie seemed made for it. Jun knew they'd won award after award in the past year for their Kona brew. Through her open window, she smelled the smoky goodness of barbecue being roasted from somewhere nearby.

As Jun looked for a place to park, she saw

brake lights flash on a new Jeep and then Kai stepped out.

Her heart thudded as she watched him move, wearing easy khaki shorts, a button-down and flip-flops. She tried not to stare at the muscles in his chiseled forearms. If she thought he looked good shirtless, he was somehow even sexier in clothes. He wore his thick dark hair in waves back from his forehead, and she itched to run her hands through it.

"Kai!" Po shouted out the open window.

Kai turned and spotted the boy, and his face split into a wide grin. Jun was barely out of the car before Po had wiggled out of his seat belt and gotten the door open. He was getting *too* independent, she thought as he bounded up to Kai. The surfer swept the boy up in the air, and he squealed in delight. Jun felt warmth in her stomach that she quickly pushed aside. She didn't like Po getting attached to people who weren't going to stick around.

Kai gently put Po down on the ground and then looked at Jun. "Glad you came."

"Again!" Po cried, holding up his hands and asking to be picked up.

"Po," Jun warned her boy, putting a hand on his shoulder. As they stood near the front porch of the farmhouse, the door slapped open and Dallas came out, a big grin on his face.

"Good to see you, man," Dallas said, shaking Kai's hand. His Texan drawl gave away that he wasn't born on the Big Island, which Jun knew already.

"Jun, welcome," Dallas said, holding out a hand, which she took. "And there's the little guy. High five, Po?" Dallas offered a hand that Po gladly slapped.

"Hi, everyone!" cried Allie, coming out on the porch and throwing her arms wide to give Kai a hug. Jun felt a little surge of something that felt a bit like jealousy. Until she saw the bright diamond on Allie's left hand.

"Did you and Dallas get engaged?" Jun asked.

"Yes," Allie said, beaming, and then added, "So nice of you to come!"

"Thank you for having us. This is for you." Jun handed her the gift bag, and Allie surprised her by taking it and then wrapping her in a warm hug. She already felt as though she were part of a little family. It had been just her and her sister and Po for so long, she'd kind of forgotten what that was like. "We did. Dallas even managed a romantic proposal."

Dallas rolled his eyes. "The things men do for love."

"I still can't believe you're going through with it," Kai declared. "You? Settle down? The stars must be out of alignment."

"You should try it," Allie said as Dallas slipped an arm around her small waist. "You might like it." Allie turned her attention to Po as she knelt down by him. "Po! Is that you? I hardly recognized you, you've grown so much!"

Po stood a little taller, proud to be bigger. "I'm four!" he declared.

"I see that," Allie said. "I've got something that I think you'll like. Do you think your mom will let you have one of these before dinner?" She reached into her pocket and drew out a small wrapped piece of mango candy.

Jun thought about saying no. But one little piece wouldn't kill him. And she was touched Allie remembered it was Po's favorite. "Okay, but tell Miss Allie thank-you."

"Thank you!" Po almost shouted as he grabbed the candy and immediately began tearing into the wrapper.

"Is that Kai? He owes me twenty bucks." A petite brunette walked out of the house then.

"Hey, sis," Kai said, and pulled the woman into a hug. Jesse, Jun assumed. She didn't know what she'd been imagining, but this no-holds barred woman wasn't it. Somehow Jun liked her instantly.

Jesse pulled back from her brother and smiled. "*You* said the customers at Hula Coffee would hate the new coconut latte, but they *love it*, so pay up. It's becoming the most popular drink on the menu." Jesse held out her palm and Kai reluctantly dug out his wallet, pulled out a twenty and slapped it on her hand.

"Okay, okay, fine. You win."

Jesse glanced over at Jun. "Where are my manners! I'm Jesse, Kai's sister. *You* must be Jun. I've heard so much about you." Jesse held out her hand and Jun shook it. Kai had talked about her? But he hardly knew her. "And Po! I heard you like Spider-Man."

The boy, mouth full of sticky candy, nodded and mumbled, "Mrghf!"

"I think he's saying that's his favorite," Jun translated, and the others laughed.

An older woman wearing a pink muumuu over her ample frame poked her head out of the front door, her silver-streaked black hair up in a large bun. "I hear a big racket out here!"

The others laughed and then Kai turned to introduce Jun and Po.

"This is Aunt Kaimana," he said, and it was then Jun remembered Kaimana from the day at the hospital when she'd visited Kai. She did have a distant memory of meeting this woman, a warm grandmotherly presence, who had been visiting the same day. Now that Jun got a good look at her, she could see some family resemblance. Kai's aunt had the same warm brown eyes, with just a hint of mischief in them, as if she were sitting on a very good joke.

"Oh, yes, Ms. Mahi…"

"Ms. Mahi'ai, but you can call me Kaimana. Everyone does."

"Kaimana," Jun said, and it felt right.

"Kai! When will you fix my cabinet hinge? My doors are falling off!" Kaimana teased Kai, who shrugged.

"Tomorrow, okay? I'll do it tomorrow!"

"*This* must be Po," Kaimana continued, ignored her nephew's promise. She knelt down so she was almost eye to eye with Po, who blinked at the older woman.

Kaimana studied the boy for a beat.

"Po, you look hungry," Kaimana said. "Why not come in and eat some *real* food!"

"I'm *starving*!" Po managed after swallowing his candy. Jun liked how Kaimana warmed to the boy at once, and how Po responded in kind. Her gut told her Kaimana would be a great babysitter. *One hurdle down.* She wasn't sure if she felt disappointed or glad.

"Why is Auntie acting like this is her house?" Kai asked Allie, who shrugged.

"You know better than I do that woman does exactly what she wants *when* she wants." They shared a grin.

"Why do you say that?" Jun asked, curious.

"She's known to speak Hawaiian and pretend not to know English if she doesn't like what's being said," Allie said. "She did that to me when I first moved back to the island and wanted to sell my share of the coffee plantation."

"She did?"

"She's done worse. But it's because she always knows best," Kai said and winked at Jun.

Jun tried to fight off his charm but was failing miserably. She found instead of making her like him less, meeting his family made her like him more. *He's a playboy who doesn't take anything seriously.* But looking at his warm brown eyes, she had a hard time believing it.

"Come in!" Aunt Kaimana prodded the group again. "Dallas, you have work to do on that grill!"

"Yes, ma'am," Dallas drawled, standing at attention.

Dallas, Allie and Po went inside, and Jun followed them. Kaimana stopped Kai right behind her at the door. Jun didn't mean to eavesdrop, but as she'd just turned the corner, she wasn't out of earshot and overheard their conversation.

"When you going to quit this crazy surfing? *He'e nalu!*"

"Auntie…" Kai breathed a long sigh.

"Thought you were going to retire!"

"I'm not ready yet. I'm going to do it whether

or not Jun helps me, and if she helps me, then I have a better chance of not drowning."

Kaimana made a disapproving sound in her throat. "You stubborn. Too stubborn."

"That's why you love me."

Jun heard Kaimana chuckle and shuffled away from her eavesdropping point, feeling even more that she ought to take the job, despite her reservations. If she could help him, shouldn't she try?

"Can I get you a drink?" Allie asked, swinging by, holding a pitcher of sangria.

Just then Dallas slid his arms around his fiancée's waist, giving her a hug from behind that made her squeal.

"Dallas McCormick! You're going to make me spill." Dallas lay a light kiss on her shoulder, her aqua-blue sleeveless sundress showing off her collarbone. He shrugged, unconcerned. The easy way those two moved together made Jun think they were made for one another. She felt a pang suddenly. She'd like to have that.

Only it wasn't going to happen. Not while she had Po to think about. He was more important.

"Jun? A drink?" Allie held up the pitcher.

"Oh, no, thank you." Jun wasn't going to drink, not when she had to drive Po home. She watched her little boy as he trailed Dallas to the barbecue out back, where he was shown the fine art of flipping a steak.

Jun saw Jesse at the kitchen counter slicing mangos. "Can I help?" she asked, walking to her.

"Oh, no, I'm fine, but I'd love the company. So, Kai thinks you can help him. He says you've got a way to rehabilitate the knee."

"I don't know about that. I *think* I can help him, but I'm just a little uncomfortable with…"

"Working for an egomaniac who parties all the time and thinks he's always right?"

Jun gaped, but Jesse laughed and then Jun felt safe laughing, too. "I guess so!"

"He's my brother, and I love him, but he's a mess." Jesse swept sliced mangos into a big bowl and then wiped her hands on a nearby tea towel. "He's also bossy, so don't let him boss you around too much. If you don't want the job, you don't have to take it, even if he bugs you to death."

"He said if I came to dinner and *still* didn't want the job, he'd leave me alone."

Jesse quirked an eyebrow. "And you believed him?"

Jun laughed. "No, I guess I didn't."

"Are you two talking about me?" Kai asked, popping over and stepping between them. "Jun, don't believe anything this girl says. She's still holding a grudge about the time I borrowed her bike."

Jesse added some more fruit to the bowl and then grabbed a spoon to stir it in. "*Crashed* it, you mean! I don't know how you bent the front wheel, but you did!"

"I didn't..." Kai protested.

"Oh, you did, all right," Allie said, leaning into the kitchen from the dining room. "I remember that. Bent the front fender and everything."

"See?" Jesse said, triumphant as she waved the wooden spoon in Kai's face. "You definitely don't want to work for this man."

"Jesse! You're not helping!" Kai threw his arms up in mock frustration. "You're supposed to convince her to take the job."

"Run! Get out while you still can!" Jesse stage-whispered, which made Jun laugh. She found herself liking everyone, and who wouldn't? The warmth and love seemed evident everywhere she turned. She remembered her own strict upbringing, her mother's perpetually sour face and an overwhelming feeling that she was always doing something wrong. This house was full of joy and laughter, and she liked it. Maybe a little too much.

"Steaks are ready!" Dallas called as he brought in a plateful of seared monsters. "I hope you're hungry," he told Jun, who couldn't help but stare at the two-inch-thick steaks. Kai had been right: he'd made too many. Yet they smelled delicious.

Soon enough they were all seated around a big farmhouse table, happily eating and chatting. The lively buzz of conversation and good food warmed

Jun, made her feel as if she belonged. Even Po cheerfully gobbled up some of his fruit and vegetables, which normally required a nightly fight. She nodded at him and he grinned back, mouth full of mango.

"So, Jun, are you single?" Kaimana asked out of the blue, causing conversation to screech to a halt.

"Auntie!" Jesse exclaimed.

"You don't have to answer that," Kai said.

"Uh…" Jun glanced at Po, worried about having to explain what *single* meant, but the little boy didn't seem to notice the conversation at all. If it wasn't about Spider-Man, he wasn't interested. "Yes, I am."

"Auntie," Kai groaned. "You know if these were interview questions, you could be sued for harassment."

Auntie waved her hand as if she didn't care. "I am just getting to know her! Woman-to-woman."

"And the whole dinner table," Kai pointed out. Jun laughed.

"Okay, so you want to talk about your personal life, then?" Kaimana challenged.

Jun was relieved to have the spotlight off her but also dreaded what a talk about Kai's personal life might dredge up. She worriedly glanced at Po again. She didn't think he needed to find out the meaning of *random hookup* just yet.

"What personal life?" Jesse said. "All the women

he dates put it on Instagram." Jun got the reference immediately. She guessed she wasn't the only one who saw Kai with women.

Kai suddenly flushed. "Did you see...?"

"The hot-tub picture?" Allie said, and Jesse laughed.

"Everyone's seen that," Jesse added. Jun didn't know where to look. "Right, Jun?"

"Well..." Jun felt uncomfortable.

Kai turned to Jun, most likely, she thought, remembering how she'd *seen* those two women at his house. Now he blushed fiercely, which somehow made Jun like him more. He was actually embarrassed. This, she had not expected. Why would an unapologetic player be...uncomfortable about his exploits?

"Nice work, man," Dallas said, and clapped his friend on the shoulder.

"Hey! You *better* not think that's nice work," Allie said, waving a fork threateningly in Dallas's direction. Dallas put his hands up in surrender.

"I was being sarcastic," Dallas protested.

Jesse fixed Kai with a look. "You've really been the talk of the island lately. That picture is only the least of it, from what I heard."

The Big Island was the biggest in Hawaii's chain, yet gossip still traveled faster than lightning. Among the locals, secrets were never safe.

"You've officially surpassed my record for

Island's Biggest Tourist Magnet," Dallas said. "Congratulations."

"If you don't watch it, you're going to end up as a stop on a bus tour," Allie teased.

"I'm not that bad," Kai protested.

Jun had the good sense to stay absolutely silent and become suddenly fascinated with the food on her plate. Po, who'd finished his dinner, began fidgeting on his chair. He wasn't going to last long before needing to move around. The boy was an endless ball of energy. Jun was already wondering if she'd need to plan a quick escape before he started running circles around the table. She might, especially if this discussion got graphic.

"Po? Do you like bubbles?" Kaimana asked the little boy. "I've got a new bottle I want to try out. Want to help me?" Then Kaimana pulled a full bottle of Spider-Man bubbles from her pocket. "Do you like Spider-Man?"

"Spider-Man!" Po blurted in excitement. He clapped his hands in joy and then turned to Jun for permission. She nodded and he took the bubbles, then gleefully clomped out to the backyard to open them.

"Thank you, Kaimana," Jun said, grateful for the distraction and the discretion. Jun stood to take her plate to the kitchen and then followed Kaimana out back, watching her help the boy un-

wrap the bubbles. She was good with kids. Kai
had been right about that.

Now more than ever, she felt as if she should
take the job. More money. A great babysitter. Why
was she even hesitating?

"Hey." Kai stood beside her at the porch door,
his muscled tall frame all coiled energy. *That* was
why. She felt his magnetic pull even now and had
to fight the urge to wrap her arms around his
neck and beg to be kissed. She could almost feel
the thought moving through her brain, warm and
tempting.

"Uh, hi." Jun straightened up, as if he could
read her mind, and tried to shake off the attraction she felt.

"So, sorry about…well, dinner."

"Sorry?" Jun was shocked. "Why?"

"Aunt Kaimana asking you…about…" Kai
shifted uncomfortably. "She doesn't have an edit
button."

"No need to apologize," Jun said and meant it.
"I like her—and your sister. And Dallas and Allie.
Dinner was really nice."

"It was?" Kai seemed genuinely surprised.
"Well…uh, good."

Jun glanced up at Kai's face and instantly realized that was a mistake. His eyes studied her
intently, and the draw she felt to him intensified.
He was handsome, yes, but beyond that, there was

something to him, something about the way he looked at her. *Maybe that's how he looks at every woman he meets*... Yet she couldn't look away. No matter how hard she tried.

"Jun," Kai said, voice low and serious.

His eyes were just so...intense. Jun couldn't look away from them. Was he coming closer? She thought he might be. Her heart sped up a bit. "Mmm-hmm?"

"This might seem...forward."

Nothing could seem too forward at this moment. Jun was already halfway to make-out mode. "What?"

All she could feel was the electric energy snapping between them. She half hoped he'd pull her into his arms and kiss the life out of her.

"Have you thought more about taking the job?"

Job? It took a second for Jun to recalibrate from the teen-make-out-party thoughts jumbled together in her brain.

The job! She felt suddenly dumb. Of course. The whole reason why she was here in the first place.

That was not where Jun had thought he was going. Not at all. Still, she felt off balance and a little winded, and she wondered why she couldn't at that moment come up with a single good reason not to say yes.

"Are you serious about this?" Jun asked, voice coming out slightly hoarse.

"More serious than anything," Kai said, taking one step closer, causing her brain to freeze. She was close enough now to feel his body heat, warm and inviting.

"Okay, I'll do it," Jun said, worrying as soon as the words were out of her mouth that she'd regret it. But the sheer joy on Kai's face banished the doubt.

"You will?"

"On one condition—I make the rules. You break the rules, I'm outta there," she said, trying to set some boundaries to regain some measure of control. Her heart, beating madly in her chest, told her she'd already lost the battle. At least where her hormones were concerned.

"Of course. You make the rules." His mouth curved up in a teasing smile, and she questioned whether he was capable of following any rules, ever.

"The first rule is, Po doesn't come with me on the first day."

"Why not? He loves Aunt Kaimana."

Jun looked over at her boy playing with Kai's aunt. "Yes, he does, but the first day, I…" *I want to be alone with you.* The thought popped into her head like a searing-hot admission of guilt. Was that what she wanted?

"I...don't want any distractions."

Kai raised a quizzical eyebrow. "Okay."

"You'll be ready at eight Saturday morning?"

Kai gave her a knowing smile. "Oh, I'll be ready. Will you?"

Jun's stomach lurched as she wondered if she'd just made the best—or worst—decision of her life.

# CHAPTER EIGHT

JUN ARRIVED AT Kai's beach house promptly at seven fifty Saturday morning, dressed in her best red-and-black-striped trainer's outfit and matching running shoes, prepared for the worst. She'd left Po in her sister's capable hands for yet another day. Her stomach felt alive with butterflies. Why hadn't she insisted Po come with her that first day? Was it that she wanted Kai all to herself? Alone, at his beach house?

Was she going to cross a line already?

Her phone buzzed in her hand with an incoming text message from Tim.

Wish you'd reconsider working for that guy, he'd written.

He'd nearly gone through the roof when she'd told him about Kai's job offer and her intent to take it. She didn't blame him, as it left him one trainer short on not much notice, but it was more than professional annoyance at the root of his anger.

But she actually felt relief that she could leave. It was getting harder to ignore Tim's advances and she dreaded having to tell him she just didn't think of him that way.

"You can take a leave of absence without pay," he'd said. "But when it doesn't work out, you come back, okay?" The look of hope on his face had made her chest feel pinched. His crush just made her uncomfortable. Still, she hoped maybe she'd dodged a bullet. If Kai's job worked out, she never had to go back to the gym.

Kai.

Her savior—and her tormentor?

His brilliant smile haunted her thoughts even now, as did the memory of his lean, muscled surfer's body doing lunges in the gym. Something about *him* just drew her in. She'd worked out with plenty of guys who were in shape. Tim was, by objective standards, nearly a perfect male specimen, and yet she felt something intangible about Kai, some kind of magnetism, that just made him different. It had been so long since Jun had even experienced desire for a man that she had a hard time figuring out what to do about it. Up until now, ignoring men had come easy. But nothing about Kai was easy.

She wondered if she'd made the right decision working for him.

*He saved Po. You owe him.*

She just wished she could pay him back some

other way, a way that didn't involve handing her livelihood—her very independence—over to him.

But then, she'd seen how weak his knee was at the gym. He'd gotten hurt in the first place because he'd stayed behind to help Po. If he'd selfishly saved himself, he'd have had two working knees right now and would probably have been at the top of his surfing game. But *could* she heal him? Could she make him strong enough to compete?

Some injuries, she knew, were just too devastating for the body to fully recover from.

Yet she knew she had to try.

She grabbed her gym bag and headed to Kai's front door. She rang the bell and waited. And waited some more.

Where was he?

She checked her watch. She wasn't late. She was a few minutes early.

She peered into the floor-to-ceiling glass windows but saw no movement inside. A T-shirt lay over the top of his sleek modern couch, as did a hastily discarded pair of flip-flops. No half-naked women visible in the foyer anyway. That was a good thing. She glanced to the back of the room and saw that the retractable glass walls that would seal off the lanai from bad weather were wide-open. Of course they would be; the only neighbors around were the ocean and the lava rockface back there.

She tucked her bag on her shoulder and made her way around the house to the back patio. She couldn't help but notice the magnificent view of the Pacific. When she turned, she could see the rest of the island rising up, the distant peak of Kilauea, one of the island's active volcanoes, just visible. A mile or two down the shore, Jun noticed a couple of luxury hotels, including what she thought might be the Four Seasons.

She walked past the square pool on his massive patio and the outdoor kitchen with its impressive grill and stainless-steel countertops, then continued past the outdoor plush sofa on the lanai and straight into Kai's house.

"Kai? Are you here?" she called from the doorway, and then took a step in. "Kai? It's Jun. Here for your training session."

There was an empty beer bottle on his coffee table. How could he drink beer and still stay fit enough to surf? His phone lay on the table. While she was staring at it, it dinged with an incoming message and the screen lit up.

She didn't mean to snoop, but the message popped up right there for her to see.

Had a great time last night! the text read, beneath a photo of Kai with his arm around a pretty redhead's shoulders. The redhead was wearing a bikini top and short shorts and they were at some open-air bar, an upscale one, by the look of the oversize lanterns hanging from the ceiling and the tasteful decor.

What had he been doing last night? *Partying?* With tourists?

Was this how Kai spent *every* night? She'd told him to be ready to train and he was out partying the night before? Doing God knows what with perfect strangers?

She was angrier than she ought to be, she knew. She was taking this far too personally, but she'd agreed to train him, and he'd gone off and stayed out late and hooked up with someone new…and she had red hair! Did he even have a type? First blondes and now redheads. The man seemed to say yes to whoever was standing in front of him!

Jun shook her head. She thought about leaving. She could. She could turn around and head right back out again. She should have, too, but something stopped her. She'd made a promise to *try* to help him, and *try* she would, even if he clearly had other ideas about what *try* meant. Then she saw the empty wine bottle on the counter.

She grabbed a trash can from the corner and threw the bottle in it. Then, on a whim, she started throwing in full bottles she saw on his small glass bar. She knew some of the labels of whiskey were probably expensive, but she didn't care. He needed to get *rid* of this if he was going to train. When the trash can was full, she set it down.

"Kai!" she shouted louder, heading up the massive open staircase. She found the master bedroom soon enough. The room was darkened by heavy curtains blocking the sunlight, so she could just make out Kai in his massive king-size bed, his bare shoulders visible above his single sheet.

Jun flung open the curtains, and the bright Hawaiian sun flooded the room.

"Rise and shine!" she called.

"Mmph," he grumbled, and pulled up the sheets, covering himself and his head.

"Kai!"

He refused to budge from under the thin sheet. Jun didn't know which was worse, the vague smell of man that still hung in the room or the empty bottle of wine on his nightstand. She marched back down to the kitchen and was irritated to find *another* empty wine bottle there on the counter. She opened his sleek white cabinets until she found a glass pitcher. She filled it with ice and tap water and carried it back up to Kai's bedroom, where she proceeded to dump it on him, ice cubes and all.

"Ah!" Kai screamed and jumped out of bed, dripping wet and, much to Jun's shock, 100 percent naked. She couldn't help but stare, frozen on the spot, as he shook the water off his head.

She fixed her attention on his flawlessly chiseled chest, the ripples of his hard abs and the perfect muscled V making an arrow straight to…

Only after she'd gotten an eyeful did she gain enough control of her senses to turn around. She felt a hot blush creep up her cheek. The man made average look small. How did he surf with that much…well, *there* there?

"Get dressed!" she mumbled, still flustered as she hurried out of the bedroom. "You've got five minutes."

"You dumped water on me! On my bed!" he protested.

"I'll do it again if you're not down in the kitchen in five," Jun called over her shoulder. It was easier to step into her Terminator Trainer persona. It helped her focus on being less embarrassed about seeing Kai in the buff. His bright white short-shorts tan line might have been burned into her memory for all time.

"What time is it?" Kai yelled from inside his room, sounding annoyed. She stood in the hall-way waiting and thought if he was angry, let him be. He'd hired her to do a job, and she planned to do it, whether he liked it or not.

"You hired me to train you, and I can't train you if you are sleeping. I said be ready at eight, and you weren't."

"What time is it?" Kai grumbled again, trudging out of his bedroom wearing board shorts hanging around his hips and nothing else as he ran a hair through his matted hair.

"Past eight," Jun said, trying to regain her composure. Jun turned and trotted down the stairs. In a daze, Kai followed.

Kai looked at the bar and the trash can nearby, filled with full bottles of Scotch and vodka.

"Hey, what are these doing here?" he asked, bending down to inspect the bottles.

"I threw them away."

"You *can't* throw them away. This is a $200 bottle of Scotch!" Kai pulled it out by the neck and put it back on the counter. He looked flabbergasted. Good. He needed a wake-up call.

"No alcohol," she said.

"What are you talking about?"

"That's my first rule. You said I made the rules."

"Yeah, but…"

"Drink this."

Jun handed Kai a clear plastic container with a screw top she'd pulled from her bag. It was filled with a thick green liquid. He peered at it suspiciously.

"What is it?"

"Kale smoothie. We're going to get your body chemistry right. Start working out all of the acids you've been putting in it. Like wine." Frowning, she picked up the bottle and dumped it in the recycling bin beside his stainless-steel refrigerator.

Kai lifted the lid and sniffed it and winced. "I prefer Kona coffee."

"Coffee is not as good for you!" Jun insisted.

"It smells healthy." He wrinkled his nose.

"It is. Drink it." Jun took the contract she'd signed from her back pocket. "I make the rules, remember?"

"About everything I eat?"

"About *everything.*"

Kai sipped at the drink and then made a face. "It even *tastes* healthy. Blech."

"Drink it all, and then we'll talk about the other rules."

Kai sipped at the drink some more. "Why do I have the feeling that drinking this is the best rule on that list?" His dark eyes studied her and she couldn't help smirking a little. It was true. The kale-and-green-apple drink—one of her favorites—was probably the least painful thing she was going to ask him to do today.

"You hired me to get you into shape for the surf competition and that's what I'm going to do." Jun put up a whiteboard on an easel on his white marble countertop. She uncapped her marker and began writing.

Kai took another sip of dark green smoothie

and his face puckered. "I think this is making my hangover worse."

"No drinking," Jun said, her marker making squeaking sounds as she went. "That's the first rule."

Kai sighed, as if he'd expected it. "Okay," he said.

"Two—no junk food. That means no processed foods. We go all fresh."

Kai eyed the kale smoothie with distrust. "As long as we get some meat in there, I'm okay with that."

"Protein is an important part of building muscle," Jun agreed. As if she'd cut meat out of his diet. She wasn't so far out there in her alternative-medicine approach that she thought a vegan diet would work for a pro surfer. "But you'll eat *healthy* protein." Jun furiously scribbled on the whiteboard. "And last but not least…" Jun took in a breath as she wrote, in all caps, "NO SEX."

Kai gagged and nearly spit out kale smoothie on his kitchen floor. "Excuse me?" He glared at her as if she'd just insulted his mother. Jun wondered if she'd gone too far, but she knew he had to do it. He had to get his mind right, and chasing hot women in bikinis wasn't helping.

"You are depleting your Chi every time you hook up with one of those tourists. Every time you…" Jun cleared her throat as her cheeks grew hot. None of this had seemed nearly so…embarrassing…in her alternative-medicine classes. There her professor and the other students talked about bodies and bodily functions clinically. Yet with Kai, shirtless, his dark eyes boring into hers, she suddenly realized talking about what he did with his body was *not* clinical. Not in the least bit.

"No sex? For *four* months? That's…an eternity." Kai, exasperated, began to pace the kitchen anxiously, as if she'd just asked him to give up air for a week.

"Four months isn't so long." She hadn't had sex since that brief fling when Po was about two, before she decided being a mom of a toddler and dating were just too hard to combine. At the time, her boyfriend hadn't understood why she'd drop everything for Po but not for him, and in the end, jealousy over the time and attention she spent on her son sank the relationship. That was fine by Jun. She had enough complications in her life without worrying about how to fit a man into the picture.

"Four months is…forever. I haven't even gone four *weeks* without." Kai considered this a moment, thoughtful. "Maybe, actually, four *days*."

"Please," Jun exclaimed, suddenly feeling woefully inadequate in the hooking-up department. What would he think if he knew the only thing she'd been up close and personal with in nearly two years was a vibrator?

"You spent a lot of energy chasing after...that." Jun was hoping to keep her voice calm, but it came out sounding shrill.

"Hey, women come on to me. I'm just being nice. Showing them the hospitality of the islands."

Jun scoffed. "Right. Nothing in it for you."

"Of course there's something in it for me." Kai took a step closer, and Jun was suddenly aware of the wide swatch of bare chest in front of her. If he got closer, her brain might start malfunctioning. He gave her a lazy grin. "I believe in *mutual satisfaction*."

Kai's meaning was clear, and for some reason it caused Jun to flush. The temperature in the room instantaneously ticked up about ten degrees. Kai's impeccably formed chest was now so close to her that all Jun had to do was reach out to touch those washboard abs. She had to curl her fingers up, pressing her nails in her palms, to stop from doing so. *Focus, Jun.* She shifted away from him uncomfortably.

"We...uh, need to focus," she murmured, not meeting his eye. "And training means you don't get to give out your number to every redhead who asks."

"Redhead?" Kai looked puzzled.

"Someone had a good time last night. She was

trying to reach you this morning." Jun looked toward Kai's phone.

"You were snooping?" Kai's face was unreadable as he picked up his phone.

"I'm sorry. I overstepped." Jun awkwardly shifted her weight between her feet, losing all the fire in her argument. "I mean, I didn't snoop. I just happened to be there when the text came in."

"That's snooping," Kai said, eyebrows raised.

Why was it that just when she thought she had the upper hand with Kai, he managed to shift the balance of power? Yin and yang, female and male, were supposed to work in harmony, equal but opposite forces keeping the universe in balance. But why did she feel as if he had all the power and she had none?

"Snooping is…wrong. I wasn't snooping. I just…"

"Apology accepted," Kai said, waving his hand. The high-and-mighty way he said it grated on Jun's nerves a bit.

"The no-sex rule is the most important," she said, trying to turn the conversation back to steadier ground. "You need to focus if you're going to be ready to compete. Your *friends*, like the one texting you, are distracting you."

Kai laughed. "You *did* read a text on my phone. That's snooping."

Jun let out an exasperated sigh.

Kai studied her for a beat.

"You're jealous."

"I'm not," she exclaimed, even as her heart pounded in her chest and all the blood rushed to her face. She felt as though someone had told her the clothes she wore were actually transparent. She wasn't jealous, though. Was she? "I just notice that you fall into bed with anyone. You don't even have the decency to have a type."

"I do have a type, as a matter of fact," Kai growled, voice low. He moved closer and his shoulders seemed to take up the rest of the space in the kitchen. Jun sucked in a breath and held it. She felt rooted in place. Jun could focus on nothing but Kai as he held her gaze. When he stepped even closer, there was hardly room to slip a piece of paper between them.

"My type is feisty Asian girls who aren't afraid to boss me around." Kai grinned then, like a wolf. Except Jun had never seen a wolf look quite as charming.

"Uh…" Jun backed up but bumped into the counter behind her. She was pinned there with Kai looming over her, eyes sparkling with mischief, as if he knew she wanted him to lean in and kiss her. Even as the thought crossed her mind, she found herself glancing at Kai's full bottom lip, wondering what it would taste like. She felt red-hot and cold all at once, hormones rushing through her veins like a drug.

Then she thought about the redhead on his phone. Had they kissed last night? More than kissed? Yet the idea somehow didn't repulse her as much as it should have.

Kai slowly set down his half-drunk kale smoothie, and the small click of the cup on the counter shook her out of the spell.

"You're just trying to get out of drinking your kale," Jun offered weakly. Kai glanced sideways at the cup on the counter, and the distraction was long enough for Jun to skip away to a safer distance, her heart pounding as she questioned whether she was glad to get away or disappointed. *No*, she told herself. *Got to get control. Sex with the island's sexiest surfer is not the answer. It'll only bring more problems.* She thought of the last time she'd let her hormones do the decision making, when she'd fallen into bed with Po's father, throwing caution and all her good sense to the trade winds blowing off the ocean. While she would always be grateful for Po, she had no intention of ever letting her desire drive her again. *Mistakes happen when you're not careful*, her mother had told her at the time. *You weren't being careful.*

"You hired me to help you," Jun reminded him. "You told me I set the rules."

"That was before I realized you were such a hard-ass."

Jun glared at him. Kai glared back.

This was going to be harder than she'd thought. He was so used to getting his way with little effort. It was about time someone showed him what it meant to work for something. "Drink it," she prompted, nodding to the smoothie. Kai just shook his head, looking sheepish at his defeat, and downed the rest of the green shake.

"*That* was disgusting," Kai groused, wiping his mouth with the back of his hand.

"*That* was healthy," Jun corrected.

"Healthy and disgusting." Kai stuck out his tongue. "They're not mutually exclusive."

Jun just laughed a little. "Wait until you taste the spinach-lemon one."

"Gross!" Kai made a sour face like the one Po made when Jun asked him to finish his broccoli.

Jun produced a manila folder out of her gym bag and pushed a crisp sheet of paper and a pen in front of him. "Now you'll sign this. It's a contract outlining all the rules I've just laid out. It's a promise that you'll uphold these rules. And that if you don't, I walk."

"How many strikes do I get?"

Jun couldn't hide her surprise. "Strikes? This isn't baseball."

"You know, how many mess-ups do I get before you pull the plug?"

Jun stared in disbelief. Her mom would have laughed out loud at the concept of getting three chances. *You follow the rules, or you don't.* That was what her tiger mom would've said. She never got *a warning.* She just got punishment, swift and decisive, anytime she stepped off the straight and narrow. She could almost still feel that slap her mother had delivered the day she told her she was pregnant with Po.

"You don't get *any,*" Jun said. "No strikes. Break *one* of these rules, and I walk."

Kai looked at the paper solemnly. "No strikes? Really?"

Jun shook her head emphatically.

Kai glanced at the list. "No drinking. No junk food. No sex." He sighed. "What counts as *sex*? I need parameters."

"What do you mean?" Wasn't there just *one* kind of sex? Then again, she'd had only two sex partners her whole life. She wasn't exactly as experienced as Kai. She doubted anybody was.

"Do blow jobs count?" Kai quirked a mischievous eyebrow, and Jun couldn't tell if he was teasing or not.

"What? Yes! Of course they do! You're losing Chi when you…" Jun swallowed, hard, imagining *that*. Was that what the redhead had given him last night?

"Okay, how about making out?"

"Kai, you have to stay focused!" Jun slapped her hand on the countertop in frustration.

"That wasn't a no." Kai grinned.

"You can't give away your Chi." Jun crossed her arms across her chest and frowned.

"Is that what we're calling man juice these days?" Kai teased.

"Kai!"

"What? I can't even talk about…Chi?" His grin grew bigger.

"Just sign the paper." Jun grabbed the pen and thrust it at him.

Kai looked at her and then at the paper and grabbed the pen. He hesitated.

"You're asking me to give up sex for four months. But have you ever done that?"

Jun scoffed. "Please. Four months is nothing."

Kai raised an eyebrow, his curiosity clearly piqued. "How long?"

"How long what?" Jun felt her guard coming up. This was not where she wanted the conversation to go. Not at all.

"How long since you've had sex?" The intensity of his interest made her uncomfortable. Plus, she didn't want to admit it had been two years. She knew he'd judge her and probably find her wanting.

"None of your business."

"It *is* my business if you're asking me to give up sex. How long have you gone without?"

Jun pressed her lips together, as if she feared the answer would pop out on its own.

"Six months? A year?" Kai's eyes widened in shock. *"Longer than a year?"*

Jun couldn't meet his gaze as she shifted uncomfortably from foot to foot. Kai took her silence as confirmation, which, she hated to admit, it was. She'd never even thought it was a bad thing. In fact, she'd never really thought about her sex life at all, until recently. Kai's bare chest had everything to do with that development.

*"Two years?"* Kai was practically shouting now as he put both hands on the counter as if to brace himself. "But you're…" He gave her a quick once-over as he digested his shock. "I mean, you could have it anytime you wanted it." The sweetness of the compliment temporarily soothed her humiliation. But the feeling was soon trampled by the judgmental shake of his head. It brought Jun right back to the time she'd admitted to Po's father that, at nineteen, she hadn't slept with anyone yet. He hadn't thought it was sweet. He'd teased her about it.

"It's not healthy to go so long without," Kai

said, and the way he said it sounded as if he'd be glad to end her drought.

She swallowed, hard.

"You're denying yourself too much," Kai said, and the criticism sounded exactly like what her sister would say. She felt herself bristle.

"And you don't deny yourself *enough*," Jun countered. He was busy drinking and having sex when he ought to be training. She remembered all too well how his knee gave out in the gym, like a weak toothpick snapping under the least bit of pressure. "I saw you at the gym. I know the knee's far from 100 percent. You need all the Chi you can get, and you know it."

Kai froze, pen in hand, and just stared at Jun. All humor fled his face, and red flames of anger danced up his neck. She'd hit his sore spot, she knew it, but it couldn't be helped. The man needed to see how serious this situation was.

"You don't know what you're talking about." She saw how quickly his defenses came up, which only proved that he knew as well as she did just how far they'd have to go to get him ready to surf competitively.

Kai dropped the pen on the counter. "I'm not signing this," he declared, folding his arms across his chest. Jun wanted to shake Kai, hard. If he were Po, she'd have given him a time-out, but he was a grown man and there wasn't much she could do.

"If you don't, then I'm leaving." Jun hoped she was calling his bluff.

Kai shrugged, and she felt as though he'd popped her balloon.

"You recruited me, remember?" Just yesterday he'd been willing to do anything to hire her, and now, at the very first challenge, he was giving up? Maybe he couldn't be saved. Maybe he was a lost cause.

"That was before I realized you'd ask me to give up *sex*. Why not ask me to give up breathing? I made a mistake asking you. That's all this is."

"Fine." Jun grabbed her gym bag and threw it over her shoulder angrily. "So, just so we're clear, if you care more about getting laid than surfing, you won't ever get back on that board."

Kai just glowered at her. Jun had no choice but to leave, and she felt Kai's stare burning into her back as she strode toward the door.

The man couldn't be helped, and she'd been a fool for even trying.

# CHAPTER NINE

LATER THAT EVENING, Kai gripped the steering wheel of his Jeep, blood still boiling after his run-in with Jun. She had some nerve reading his texts, spying and ordering him around. She was his personal trainer, not his *wife*.

Kai still couldn't believe Jun thought he'd give up sex just like that. Sex wasn't his problem. His *knee* was the problem, and he could live like a monk and still not get any better at surfing.

Chi had nothing to do with surfing. Surfing was about strength and balance, and the tsunami had taken both of those things from him.

Her out-there alternative-medicine ideas were crazy. *Probably because she hasn't had sex in so long. All that built-up tension is rotting her brain.* He'd seen how uncomfortable she was about the whole topic and knew there had to be a story there. He also realized that he'd made assumptions about her he probably shouldn't have. He knew she'd gotten pregnant young and had Po out of wedlock. He'd assumed that was because she had sex, and lots of it. He wasn't sure how he felt about this new information.

But it didn't matter now. She wasn't going to work out, and that was that. He turned off the two-lane road to his aunt's house, the small, modest one-story where he and Jesse had grown up.

Their aunt had raised him and his half sister as her own after his mother died. They would've been orphans without Aunt Kaimana's guiding hand, and thanks to her, he and Jesse had always felt love. Kai had sketchy memories of his biological father, the most vivid one when he came to Hawaii for his mother's funeral. He'd come to ask Kai if he wanted to go home with him to the mainland, where he'd moved when Kai was just a baby. Kai was eight at the time, too little to make the decision, really, but he didn't want to leave his Aunt Kaimana's side, or Jesse, who was just five. His father didn't really want him anyway, letting him go with no fight. After that they had a distant, barely there relationship of an occasional Christmas or birthday card, sporadic support checks to his aunt and one plane ticket to the mainland during high school, where Kai discovered that his father had a steady job and a loving new family in Chicago, a boy and a girl, whom Kai had no desire to get to know—then or now.

Unfair, perhaps, but the fact that his father had run away from him, only to go start a new family, rankled, even to this day. He still remembered the #1 Dad mug in the kitchen and the way those little kids worshipped the man and how he catered to their every need, giving them bouncing shoulder rides and bandaging up skinned knees. The revelation hurt him more than he ever admitted, even to himself. He was an amazing father to them, but not to him. Why did *they* deserve it and he didn't?

Kai was seventeen on that trip, and it was the last time he'd ever visited his father.

When he returned home, he redoubled his efforts to become the best surfer he could be. The bigger the waves, the better. Anytime he surfed one, it felt like a little battle won against the powerful emotions raging inside him. If he could keep upright, he thought, it would be a little victory against his father. That was why he'd surfed waves more than eighty feet high at the most dangerous breaks in the world: Teahupo'o, Ghost Tree, Mavericks, and of course, Jaws.

Not that his aunt approved. Or his sister, for that matter. They both thought he was crazy for doing it, and maybe he was. But surfing monstrous waves was the only way to keep the typhoon inside him contained.

He pulled up to his aunt's house and cut the engine.

He'd promised he'd help her fix a cabinet that had come loose in her kitchen and now here he was. She'd be asking questions about Jun, too, about when she should look after Po. Now what was Kai going to tell her? She'd been looking forward to the babysitting. Well, she'd have to find another part-time job.

His aunt, wearing a billowing flowered muumuu, poked her head out of the screen door and waved. "How did the first day of training go?"

"Not so well." He dragged his heavy toolbox out of the back of his Jeep and carried it up to the back porch.

His aunt frowned. "Why? You scared her off already?"

"No. She's crazy." Kai brushed past her and went into her house, which always smelled like tropical flowers. He made a beeline for her kitchen and set the toolbox down on the counter. He opened the loose cabinet door—second from the sink—and studied the loose hinge.

"Why?"

Kai dug around in his toolbox to come up with a screwdriver.

"She won't let me drink. Or have sex. Or…"

Kaimana burst into laughter. "Sounds like she *does* know what she's doing, then."

"Ruining my life, you mean?" Kai grumbled as he went to work on the hinge.

"You should give Jun one more chance. Let me babysit her little one for one week."

He focused on his work.

"But, Auntie, she has crazy ideas about kale shakes and Chi and… No. I can't work with her. I just can't."

"Can't or won't?" Aunt Kaimana challenged him.

"Does it matter?"

"Only if you want to surf." Aunt Kaimana shrugged. "I'd be happy if you didn't, but you might feel differently."

In a few more seconds, he'd finished fixing the door. "There," he said. "Good as new."

Aunt Kaimana inspected his work and nodded her approval.

He went to her fridge and opened it and grabbed a beer from inside, twisting off the cap.

"You drink too much," Aunt Kaimana said, jabbing a finger into Kai's chest and then stealing the bottle.

"Hey, that's mine!"

"It's *my* fridge, so it's mine." Aunt Kaimana grinned, mischief on her face, as she happily took a swig of the beer. "There's more to life than surfing. Maybe you should think about retiring. When are you going to quit this young man's game? You're too old to be helicoptering into waves."

"I only helicoptered in a few times. Most of the time, I get towed in by a Jet Ski."

"Same difference. It's all suicide, if you ask

me." Kaimana took another swig. "Did you find a new tow partner yet?"

Kai thought about Bret and the furious look in his eyes when he'd stalked out of Kirk's office. Kai deserved every last bit of that resentment, too.

"Not yet. Still looking," Kai said. *Might never find one.* The thought of big-wave surfing was scary enough, but without Bret, could he really do it? The two had been so close they could almost read each other's minds. Kai knew he'd never find that in another tower. But, he couldn't blame Bret for quitting on him, either. If Kai had been in his shoes, he would've done the same.

"You're too old for this extreme stuff," Kaimana said again.

"If I'm old, what does that make you?" Kai teased, and his aunt just gave him a playful shove.

"Old enough to tell you what to do!"

"You got me there." Kai knew she had a point about his age. He was thirty-three. The guys who were up and coming now topped at eighteen or nineteen. Too young to figure out they were in a crazy sport where people sometimes died.

"You need to stop this risky surfing, Kai. Focus on your other businesses. Stop trying to kill yourself."

Kai thought about the tsunami, about how close he'd come to dying that day. Still, he wasn't ready to walk away from the ocean. Surfing was all he'd ever wanted to do, and he'd been lucky enough to make a fortune doing it. Giving it up just wasn't in him. It was too much an ingrained part of his identity to let go. Plus, the idea of figuring out something else to do terrified him.

"I'm not quitting," he managed. "Surfing is my life." Kai put his arms around his aunt's shoulders and squeezed. He knew she loved him and wanted to keep him safe. "And I know it's just because you want me to come work on your house every day."

"Got me," Aunt Kaimana said.

"But I like what I do. I don't want to change."

"The only thing constant about life is change," Aunt Kaimana said, taking another sip.

Kai sighed. "I'm not ready to change yet," he said, holding out the rumpled contract Jun had left in his place, the one asking him to forgo sex. "Not *this* kind anyway."

Aunt Kaimana picked up the crumpled paper and read it with interest.

"Sometimes change comes whether you're ready or not," she said, finishing off his beer. "Like, first your bottle is full, and now it's empty."

THAT EVENING, JUN lay in bed trying to sleep, still rattled by her day with Kai. She'd signed his contract, but he refused to sign hers. He'd fired her after she'd worked barely an hour, and according to the contract, he owed her six months' pay. Not that she'd take it. She'd thought she could take the money, but now she realized she couldn't accept money for a job she hadn't done. It was a matter of pride. Besides, she already owed him enough. Even Kai's being pigheaded, shallow and wrong wasn't going to change the fact he'd saved Po, and she still owed him a debt she probably could never repay. Still, she wanted to shake some sense into his sex-obsessed brain. How could he possibly think that sleeping around could *help* his surfing career? Men were all the same, she thought. They always believed they could compartmentalize everything so nicely, yet the fact was, no one could really live a life divided. If there was one thing alternative medicine had taught her, it was that a person's mind, body and spirit were all connected in often surprising ways.

Right now her mind and body were at odds: her body wanted to sleep, but her mind was having no part of it. She flopped over in her bed and glanced at her phone. Two in the morning. Po would be up by six thirty. She'd be lucky to get four hours of sleep, and tomorrow would be another busy day: she'd need to call Tim, a task she dreaded. Being free of his unwanted advances had been a relief.

Then there'd be a new round of calling day cares. She'd yet to find one without a waiting list, and she'd tried every single one within a thirty-minute drive. She'd have to increase her range, but that would mean an hour or more commuting back and forth from work to day care each day. Jun's sister had been nice enough to watch Po on her days off, but she'd be back to work tomorrow, and there'd be no way Jun could ask her to take a sick day to watch her nephew, especially since she lived an hour away.

*Why does every day feel like I'm climbing Mount Everest? Why does it all have to be so hard?* Just as Jun began to indulge in a rare moment of self-pity, she heard a strangled cry come from Po's room.

Instantly, she was on her feet, headed down the narrow hallway in their small two-bedroom condo. Was he having another nightmare? That would be the third night this week. Neither one of them had been sleeping well and now it seemed the nightmares were becoming more frequent. *Just when I think we've put the tsunami behind us, here it comes again.* Jun heard a sudden crash from Po's room, followed by a scream, and she sprinted the rest of the way to his door, her heart in her throat as she worried he'd fallen out of bed—or worse.

She saw Po, eyes wide and scared, tears streaming down his face. He was standing in the middle of his room, the covers of his bed and his pillow tossed on the floor. He'd knocked over the small wooden step stool near his bed, along with a stack of picture books and a crate of oversize blocks.

"Po, honey? Are you okay?" She went to him and tried to put her arms around him, but he screamed in fear.

"Po! Po, honey!" Jun's blood ran cold as her little boy fought her and screamed and cried. It was as if he didn't even recognize her, as if she weren't there. He slipped from her grip and managed to wander over to the other side of his room in a kind of daze. Jun let him go and tried to calm her voice. He was clearly terrified, yet he didn't want her to comfort him. He bumped into things in his room as if he wasn't even seeing them. As if he was asleep with his eyes wide-open.

"What's wrong, Po? What's...?" She ran after him, trying to hug him, but he shrieked again, kicking and hitting. She tried to hold him, but the tighter her grip, the more he fought her. Her heart pounded. What was wrong with her boy? She felt helpless and scared as she let him go again and backed away.

He stood, swaying a little on his feet, staring at her but not seeing her. Was he having a fit? A seizure? He'd never had one before. Helplessly, she stood there trying to figure out what to do. Touching him only made it worse.

"Po!" she repeated, but even the sound of his own name made him scream and thrash, knocking over his big stuffed bear from a chair and crayons from the table. They clattered to the ground with the spilled blocks.

"Water!" he shrieked, and cried. "Sharks!"

She glanced all around the room, but of course there was no water. Nothing but his toys and books and small dresser filled with clothes. The only water was the huge frothy wave on the poster he had of Kai Brady hanging in his room, mass-produced and signed with his big looping *K*. He must be having a nightmare, and yet his eyes were wide-open. She took a deep breath, trying to remain calm, all the while her mother brain firing off intense messages of panic: *What's wrong with him? Do I need to call 911?*

"Sweetie," she whispered, voice low. "Let's settle down."

The soft sound of her voice seemed to steady him a little, or at least, he didn't scream, so she started talking some more, careful to avoid his name. "Let's just calm down. You're in your room. You're not in the ocean. Nothing to be afraid of. You're just having a dream..." Jun tried to clear a path, moving toys and crayons away from his feet so he wouldn't trip. He sobbed, tears rolling down his small cheeks, breaking her heart because she so badly wanted to wipe them away and hug her son but feared that touching him would set him off again. She kept talking, keeping her voice soft, and he slowly started to calm down. After what seemed like an eternity, he eventually stopped crying.

His hands flopped to his sides as he took deep breaths. Po's head began to lull forward. She crept to his side and saw his eyelids growing heavy. Cautiously, with her pulse thrumming in her temples, she took a step forward and gently put her hand on his back. He didn't scream or twist away from her. "Let's get back to bed now," she said, ever so gently pushing him toward his single twin bed. She pulled back his Spider-Man sheets and he climbed peacefully into them, lying his head down on the pillow and snuggling into his comforter.

She sat by his bedside for another twenty minutes, watching as he slept, with a deep nagging feeling that something was wrong with her boy. Her gut told her it had everything to do with the tsunami and had been triggered, probably by that teacher who'd tried to force him to swim. But she didn't know that for certain. All she knew was that her son had gotten up in the middle of the night screaming and knocking things over in his room and shrieking whenever she even touched him. They'd made so much progress in the past year, but his nightmares were back, and now... this. Would Po ever get better?

# CHAPTER TEN

PO WOKE UP fine the next morning, full of energy and acting as if nothing had happened the night before. He didn't even remember waking up in the night screaming or knocking over his toys in a panic. Looking at him now as he happily ate Cheerios—no milk—from a bowl, Jun almost thought she'd imagined the whole episode. And yet she knew she hadn't. She should make an appointment to take him to see the pediatrician, she decided, a nagging fear telling her something was wrong, and it wasn't something a dose of ibuprofen could fix.

And then what about her job?

Tim wouldn't be at the gym today, but she could probably text or call him. She'd need to get on with finding a new day care, and her to-do list seemed unbearably overwhelming. She glanced down at her own uneaten bowl of cereal, which had grown soggy as she worried, and pushed it away.

*Gotta just do it*, she thought, gritting her teeth. No point in complaining. Her mother once told her that the trade-off for having a purpose and being meaningful was stress. *Worry is just the price you pay for being needed*, she'd often say. Memories of her mother always brought her a sharp pain of regret. She'd died before they'd had a chance to reconcile, before she'd had a chance to prove to her mother that Po was no mistake, that he was the best thing to happen in her life.

A knock at the door made her jump. It was nine in the morning and she wasn't expecting anyone. Her condo door faced an open walkway and, beyond that, the parking lot. She thought it might be the super for the building, perhaps finally come to look at her leaky kitchen sink.

When she peered through the peephole, however, she saw Kai's aunt Kaimana on her porch. What was she doing there?

Her first thought was Kai. Was he okay? Had something happened?

She swung open the door.

Aunt Kaimana wore a white-and-brown muu-muu and brown sandals, a wicker purse hanging on her thick forearm.

"Aloha."

"Is everything okay?" Jun asked.

"Yes, yes, everything's fine. Kai asked me to come pick you up."

"Pick me…up?" Jun struggled to follow. "Why?"

"Training!" Aunt Kaimana declared. "Second day of training."

Jun felt disoriented as she struggled to process this. He'd fired her!

"Uh… Kaimana. I'm not working for Kai anymore. He let me go yesterday, so I'm sorry you made the trip out here, but there's no reason to stay."

"No, no, no." Kaimana shook her head. "He didn't fire. No fire. You work for him." Was it her imagination or was Kaimana's accent growing thicker? "He sent me as… How do you say it? A papaya branch?"

"Olive, I think."

"Papaya would be better than olive!" Kaimana exclaimed, and then shrugged. "Kai asked me to come right over. He wants you and Po over at his house this afternoon. I'll watch Po and you can help Kai train."

"This afternoon? This is the first I'm hearing of it." Why had Kai not called her? He'd decided to hire her back and thought she'd just know by osmosis? Besides, he had some nerve. Who was to say she'd even take the job back? After he'd kicked her out? Laughed at her methods?

"Kai is stubborn and proud, but he does want to apologize. He sent me to feel you out. I'm happy to give you a ride now, if you're free…"

"I don't know." Jun hesitated. Part of her was

tempted to go and see if Kai really was ready to
work. Was it possible that he wanted to apologize?
She couldn't imagine it, yet his aunt seemed so
certain. "Kai wants me back? But he was so adamant yesterday." Jun felt doubtful.

"The boy's always been fickle. He can't decide what he wants to do so often! But when he
decides, he goes for it. Sometimes when he was
little, he'd run out of the house with just one shoe
on."

Jun almost smiled at that, the image of Kai as
young as Po, so eager to get outside he'd run out
in one flip-flop.

"Boys are always leaping before they look," Jun
agreed. The two women shared a moment, both
understanding all too well the unruliness of raising little boys.

"He wanted me to give you this." Kaimana dug
a crinkled piece of paper out of her wicker bag.
"I'm sorry about the folds in it. He was a bit angry
before he calmed down and saw reason."

Jun stared at the contract in disbelief. An illeg-
ible black scrawl formed a signature above Kai's
name. She recognized the large loopy K from the
poster in Po's room.

Just then Po poked his head out from around
Jun's side.

"Hello, Po," Kaimana said, smiling in a genuine and loving way that immediately put Jun and

Po at ease. She could always tell the people who faked it.

Kaimana glanced at Jun. "Is it all right if he gets a little treat? I remember that his favorite is mango candy."

"Can I, Mommy? Can I, please?" Po looked so excited she couldn't tell him no, especially not after seeing him so terrified the night before. Besides, she was so stunned to be holding Kai's contract in her hands that she found herself simply nodding.

Kaimana reached in her bag and pulled out a handful of his favorite mango candy. He greedily took them.

"Po, what do you say?" she admonished.

"Thank you!" he shouted gleefully, and then ran back inside, probably to devour every last bit in one sitting, but Jun felt too disoriented to chastise him. Should she give Kai another chance? She thought about having to work for Tim again in close quarters. She didn't want to do that. But was Kai the answer?

"Kai can be pigheaded, believe me," Kaimana said. "Most of the time he doesn't know what's best for him. But from what I can see, you're good for him. I know you don't owe him another chance, but would you think about at least hearing him out?"

Jun appreciated the older woman's praise, yet

wondered if what she said was really true. She looked at the crumpled contract in her hand. If he'd come to see that getting serious about training was the only way forward, maybe she had to do it.

"I'll come and talk to him," she said, and Kaimana's face lit up in delight. "But I'll drive myself."

"Wonderful," Kaimana said, clapping her hands together.

JUN PULLED UP to the driveway of Kai's beach house.

"Whoa!" Po exclaimed from the back, his eyes bulging. "This is where Kai lives?"

The boy had never seen a mansion up close before. They'd driven by plenty on the Big Island, but he'd never stood before one.

"Does he have to share it?"

"Share it?" Jun asked.

"Yeah, with neighbors."

Po knew all about neighbors. She was always telling him to walk softly and not run in the apartment so he wouldn't disturb the woman who lived downstairs. Not that it helped all that much. Po had only two speeds: dead stop and full tilt. Asking a four-year-old to be quiet was like asking an elephant to tiptoe.

"No, he lives here all by himself."

"Whoa," Po exclaimed again.

Jun got out, opened Po's door and helped him slide out of his booster seat. She felt uneasy as they walked up to the house. Kai was the one who wanted her here, had sent his aunt to beg her to come, yet butterflies relentlessly beat their anxious wings in her stomach. What was she scared of? He'd already fired her once. That was pretty much the worst he could do.

*Or he could really be sincerely sorry and hire you on for good.*

She was beginning to think that was exactly what she was worried about. She wasn't sure she *could* help him. The way he looked at her, the way he seemed to know more about her than she knew herself, made her feel as if she were always on her back foot. Jun still remembered how he'd challenged her about her own sex life, turning the tables in a way that made Jun think long and hard about some of the decisions she'd made in her life. Something about Kai's confidence made her question her own life. *Which is hilarious, considering his is such a mess!*

She shook off the insecurity. She had to dig deep and find her own confidence. She *knew* she was right. If he cut out the distractions, he would be more focused and stronger out there on his surfboard.

Po excitedly skipped ahead and ran to the

front door, where he eagerly pressed the doorbell. There was no keeping her little boy away from any button—elevators or doorbells.

"Just once, Po," she admonished, and he dutifully nodded and stepped back. Though she could tell it took quite a bit of effort for him not to hit the glowing button once more.

The door opened and Kaimana stood there. "So glad to see you," she said. "Come on through to the back."

Po followed Kaimana through the sleek foyer and living room, eyes bugging out at the size of Kai's flat-screen TV and the impressive open staircase leading to the bedrooms upstairs. Then, as they walked to the open lanai, he saw the pool in the backyard, crystal blue and square, its surface almost completely flat like a mirror.

Po stopped in his tracks. "I don't like swimming," he told Kaimana solemnly.

The old woman nodded. "Me neither," she said, and Jun watched as Po's face magically relaxed. She felt grateful Kaimana had said that and hadn't, like so many other adults, tried to convince Po he was wrong. There was no shortage of people out there who felt as if they could raise her son better than she could, but Kaimana seemed not to be in that camp. Kaimana put her wrinkled hand on the boy's shoulder. "Do you want to take a walk on the beach? I think there's a tide pool out there and I saw urchins and a crab in it this morning."

"A crab?" exclaimed Po, enthusiastic.

"A fast one with big claws," Kaimana promised.

"Can I go? Can I?" Po asked Jun, who nodded.

Kaimana and Po were out the back door and headed to the steps leading to the beach when Jun heard Kai's voice behind her.

"Jun?" He sounded surprised.

She whirled.

"K-Kai." No matter how good-looking Kai was in her memory, seeing him in person always jolted her a little, always reminded her that her recollections didn't do him justice. It could have been his broad shoulders filling out that tightly fitting light blue T-shirt or the way the khaki shorts he wore showed off athletic, muscled legs. Charisma, she thought. It was no wonder he could sell whatever he wanted and that he had companies lining up asking him for endorsements. Who wouldn't buy yogurt from a man with this kind of smoldering intensity?

"What are you doing here?" Kai frowned, looking almost…annoyed. But he was supposed to be the one ready to apologize. Why did it seem as if he had no intention of doing that?

"I'm here to hear your apology," she said, confused as she struggled to understand why Kai looked so ticked off. His mouth was in a thin line, and his dark eyes now flashed fire.

"My apology!" he barked, sour amusement tugging at the corners of his mouth. "Why would *I* apologize? You're the one who owes *me* an apology."

"Excuse me?" Jun felt her blood simmer.

"You can't just come into a man's home, throw away his stuff and snoop through his phone."

"You said I made the rules!" Jun had lost track of why they were even arguing. Hadn't he invited her here?

"What are you doing here, really? Here to get your severance check?" Kai crossed his arms and looked at her suspiciously. "I can write it for you now."

Jun looked for Kaimana, who had already disappeared to the beach. "But Kaimana said you wanted us here. You signed this!" Desperately, Jun dug the contract out of her bag. Kai just blinked at it and then laughed.

"I never signed that."

"But your aunt…" Jun was flustered. Had she misunderstood somehow?

Suddenly, Kai's annoyance disappeared, and a strained cough broke from his throat. "Auntie strikes again!" he declared, shaking his head. "Where is she? I'm going to give her a piece of my mind."

"She took Po for a walk on the beach," Jun said, pointing and now growing worried.

Kai just sighed. "They're probably halfway down the shore by now, knowing her."

"What? Do I need to...?" Jun suddenly feared the nice elderly Hawaiian woman might have kidnapped her son.

"Oh, don't worry. They'll be back." Jun felt her shoulders sag in relief. "This is just her way of getting us alone together."

Jun's cheeks grew hot. Alone together? "What are you talking about?"

"My aunt thinks you're good for me. She thinks you should train me, and when I said no, she tricked you into coming over here. She does that a lot with people who don't mind her advice." Kai shook his head and chuckled softly. "I should've known she'd try something like this."

"So you're not going to apologize?" The truth was still sinking in, and Jun was embarrassed and angry at the same time.

"No."

"So you don't want me to work for you?" In that moment, Jun realized how much she'd been hoping that Kai would apologize, that he'd offer her the job back, that it would be the answer to at least half of her stress: money, child care, how she and Po were going to ride out the next couple of months without Tim's roaming hands making her uncomfortable at work. And then she hated herself for feeling so desperate. Hadn't she always prided herself on being independent? On taking care of Po and herself, no matter how hard or impossible it seemed. Yet disappointment struck her like a swift kick to the shins.

With Po's nightmares getting worse, and then with the episode last night, it just seemed as if she wasn't balancing on the tightrope anymore, that somehow they were all falling. Even worse, Jun felt her throat constrict as tears threatened to spill. Now she was going to cry? She never cried. But she was running on fumes: hardly any sleep, and she'd barely had time to eat today. That must be it, she thought. It had to be it.

Kai hesitated a bit. "I can write you the severance check," he offered. "A deal's a deal."

"I can't take it," Jun managed, swallowing the lump in her throat. *I will not cry. I will keep it together. What is wrong with me?* "I'll just…go get Po." Jun walked away from Kai stiffly and headed out the back door and past the pool. She didn't care whether Kai followed her or not. She just needed to get her son and get out of there. The salty breeze off the sparkling Pacific Ocean ran through her hair as she jogged down the wooden steps built over the black lava rocks dotting the beach. Tourists lay on the sand of the narrow beach with towels and umbrellas, and she wandered through them. All beaches in Hawaii were public land, so even houses built near them had to share. The scent of coconut sunscreen filled her nose as she strode past.

She saw Kaimana and Po about a hundred feet away, walking surprisingly near the water line. Jun couldn't believe Po was all right with being so close to the water. She hurriedly made her way toward them, anxiety knotting her stomach. After last night's nightmare, she didn't think it was a good idea for Po to be that close to the tide. Unlike the day-care and preschool teachers, she didn't think throwing him into the water was any way to help him overcome fear.

"Jun!" Kai called from behind her. "Jun, wait." She turned but didn't slow her steps. The last thing she wanted to do was get in a prolonged conversation with Kai about how she ought to take a severance check or other such nonsense. She just wanted to get home. Jun glanced back at Po and saw, miracle of miracles, that Kaimana had somehow gotten the boy to wade into the surf up to his ankles. She froze, amazed. Po wouldn't even take a bath, much less step into the ocean. Kaimana was showing him a small crab, about the size of a silver dollar, that had darted back into the surf and then out of it again, looking for lunch. Jun realized that Po was so distracted by chasing the crab that he'd stepped into the water without thinking about it. Kaimana held his sandals in her hand, and she also kept her hand on the boy's shoulder.

"Po!" Jun called, holding up her hand. Her boy beamed up at her and waved back, his jet-black hair ruffled by the wind. Kaimana, up to her knees in the surf, glanced up, too, turning her back for a second to the ocean. It was Jun who saw the big blue rolling horizon behind them, twice as high as the others.

"Look out!" she shouted, but too late, as the wave came crashing into Kaimana's side, drenching her, then knocking Po straight off his feet. Next thing she knew, Po was flailing and screaming hysterically. Her heart raced as she tore down the beach to him.

## *CHAPTER ELEVEN*

KAI RAN AFTER JUN. It had all happened so fast; one second the boy was standing with his auntie in the surf, and the next he was flat on his butt, head dunked down in only about two feet of water, his mother bolting to him in a panic. At first he thought she was overreacting. After all, Po just needed to find his feet again and stand up, and he'd be fine. There was no chance of drowning, and his auntie was already bending to help him to his feet. But then Po screamed in terror, a primal kind of shout. Even when he managed to regain his footing, he didn't stop. He kept screaming.

That was when Kai realized something was wrong. Something was very wrong.

Kaimana was holding him upright, but the boy was thrashing, fighting back, kicking and shrieking, as if the very touch of water on his skin brought him pain. Jun was there, too, running out into the surf with her cross-trainers still on, not caring if they got wet. She snatched up Po in her arms, but he fought her, too, flailing as she tried to get him to the dry sand. She struggled with the thrashing boy as she walked, and then he bit her, hard, on the arm. Jun cried out in pain and, stunned, dropped Po to the sand. He took off running, but Kai intercepted him. He was in front of Po in seconds, arms on the preschooler's shoulders.

"Po! Po, you're all right. Stop." The boy's eyes were wild with fear. Kai recognized the panic. He knelt down.

"Po. Look at me. Calm down. Deep breaths. It's Kai, okay? Remember me? I'm here, Po. No need to be scared. You're not going to drown. You're fine. You're *fine*." Distantly, Kai remembered it was close to what he'd told him after the second wave hit, when they were floating in dangerous debris in the street. "I'm not leaving you, okay? You're fine."

Po blinked at Kai, as if seeing him for the first time, and then recognition flittered across his face. "Kai!" he cried and he threw his arms around Kai's neck and squeezed hard, holding on for dear life. Kai glanced up and saw Jun, holding her bitten arm, looking somber. Po didn't want to let go of Kai's neck, so he picked the boy up and he clung even tighter to him.

"I don't know what happened," Aunt Kaimana said, bewildered. "I…"

"He's afraid of the water," Jun said. "Ever since…" Her voice trailed off as she guiltily looked at Kai. Understanding dawned on Aunt Kaimana's face.

"I'm sorry. I didn't know! I just thought he didn't like to swim. I didn't think getting his feet wet would…" Regret pinched her features.

"It's okay." Jun reached out and touched her shoulder.

"Let's go inside," Kai said, suddenly feeling the weight of the moment. He realized now he wasn't the only one who hadn't healed from the tsunami, that Jun and Po carried their own kind of baggage.

Once inside, Kai grabbed a towel and wrapped Po in it. He sat the boy on the couch. Aunt Kaimana got some crackers from the kitchen and fed the boy a few. Kai went to the bathroom for more towels and Jun followed him there.

"We should go," she said, still clutching her bitten arm. "I…"

"Let me look at that," Kai said as he took a step closer to her.

"It's nothing." Pain flashed across Jun's face, and Kai didn't know if it was from the physical wound or the emotional one, the chagrin of being bitten by her own son.

"Let me see." He touched her arm and she jumped a little. He almost expected her to shove him away, but instead she cautiously reached out to him. He examined the bite mark. Po had barely broken skin, but an angry circular red mark told him she'd have quite the bruise tomorrow.

"Ouch," he said, studying it, and noticed how smooth her skin felt beneath his hands. Her arm was so small, so delicate. He glanced up and saw her gazing at him steadily, never having looked so pretty. Her dark hair was a bit windblown, her pink puffy lower lip so very kissable. *Down, boy*. He glanced back down at her arm.

"So, the teacher isn't the only one he bites. Has he done this to you before?"

"No. Never." Jun shook her head resolutely.

Kai opened the mirrored cabinet in the sleek granite bathroom and pulled out a first-aid kit. He took out bandages and some antibiotic cream.

"I've tried everything, but he still bites." Jun sighed. "And his fear of water is getting worse, not better. I just don't know what to do anymore."

The helpless frustration hit a nerve with Kai. He'd never seen Jun this vulnerable. She'd always been the one who had all the answers, with her no-nonsense "just get it done" attitude. He'd never have guessed sometimes she could feel like throwing in the towel. The frustration in her voice made him feel an urgent need to help. He felt… responsible somehow. He remembered how Po had seen his face and instantly calmed down. He knew, on some level, he could help that boy. He just knew it. But he wouldn't get a chance if Po's mother left now.

"He won't even take a bath, much less go swimming, and now he's waking up in the night screaming about water." She sucked in a shaky breath.

He wanted to pull her into his arms right at that moment. The urge was so strong it took him by surprise. He almost acted on it but stopped himself at the last moment.

"I don't know." Jun shook her head, the weight of her worry evident in her face. "Maybe we need to leave the islands."

"No," Kai said, more forcefully than he intended, as the thought of Jun and Po leaving filled him with a strange kind of disappointment. "No, it's not the island that's the problem."

"But a boy scared of water might do better on the mainland. Sometimes I think if I saved up enough, maybe we could move. Maybe if we lived in a place where there *couldn't* be tsunamis, he'd calm down. Be less afraid."

"You can't run from water," Kai pointed out. "On the mainland, they have lakes and streams and swimming pools. And they have tornadoes and hurricanes and earthquakes. There's always something to be afraid of. Do you have family here?"

"My sister. Her husband and daughter."

Kai thought about when his mother had died. If Aunt Kaimana had shipped him off to his biological father on the mainland, his life would've been completely different. He never would've learned to surf. He'd never have this bond he had with Hawaii, a place like nowhere on earth.

"When my mother died, my aunt asked me if I wanted to go live with my father on the mainland or with her. I picked her, and I would again." Kai remembered his father and the new family he so lovingly protected. He couldn't imagine being raised by him, in the Midwest, being reminded every day that he was a mistake, an afterthought. And without his surfboard to help him cope, he would've been a delinquent in jail or worse.

"Your mother died? When?" Jun looked at him with surprise.

"When I was eight," he said.

"Eight! That's…horrible." Jun shook her head. "Mine died when I was twenty. When Po was just a baby."

"It's hard to lose your mother at any age." Kai held Jun's hand and squeezed it. She sent him a weak smile. He knew it was true. It was impossible to explain what it was like to lose a parent to anyone who hadn't lost one.

"She was…disappointed with me that I got pregnant so young. Sometimes I feel like she's still disappointed with me. That she'd think I'm a bad mom." Jun shook her head, biting her lip, her face flushed with emotion as she looked at the floor.

They were standing so close now. Every inch of her body seemed to scream out to him to be comforted. He wanted so badly to do it, to wrap her in his arms and make all the worry go away. The desire to do so was so intense he had a hard time fighting it.

Kai shook his head. "Hey," he said, tucking his finger under her chin to raise it. "You're the best mom I know. Po is lucky to have you. You're strong and smart and you'll figure this stuff with him out."

Jun blinked back tears, and Kai could see a grateful look pass across her eyes. Her shoulders relaxed a little. "You really think so?" Her vulnerability, her doubt, shook him. Made him see her in an entirely different light. She wasn't someone with all the answers, a know-it-all. She was just like him: struggling with problems she wasn't sure she could solve.

"Yes, I do. And it will be easier for you to do with *'ohana*," he added, using the Hawaiian word for family. "Not just *'ohana* by blood, but…" He realized he'd been about to say something about *him*. It had dawned on him just today when he'd carried that boy across the beach how he'd started to feel as if Jun and Po were *'ohana*, his *'ohana*. But that was wrong. They weren't his.

He took a step back from her and dropped her hands. "...but, you know, Hawaii is a special place. Locals look after one another."

It was true and always had been. The island might have tsunamis, but the locals lived in a special kind of tribe, doing favors for one another, making sure they all got by during difficult times. The spirit of Hawaii radiated through smiles and nods, the ushering of locals to the head of the luau line, and the delivery of fruit baskets to grieving families. Kai also remembered how the entire island had come together after the tsunami to help rebuild what the ocean had taken away. He glanced up and realized that by stepping back, he'd broken whatever moment they'd been sharing. She nodded, recovering her composure, the wall protecting her vulnerability once again going up.

"You're right." Jun smiled bravely, her can-do spirit back again.

"I think Po can learn to overcome his fear," Kai said.

"I should be spending more time with him, but with two jobs..." Jun abruptly buttoned up. It was obvious she wasn't going to ask him for what he owed her from the contract, even though it was clear she desperately needed it.

"I owe you your severance," he said, opening the wrapper of the bandage.

Jun shook her head, tilting up her chin in subtle defiance. "I'm not going to take that."

"You need it."

"I didn't earn it." Her dark eyes flashed, and Kai had to admire the fire in them. Most people he met, especially all the tourists, were happy to let him foot the bill for everything. None of them had second thoughts about spending his money. And here was Jun, who'd signed a contract that said he owed her, and she wasn't going to take it! Inwardly, he shook his head, appreciating her stubborn independence as he stuck the bandage on. Then he knew what he'd have to do. He really didn't have a choice.

"I'll hire you back," he said.

"You don't want to hire me," Jun pointed out as she pulled back her arm. "I'm not going to be a pity case."

"You're not going to be. I need your help and you need mine. It's an equal trade."

Jun just stared. "You'll sign the contract? For real?"

He'd almost forgotten about that. In his mind, he groaned. No sex. No alcohol. And no junk food. Well, what was four months, really? He could handle it. It was a small price to pay to make sure she and Po were set. That they didn't have to worry about money for a little bit. They had enough to worry about—that was plain to see.

"Sure."

"Promise?"

"It's a promise," he said, hoping he could stick to it.

## CHAPTER TWELVE

WHEN JUN DROVE to Kai's house the next morning, down the beautiful shoreline highway, she wondered if she was making a mistake. Po, however, was beyond excited as they pulled up to the curb.

"Kai's house!" Po exclaimed as Jun helped the little boy out of his car seat. She winced a little about how thrilled he sounded. Po worshipped Kai, and the worship had only grown after yesterday. Jun remembered the seemingly magical touch the man had with her son, calming him down when even she couldn't. Inside, she felt torn—grateful to Kai for the help but nervous that the gratitude could turn into something like dependence. In her world, when you started depending on people, that was exactly when they disappointed you.

She thought about her mother, about the cold cruelty and anger on her face when she'd told her about her pregnancy. Her mom had always been so strict, so absolute about her rules, and yet part of Jun had hoped in that moment for a little bit of empathy. She wanted unconditional love and support. She'd even thought that after her mother's temper died down, she would help her with Po. At least help her with the pregnancy and delivery, which had frightened her out of her wits.

*You won't get my pity,* her mother had said at the time, and she'd kept that promise. *You made your bed. Now you lie in it.*

But her mother's cold shoulder and stubborn refusal to have anything to do with her or her baby after that had taught her that the only person she could rely on was herself. In some ways, she thought, her mother had been right to do it. Jun was a stronger, more independent single mom now.

After her mother's reaction, she'd vowed never to need anyone again. And she hadn't.

*Except that morning of the tsunami. You needed someone then. You couldn't be there for Po. You can't be everywhere all the time.*

She pushed the thought from her mind, focusing instead on Kai's front door. She waited on his porch, holding Po's hand, telling herself to watch her son. He was already so attached to Kai. He idolized the man. Kai might have saved her son's life, but she was still going to guard the boy's heart as best she could. Po had had enough disappointments in his life.

Besides, Kai might have decided he was up for training, but Jun was still skeptical he'd see it through. She feared that he had too much quit in him, making him capitulate when things got too rough. No doubt it was because he was so damn charismatic. Gorgeous men rarely had to work hard for anything, she suspected.

She half expected Kai to answer the door hungover and with a woman hidden in his bedroom. But to her surprise, he opened the door looking bright eyed and awake, wearing gym shorts and a sleeveless cotton workout T-shirt showing off his sculpted tan arms.

"Kai!" Po cried, bursting with excitement. Kai, in a warm show of affection, scooped up the boy without hesitation.

"How's my big guy?" Kai asked, swinging him up and then putting him back down again. The boy squealed with glee.

"Is Auntie here?"

"In here, Po," she called. "Want to help me make a special necklace?"

Po shrugged. "Sure," he said, and bounded into Kai's house. Aunt Kaimana sat on the edge of the open lanai, a big teak bowl filled with dried macadamia shells in front of her. She was going to show Po how to bead. "Do you know how to count in Hawaiian?" the woman asked, and Po shook his head slowly. "Well, *that's* what we're going to learn today."

Kaimana smiled at Jun and she nodded back

at the woman. "One. *Ekahi, ho'okahi,*" Kaimana said, holding up a single shell. Po, fascinated, went to sit by her and picked up the shell.

"I have something to show you," Kai said. As Jun walked past his glass bar, she saw all his bottles of spirits were gone. "I packed them all up," Kai said.

"Every last bottle?"

"Every one." Jun couldn't help but feel surprised. He was really trying. "And I made this." She followed his broad shoulders into the kitchen, where she saw a blender full of green smoothie. He poured some into a glass and offered it to her.

"*My* kale smoothie," Kai said. "A tweak on your recipe." He offered her a sip and she took one. The lemon, kale and apple were there, but another sweeter and smoother taste followed. "Mango," he said, filling in the secret ingredient.

"It's good." *Maybe even better than mine.*

"So? What's first up today?" Kai looked so... willing as his magnetic eyes waited for her answer. She had to admit, it threw her.

"Meditation," Jun said instantly. "First we meditate and then we exercise."

JUN DESPERATELY TRIED to clear her mind of pesky thoughts as she sat cross-legged on a beach mat just feet from Kai under a lush Bodhi tree in the middle of the Paleaku Gardens Peace Sanctuary. Normally, the serene seven acres of botanical gardens in South Kona were the perfect place to meditate. Amazing views of Kealakekua Bay assaulted them from nearly every angle, and everywhere she looked seemed ready-made for a postcard. The garden was a beautiful spot, quiet and peaceful. Jun couldn't help but sneak a look at Kai and saw how much he was trying—legs crossed, hands palm up on his knees. But all Jun could think about was his muscled frame near hers, the sound of his steady, rhythmic breathing. She felt hyperaware of his body's slightest shifts, of even the breeze rustling his gym shorts.

What was wrong with her?

Usually, she could block out anything. Meditation, so good in so many ways, lowered her blood pressure, helped her feel calmer, more in control. But with Kai sitting next to her, she felt anything but in control.

"Keep your mind clear. Listen to the sound of my voice," she instructed, but the missive was as much for herself. "Deep breaths. In and out."

Kai took one deep breath and then let it go. Jun, having given up on meditating herself, opened her eyes and studied Kai. His chin was so strong, his mouth a sensual curve. He was half smiling, as she'd told him to do. A small smile could make or break a good meditation session. As she took in his smooth skin, the strong slope of his neck, she just wanted to stare at him all afternoon, like this, when he didn't know she was looking.

Then he squinted one eye open, catching her off guard. "You're supposed to have your eyes closed," Kai said, cocking his head to one side.

"I'm the teacher," she pointed out.

"I can feel you staring at me." Kai grinned, his smile lighting up his whole face. She could feel the warmth in her bones. The powerful desire she had to put her hands on him stunned her. What was wrong with her? She'd happily been man-free for two years. *Now* all of a sudden, she couldn't stop thinking about what this man's lips would feel like.

Kai glanced up. "The tree is pretty."

"It's a Bodhi, the kind of tree Buddha is supposed to have meditated under when he attained enlightenment. It's a holy tree for Buddhists, and they think the tree contains the meaning of life."

Kai studied the tree's low-lying leafy branches. "Are you Buddhist?"

Jun shook her head. "No. I'm…still working out what I believe. My mother was a staunch atheist. I respect all religions, though. I think maybe when we die, we'll figure out that somehow they all work together. That God has a bigger plan and that really everyone is right."

"It's a nice thought," Kai said, studying her.

"It's like alternative medicine and traditional

medicine. Neither one is completely right, but together, maybe we can figure it all out," Jun said. "It's why I love this garden. There are exhibits representing so many points of view. The Bodhi tree is just one."

Kai exhaled slowly, looking around them.

"Do you feel better?" Jun asked him. They'd meditated for only about ten minutes, but sometimes that was all a person needed.

"More relaxed," Kai admitted.

"Meditation lowers blood pressure, gives peace of mind and clarity, helps you feel better and focus more." She tried to think of the dozen other benefits she'd learned, but Kai staring at her made her brain feel like spaghetti.

"I can see that," Kai said. "*If* you didn't stare at me while I did it." He grinned. "You're a distraction."

"I'm not." *He* was the distraction, with those sharp brown eyes and that smooth tanned face, that rugged square jaw.

"Oh, yes, you are."

"Let's try a little bit of stretching," Jun offered, eager to get on her feet and lose the hormones buzzing in her veins.

"Yoga? I don't know." Kai shook his head. "I've never really done yoga before."

"You haven't?" exclaimed Jun, shocked. "But with surfing, it could help with your balance, flexibility and strength. Why *haven't* you been doing yoga? I would think every surfer would be doing an hour a day."

Kai shrugged. "Just never got into it."

Jun shook her head in disbelief. "Okay, let's start with Mountain pose," she said as she arranged herself. "Palms together and feet apart, stand straight." Kai stood and mimicked her. "Breathe in…and out…"

"There's a lot of breathing," Kai muttered.

"The body needs oxygen, and we don't give it enough," Jun said. "Now let's curl down for Downward-Facing Dog." Jun showed Kai what she meant, curling her back and putting her palms on the spongy grass, her body making a tentlike triangle. Kai followed her, craning his neck to keep up. Jun tried not to be distracted by Kai's bulging calf muscles. She failed.

"Now let's head up to Warrior pose." Jun straightened, took one giant step with a bent knee. Kai mimicked, but his foot was turned the wrong way.

"Out, like this," Jun said as she broke her own pose to help Kai get into the right position. "Then bend down and twist for Triangle pose." Jun put her hands on his thick shoulders and helped him twist. Yoga usually calmed her, but feeling Kai's strong muscles beneath her hands, she felt nerves prick along her skin, and her stomach was a riot of emotions. Why was she nervous? She noticed Kai staring up at her.

"I feel like a pretzel," he said. Jun felt warmth grow in the pit of her stomach.

"You don't look like one," she said. *You look amazingly, heart-stoppingly sexy.*

Kai met her gaze, twisted as he was, and wobbled, nearly losing his balance. Jun tried to save him by grabbing his shoulder, but she overcorrected, and Kai's weak knee wasn't able to compensate. They both went tumbling down into the grass, Kai on his back and Jun right on top of him.

"Are you okay?" Kai asked, grabbing Jun's shoulders, concern on his face.

"I'm…" Jun was about to say *fine*, but then she realized she was pressed against Kai, their noses nearly touching, his rigid stomach and muscled chest firm beneath her. She didn't want to move, yet she wasn't sure she should stay still. She was deliciously uncomfortable.

She felt as though she were drowning in his warm, rich eyes, as they'd grown suddenly and irrevocably serious. He wasn't letting go of her shoulders, and she didn't want him to. If she'd thought sitting next to him had been distracting, lying on top of him was a whole other level of irrational thought. Unable to help herself, she glanced at Kai's lower lip, full and just millimeters from her own mouth. She could feel the hormones zinging through her veins, lighting her blood on fire. The only important question was: *What do his lips feel like?*

She didn't know whether she was moving closer to him or he to her, but before she could regain control, her lips touched his, igniting a spark she knew immediately she wouldn't be able to control. Jun had wondered if she even remembered how to kiss a man, but with Kai, it was as if she'd always been meant to kiss him. His lips gently explored hers, tasting like the mild trade winds off the sea. Jun's lips parted and she felt his tongue, the warm wetness of it, and suddenly the blaze in her mind ran so hot she felt she might faint from the heat. All she wanted was more of him. His arms tightened around her waist, pressing her closer into his body, and she thought they might melt together. His hands ran the length of her back, and she shivered, wishing for a minute she could rip off her top, feel his hands on her bare skin.

Nothing made sense in that moment and yet everything did: she wanted Kai Brady. Had wanted him maybe since she'd first met him a year ago. Despite everything she said about not wanting to get involved with another man, despite everything that told her Kai was the last man on earth she ought to consider seriously, her body had different ideas.

*Maybe this was the way I always wanted to*

*repay him that debt.* White-hot need surged through her body as she thought about what it would be like to give herself, all of herself, to this man.

Then, abruptly, like a bucket of cold water, she heard her mother's voice in her head: *Girls who let themselves get carried away have only themselves to blame.*

Suddenly, she broke the kiss, reason bursting its way through the moment.

*I can't do this. I shouldn't do this.* Jun pulled away, out of breath, and as she did, she saw that Kai's eyes had dilated as he, too, panted beneath her, and for an instant, Jun thought he could see right through her, straight to her core. *He knows I want him.*

Embarrassed, she scurried to her feet, nearly losing her balance once more as her shaky knees almost buckled. Flustered, she frantically pushed her hair from her face.

Kai sat up on one elbow, a lazy smile crossing his face as he gazed up at her. "You okay?" he asked.

"You shouldn't have done that," she sputtered, one hand holding her waist, as if she worried the heat still spilling through her would somehow explode and she'd jump on him again. Slowly and deliberately, Kai got to his feet.

"*I* didn't do anything. *You* kissed me." The corner of Kai's full mouth lifted, his dark eyes sparkling as he stretched his muscled shoulders.

"I didn't!" Did she? Jun didn't know. Could she have kissed Kai first? All she knew was that her lips were still tingling from the contact. She put her hand over her mouth.

"Really? I thought you were just testing me."

Jun glanced up, confused. "Testing?"

"Your rule number three—no sex." Kai's smile grew bigger and Jun felt embarrassment roll up her neck and flame her ears.

"W-we should get back to your house," she muttered, not able to look him in the eye. "Time for you to do some strength training."

"Yes, ma'am," Kai said, nodding deferentially. "Just…try not to kiss me again," he added. "I'm not sure I'll be able to keep rule number three if you do."

# CHAPTER THIRTEEN

A WEEK LATER, Kai hummed to himself as he rounded the last mile of a three-mile jog down the beach, sweat dripping down his temples in the warm Hawaiian sun. He ran shirtless, the cool ocean breeze caressing his bare skin. He'd found the chink in Jun's armor, and the discovery put him in a stellar mood. He'd thought, up until now, the woman was nearly asexual, having not had sex in who knew how long and holding him to a standard of absolute abstinence, and yet *she* was the one who had kissed him. He knew he hadn't imagined it. He'd been frozen, his head flat against the dewy grass. She'd *definitely* kissed him.

They'd worked together closely for days, and he noticed in no uncertain terms that she was having a hard time not repeating her performance at the botanical gardens. He could tell how stiffly she tried to avoid incidental contact. Yesterday when she'd handed him a celery smoothie and their fingers touched, she'd nearly jumped a mile. The thought brought a sly grin to his face. He liked keeping Jun Lee off balance. She had everything—from what he ate to when he slept—under such strict control that he liked pressing her buttons and watching her react. She was so tightly wound he wondered what would happen if he got her into his bed. If she really let go, the sex would be amazing. All that pent-up coiled energy released at once? He could only imagine it. And he did. Often.

If she knew he imagined her naked beneath him—and on top of him and in front of him and beside him—she didn't let on. He jogged down the sandy beach, barefoot, his feet making imprints in the wet sand as he went. He passed two pretty beachgoers in bikinis and oversize sunglasses who craned their necks to get a better look at him as he ran by, but he barely gave them a second look. His mind was too focused on Jun. She'd sent him out for this run so he could "work out bad energy," she'd said, but it was *her* energy he was most interested in.

When he'd accidentally-on-purpose brushed her elbow in his weight room, she'd been so startled she almost stumbled. She'd banished him from his own house right after. He wondered if she'd been thinking of kissing him then. He'd been thinking of kissing her. He could hardly look at her tight little rear in those spandex capris without wondering what it would be like to peel them off her. But that would, of course, be breaking rule number three. Some rules were meant to be broken.

Besides, could she blame him for breaking the rule if *she* was the one begging him to break it?

He couldn't help but inwardly laugh at the thought. How much would he love that? The victory would be too sweet. He'd get to have her and prove to her that her silly rule didn't make a difference one way or the other.

Kai still didn't believe sex was his problem when it came to surfing.

Granted, he had to admit that the meditation and the yoga had been helping his state of mind. *And* the fact that he'd given up alcohol had allowed him to focus more. He had no doubt about that. In just a week, Jun had helped him feel stronger, healthier and more like his old self.

He jogged by the crystal-blue Pacific, sparkling under a clear blue sky, and watched the waves crash at the break at the reef about a half mile out. Foam burst up in the air as the waves rolled through.

*But you haven't been out there yet. You haven't been on a board since the last wipeout. What does any of this matter if you can't get on a board?*

It was true. His board hung unused on the wall in his garage, mocking him. Jun hadn't pushed him to go out—yet. But she'd been hinting that was coming soon. She called his first week a "detox" week and said that he'd be better equipped to tackle waves after his body had gotten used to his new regimen. Secretly, he'd been relieved. He was in no hurry to get back on the board. And that very thought scared him more than anything else.

*You're scared, and you should be. You've got no business being on that board, and you know it.*

No matter how he tried to shake it, the doubt was always there. And the minute he thought it, he felt a twinge in his weak knee. He stopped running, worried that he'd hurt it. Gingerly, he began walking at a slow pace, wondering when his knee would feel strong again, whole. When would it *not* feel like a flimsy rubber band?

Distantly, out on shore, he swore he saw a bright flash of an orange kayak. Was that Bret Jon? His old tow partner?

Kai stopped and squinted, trying to make him out. No, of course that wasn't Bret. Just some guy who had a similar kayak. Bret lived on Maui now. He'd flown to the Big Island only at Kirk's request, probably under some pretense Kirk made up, and he was probably long home by now. Kai should call him, but he knew Bret wouldn't answer. It would be one more call sent directly to voice mail.

The last time he and Bret surfed together had been six months ago, just after the doctors cleared him for surfing. He'd decided to go for it on Pe'ahi.

Pe'ahi—Jaws to the locals—broke on the north side of Maui. This wasn't regular old surfing. This was being towed by a Jet Ski into waves upward of fifty feet. Extreme surfing in the most dangerous way. They called it Jaws because it was as unpredictable as a shark attack and just as deadly.

Kai had thought he'd been ready. Bret had had his doubts.

"You sure you wanna do this man?" Bret had said, shaking his head as he glanced at the roaring waves. "You've been hitting tourist beaches, and I don't know that you're ready for this."

"I'm ready." The more Bret told him he wasn't ready, the more Kai thought he was. Kai had always been stubborn. After all, it was that stubbornness that fueled his determination to risk his life surfing waves never really meant to be surfed in the first place. Bret had said dozens of times that big-wave surfers were born, not made, so he should've known it was just something in Kai's blood.

He'd fallen a few times on regular pipes, but Jaws would *force* him to surf or it would knock him down. Either way, he'd get the kick in the butt he'd thought he'd needed at the time. Kai had been thinking only of himself. He knew that now. He hadn't considered he'd be putting his tow partner at risk when he came barreling in on the Jet Ski to save him if he busted it. He and Bret had ridden together so much, had worked together seamlessly for years, and Bret was even more of a risk taker, an adrenaline junkie, than Kai was. And he was good at it. Kai had always told Bret he didn't expect to be saved, but he should've known by then that Bret was always going to try.

Bret had stopped big-wave surfing himself at his wife's request the day after he came back from his honeymoon, but he'd kept on towing Kai, out of respect and because of their shared history. Towing was supposed to be safer than surfing. Most of the time.

But both men knew how dangerous it all was. You rode the devil, and sometimes he'd bite you. They'd lost friends out there on the reef.

"Sarah wants me to stop towing after this year," Bret had told Kai on that beach. "She's having a baby and she wants me to stop. Says no dad should be out in these waves."

"I get it, man." And Kai did. It was going to be their last season together.

When Bret started talking about maybe Kai not being ready, Kai had just thought it was the nervous soon-to-be dad in him talking. It had never occurred to him that Bret was talking to him earnestly, that he *truly* thought Kai wasn't ready.

Bret had been right. Kai hadn't been ready and he'd nearly killed them both that day.

As he looked out on the ocean, vast and blue and powerful, Kai sucked in a few deep breaths, hoping that there'd be more weights in the afternoon. Jun might want to meditate, but he didn't want to be alone with his doubts in silence. Not today.

Kai swiped at the sweat across his brow and saw his house in the distance. He'd grown up in a tiny little two-bedroom house, next door to Allie and her grandmother's coffee farm. His aunt had worked odd jobs when he was little: babysitting or working the register at gift shops or stringing leis for tourists. Kai and Jesse had always had food in their bellies and clothes on their backs, but it hadn't been easy. Now Kai had a bigger house than he'd ever dreamed of owning and more clothes than he knew what to do with, most of them with his name on the label, like the ones he was wearing. Kirk, had told him that they might be closing a deal with a big-box store to bring the line to a mass audience. That would mean even more money.

"I'm trying to close the deal before the competition," he'd said. "But they might want to wait. See the kind of press you generate after hitting Jaws again."

Kai wondered what would happen if everyone found out he was a fraud. If he wasn't a surfing champion, if he wasn't trying to break world records for surfing hundred-foot waves, then how fast would all the money go away? How quickly would Kirk desert him?

And then there was Bret. He'd warned Kai to stay off Jaws. Or else. He knew the man wasn't kidding, either.

Sweat dripped down Kai's bare back as he made his way up the stairs to his backyard, his knee protesting every step. The pain was gone, he noticed, but the strength wasn't there. Not in the least. The flimsy-rubber-band feeling just wouldn't go away.

He crested the landing and walked by his immense pool and Jacuzzi tub, wishing he could slip into the warm water and hit the jet bubbles, but his workout wasn't done yet. If he knew Jun, she'd have something else planned for him.

He noticed Po's sand bucket and shovel left near the back door, washed out but still drying, pictures of happy green sea turtles swimming around its blue base. He realized how odd it was to see children's things near his house. Yet he didn't find it unsettling in the least. He kind of liked the bucket there, lined up beside Po's tiny little sandals. So small. The boy had been an unexpected joy of the week.

Just then Po came bounding up to the back door, grinning. "Kai! Fist bump!" he shouted, as he did now every time he saw Kai, since he'd taught the boy how to do an exploding fist bump.

"Bam!" Kai said, and the boy giggled as the two bounced closed fists together.

"All right, that's enough," Aunt Kaimana said. "Kai has to train."

"For big waves!" Po cried, and then threw his little arms out as if he were catching a wave on the shiny wooden living room floor.

"Come on, little one, it's close to naptime," Aunt Kaimana said, tapping the boy on the shoulder.

"Aw, do I *have* to?"

"Believe me, kiddo, take advantage of naptime now," Kai told the little boy. "You'll *wish* you had naptime when you're a grown-up." Kai glanced around the empty living room. "Where's Jun?" Kai asked his aunt.

"In the garage, I think. Making *more lists*," his aunt warned him, "on her *clipboard*." Kaimana raised her eyebrows for emphasis, which made Kai smile. Jun's clipboard was as rigid as her regimen: she kept a no-skip checklist for him for every day of the week. Even Kaimana, who thought he needed discipline, thought the list was overkill. It had his entire day planned out to the minute.

"Do you have bathroom breaks planned in there?" he'd joked on Monday. As it turned out, she *had*.

If he thought Gretchen had been merciless, he'd gotten the shock of his life.

Now, he wandered out to the garage. He saw her standing, clipboard under her arm, glancing up at his collection of boards. He couldn't help appreciating her firm curves, and the shorter-than-should-be-street-legal shorts she was wearing certainly caught his attention. He felt his body respond in new ways. Women hit on him all the time. He'd bedded more than his fair share, and yet…something about Jun just disarmed him. Maybe it was her steadfast insistence that she wasn't interested. Everything about her stiff, determined posture screamed challenge.

And Kai was never one to back down from a challenge.

"Looking for something?" he asked, and Jun started at the sound of his voice. When she turned, a small, barely visible blush crept up her cheeks.

"Oh…good…you're back." He watched her struggle to regain her composure and put on the professional veneer that had momentarily slipped.

"See one you like?" he asked her, nodding at the wall of surfboards.

"I don't know. Which one is your favorite?"

Kai felt a ripple of unease in his stomach as he looked at the five boards, including the one, up top, that he'd used to win last year's championship. He looked at the old board, one handmade by Hawaiian surfing and surfboard-shaping legend Ben Aipa. It was waxed and well cared for, but the old logos were worn and faded from overuse. He used to think it was his lucky board, but now he was almost afraid to surf with it. Afraid his bum knee might somehow suck all the magic out of it. Kai remembered watching old clips of the master surfing when he was little. Aipa had made one championship board after another since 1970.

"That one," he lied, pointing to one of the new demos, one of the ones Kirk wanted him to be seen surfing with, a board that was fine but lacked the finesse of his favorite.

"*This* one?" Jun narrowed her eyes. "I don't believe you. *This* is the one I see you on in all the posters." She tapped the championship board, as if she saw right through the lie.

"That's my Ben Aipa board," he admitted. *The board that slices through water like a shark, almost anticipating every move the water makes.*

"Ben Aipa! We must go test it out."

"What do you mean 'we'?"

"We're going surfing. Today. Now."

"Now? But…" Kai desperately looked for an excuse. He glanced out the open garage door to the white-capped waves. "I don't know that there's good surf today…"

"It's Hawaii. There's *always* good surf." Jun grinned at him, and he knew there'd be no getting out of it. He swallowed the trepidation in his throat. *Now she's going to find out what a fraud you really are.* "Which board do you want?"

"This one," Kai said, stubbornly sticking to the Kai Brady prototype.

"Fine, mind if I borrow the Ben Aipa?"

"Wait, *you* surf? Since when? Why didn't I know this about you?"

"I learned when I was fifteen," Jun said, shrugging one shoulder. "Had a crush on a boy who surfed *every* day. I had to learn if I ever wanted to talk to him. But I only did it for a year and then quit."

Kai tried to imagine Jun at fifteen, chasing after some surfer dude on a Big Island beach. He felt an irrational flare of jealousy. Where had *that* come from?

"How long did you date?" Why did he care?

"We didn't," Jun said, and Kai felt a perverted kind of relief. "But I did learn to surf. That was something. So, can I use it? I've never surfed with one."

Kai hesitated. The old Kai would've hated to have a novice surfer out with him on the breaks, slowing him down, causing him worry, and he'd never let a novice near his championship board. Now he was surprised to find himself even considering it.

Jun studied him. "I mean, I'd like the board, if *you* don't want to use it." Kai got the impression Jun was testing him. Or trying to get him back on his favorite board. He struggled with admitting his fear of using it *and* his reluctance to let anyone *else* touch it.

"I have to see how you surf first," Kai said, hoping to buy himself some time. "Use this one, and then I'll see if you're Ben Aipa–worthy."

"Fair enough," June said.

"Should we stick to little waves?" Kai asked Jun, hoping she'd say yes and give him an excuse to take it easy, hit the small pipes. *Not that you could handle anything else.* He tried to shake the doubt from his mind, but the problem was he knew that inner voice spoke the truth.

"Sure," she said. "Let's surf."

FIFTEEN MINUTES LATER, Jun and Kai were paddling out together in the cerulean Pacific, headed toward the break. Kai watched Jun paddle easily, her muscled arms working against the current. She looked as if she knew what she was doing. Sun made the drops of water on her shoulders gleam. He'd never found her so attractive as then: black hair swiped up in a tight wet bun, makeup-free face lifted up from her board, eyes focused on the water. Kai might have found her weakness, but he wondered, fleetingly, if she'd found his. He had a hard time concentrating on the rhythm of paddling with his arms with her so close to him. She caught him staring at her and she smiled.

"Race you," she called, and began paddling up to a looming wave in the distance. She got a head start and was going to catch it. Heart pounding, he trailed her, for once not thinking about his knee as he watched her backside bob back and forth on the board. He could follow those firm, fit curves, anywhere, he thought as he doubled his efforts to catch up.

Jun turned her board at the precise right moment as the big wave came rolling in. Kai was watching her half-hypnotized as she popped up perfectly on the board. Her toned legs held her weight easily as she balanced on his surfboard. He was so busy looking at her bare legs that he hardly had time to ready himself and his own board. In a hurry, he turned and stood, steering his board after hers in the small four-foot wave as she ducked into the blue barrel of water, gliding perfectly across its face.

"Catch me if you can," she shouted.

She wasn't an expert surfer, but she had the muscle and balance to make it work. Kai was impressed. He was so focused on following her and keeping up that he didn't realize he'd been surfing for a good five minutes, that he'd ridden the wave through. Jun looked back at him and laughed, her white teeth sparkling against her smooth skin, and for a second he was lost in the gleeful moment of having fun.

Then his brain kicked on. *This is the longest you've stayed upright since the accident.* He was suddenly aware of the loose-rubber-band feeling in his knee. *It's going to give out.*

Seconds later, he felt himself tumbling into the deep blue, board sliding away from him, the security line tugging painfully at his ankle, nothing around him but stinging salt water and the rush of bubbles and cold, wet panic.

JUN SAW KAI go down but almost didn't believe it. She knew surfing wipeouts happened all the time, but she'd never seen Kai Brady lose it on such a tepid wave. Still upright, she swooped back but saw his head bobbing to the surface as the wave pushed him into shore. He got caught up in the roar of a newer, bigger wave that pushed on past hers and drove him to the beach. All she could do was hang on and ride toward him, her own wave quickly losing energy to the one sweeping Kai from her. Kai flailed in a panic, arms and legs everywhere. She watched, worried and helpless, as he gasped for air. The sea didn't seem that choppy, and yet, she knew from experience, sometimes the currents were stronger below. Jun caught up with him when he was in the shallows, board still tethered to his leg, his hair dripping wet and plastered to his head, and he himself red faced and hacking up salt water.

"Kai, are you okay?" Jun managed, getting to him at last.

"Leave me alone," he growled.

"Kai…" She reached out to touch him, but he whipped his arm away from her. And stomped up the beach. Angrily, he yanked off the surfboard tether, happy to let the board drift off to sea. Jun knew it was an expensive prototype. She grabbed the security line and dragged it behind her.

"Kai, wait!" Jun pulled two boards behind her as she followed the tense slope of his shoulders. She knew he was embarrassed and she knew why: his knee. It was the only explanation for what had happened out there. She'd seen it give way in the gym, and now she'd seen it give way in the surf. Coincidence? She was beginning to think not.

After the boards were safely on shore, she dropped the security lines and jogged after Kai. Thankfully, the beach was mostly deserted, although a few tourists had set up blankets and umbrellas.

"Wait!" she called, running after him.

When she'd gotten close enough, he whirled. "You wanted to see me surf—are you happy now?" She hadn't expected the sudden red burst of rage.

"Kai, it's okay. Let's calm down—"

"It's not okay! Did you see that out there? Did you?" Pent-up frustration boiled over in his eyes. He ran a hand through his wet hair.

"One misstep."

"Hardly. It's not one—it's *every time*."

This stopped Jun cold in her tracks. This happened *every* time he went surfing? Now she realized how far he was from truly recovered. Now she understood what was really at stake: he might not be *able* to surf. The realization hit her harder than she'd anticipated. She'd had doubts about his knee, but even she hadn't thought it was this bad. For once, she was out of options. If he couldn't stay on the board…how could she help him?

"We'll figure this out," she said. "We can do more strength exercises. We can find a way…"

"There is no way!" Kai stepped right up to her then, glaring at her as they stood nose to nose. "I'm handicapped, okay? Probably forever! Because…"

*Because of Po.* He didn't have to say it, because she filled in the blanks for him. All at once, she felt the hopelessness of the debt she owed him. Her son's life might have cost him his surfing career. Could she live with that? She knew she could, because she'd give anything to have Po live, but this thing wasn't hers to offer.

"I'm sorry, Kai." It wouldn't make things right, but it was the only thing she could think of to say.

"Why are *you* sorry?"

"Because…it's…my fault. Po's. Ours. It's…"

"No, it's not. Don't ever say that." Anger still simmered in his voice.

Suddenly, Kai's mouth was on hers. He wrapped her up in his arms and pressed her into his body, his mouth ravishing hers as his tongue whipped mercilessly into her mouth. She was so taken aback she didn't fight him. She opened her mouth to receive him and felt the rage and the passion simultaneously in his lips. He tasted like the ocean, salty and wild, and his strong hands cupped her behind, lifting her up, and her legs wrapped around his waist as he held her. She was kissing him back, powerless to do anything more, cowed by guilt and shame and regret, knowing that if it was her body that he needed, she'd have to give it to him. She couldn't imagine saying no, not now, when she grasped all he'd sacrificed for Po.

Not that it was even in her head to say no at all. Not when her body responded to his every touch.

He laid her roughly on the wet sand, his body heavy on top of hers, his hands roaming the length of her, nothing but thin swimsuit fabric between them, and he tugged on the strap of her suit as if on a mission, his hands furious. She thought in that moment, he wasn't Kai at all. She wondered if this was what he was like with all his other women. If all he wanted to do was release that anger and frustration, if it was just about losing himself for those blissful few minutes. She wondered if that was all he saw in her: another distraction. And then she could see that was exactly how he used sex: as a way to avoid his problems.

He dropped rough kisses down her neck and her body responded and she arched into him. What was she doing? He was using her…and yet she didn't care. It had been so long that she'd forgotten the sweet feel of a man's weight on her, the strength of his hands stroking her body.

Her belly came alive even as the warning bells sounded in her head: Was she going to let him take her, right here? On a public beach in broad daylight, just steps from the house where Po played? But the rational thought was pounded out of her head by the feel of Kai's hungry mouth on hers as his tongue laid claim to her.

She felt her body giving in to him long before her mind agreed. Then, as if drowning, she found herself gasping for air, trying to come up to breathe.

"Kai…wait…the rules," Jun panted as she pushed on Kai's chest.

"To hell with the rules." He pulled away from her, his brown eyes dilated with want, his face flushed above hers, salt water dripping off his chin.

"You need to get better. You need to train. For the competition…"

Kai frowned. "Is that what this is? You don't want me now that you know I'm broken?"

Before she could respond, she heard a voice calling.

"Kai!" the name came over the ocean breeze. Jun recognized it as Aunt Kaimana. They both glanced up to see the older woman frantically waving her arms.

Jun realized something was wrong. *Po!* Jun scrambled out from beneath Kai, and she took off running. She heard Kai coming after her.

"It's Po," Aunt Kaimana said, out of breath, to Jun. "Come quick."

# CHAPTER FOURTEEN

FEARING THE WORST, Kai sprinted inside his house after Jun, not caring about the sand he carried on his bare feet as he ran toward the sound, blood pumping in his temples, panic in his throat. Something was wrong.

"He was just taking a nap..." Aunt Kaimana said. "But now he's screaming and...he won't wake up." Kai saw the boy thrashing wildly, his eyes open but not seeing. Jun desperately tried to corral him, but he ran from her, shouting in absolute terror. This was the water incident times a million, except now there was no water.

Kai leaped into the room, scooping the boy up. He screamed more and fought him, but Kai was too strong, and he held the boy still in his arms. Aunt Kaimana was right. It was as if the boy was in some kind of strange trance. He wouldn't wake up.

"Call 911," Kai told his aunt.

KAI FOLLOWED THE ambulance that held Jun and Po, with his aunt in the passenger seat as she explained how out of the blue it had been. The boy had been yawning, so she'd laid him down for a nap. Fifteen minutes later, he was screaming and running around the room, bumping into things and nearly bringing down a dresser on top of himself.

"It was like he was possessed," Auntie said, shaking her head. "More than just a nightmare."

Kai pulled into the hospital parking lot and flew out of the car, his aunt not too far behind him. He felt his stomach shrink as he looked at the familiar white building—where he'd been rushed after the tsunami last year.

He'd sliced an artery in his leg. The doctors thought it was a miracle he'd lasted as long as he had in the water without bleeding out.

He still remembered dog-paddling and looking for floating debris Po could safely sit on. Then, not too long after that, darkness had come, and so had the first shark, attracted by the blood in the water. He'd been lucky not to have been eaten. Lucky that Dallas, who'd been looking for him in the aftermath, hadn't given up the search, or Kai would've died in that floodwater.

Kai took a deep breath as he swept through the automatic doors of the hospital, anxious to find Jun and Po. "I'll wait here," Aunt Kaimana said, sitting in the front of the waiting room. "Too many bodies back there will just make the doctors crazy."

Kai nodded and rushed back to the treatment rooms, just gurneys separated by curtains, where doctors examined a now-sleeping Po.

A resident in green scrubs, a stethoscope hung around her neck, asked Jun questions while the young mother glanced at her boy anxiously.

"Is this the first episode like this?" the resident asked, holding a clipboard where she scribbled notes.

Jun shook her head. "No, last week was the first."

"This happened before?" Kai asked, his voice louder than he'd intended. Jun glanced at him guiltily and then away.

"It wasn't this bad," Jun said. "The first time, he eventually went back to bed. I just thought he was having a nightmare."

The resident in green scrubs nodded and pushed up her wire-frame glasses on her nose. She put down her clipboard and resumed her examination of the boy, listening to his heart and lungs and looking in his eyes.

A nurse walked in wearing scrubs showing surfing bears in Hawaiian shirts and sunglasses. Kai's hands twitched. Something was wrong with Po and he was terrified to find out what it was. Autism? Brain tumor? Worse? Po lay still, seeming as if he was sleeping soundly on the gurney. Had they given him something? He looked at Jun, saw her tense mouth and wondered how she managed to keep it together.

"You'll need to fill out these forms," the nurse said as she handed over a clipboard.

"My insurance probably won't cover this," Jun said. "I mean, my deductible is pretty high."

"I'll cover it," Kai volunteered.

"That's generous of you, but I can't accept that." Jun folded her arms across her chest.

"Yes, you can. He had this episode at my house, and I'll cover it," Kai said, resolute. He could see fight brimming in Jun's dark eyes, but she wasn't going to win. He felt responsible for the boy and covering a thousand-dollar ER visit was the least he could do. And it had been his call to get an ambulance. He took the clipboard from the surprised nurse and began filling in his information.

"All the bills will come to me," he said, handing the clipboard back along with his credit card. The nurse took it before Jun could protest further.

"Don't fight me on this," Kai warned her. Jun, seemingly too anxious about Po to argue more, let it drop.

Po came awake, it seemed, glancing around him at the adult faces.

"Mommy?" Po asked.

"I'm here, sweetie. I'm here." She rushed to his side and held his hand.

"Hi, big guy," Kai said, taking up a position behind Jun. The boy smiled at him.

"Kai!" he exclaimed, happy.

"Po, I'm Dr. Hill," said the resident. "Do you remember what happened?"

"I was sleepy," he said. "I took a nap?"

"That's it?"

Po nodded.

"Okay, I'm going to shine this light in your eyes, all right? It will be bright."

Po nodded again, and the doctor took out the pen light and examined Po, and then she plugged the stethoscope to her ears and listened to his heartbeat.

Po lay very still, his dark hair a rioting mess around his head. "Breathe in and out," Dr. Hill told Po as she listened to his lungs through the stethoscope. "That's it. Just like that."

Eventually, she withdrew. "You did just fine, Po. Thank you." She grinned at the boy and the boy smiled back.

Dr. Hill looked at Jun. "Ms. Lee, I think Po is fine."

"But what happened this afternoon?" Kai knew what he'd seen. The boy wouldn't wake up.

"If I had to guess, what Po experienced was something we call night terrors, although that's really a misnomer, as they don't always happen at night."

"Night terrors?" Kai hadn't heard of them before.

"It's like sleepwalking, except there's intense fear involved," Dr. Hill said. "Has Po been having trouble sleeping lately?"

Jun nodded. "We both have," she admitted.

Kai glanced at her. They both hadn't been sleeping? He wondered why not.

"He's been having a lot of nightmares," Jun explained to the doctor. "And not a lot of sleep. And he's been coming into my bed but…" Jun swallowed hard. "I was raised kids don't sleep in adult beds, so I've been walking him back a lot."

"Night terrors often happen when there's lack of sleep involved," Dr. Hill said.

"What about…the tsunami? Could that be…?"

"Stress plays a factor," the doctor said, tucking her stethoscope around her neck and putting her hands in the pockets of her white coat. "This could be residual from that event, but children are usually amazingly resilient. Have there been any other stressful events lately?"

Jun recounted the day-care biting incident and, of course, the teacher nearly throwing him in the pool, and then the close call with the waves near Kai's house. Dr. Hill nodded her head sympathetically.

She smiled at Po. "So you don't like the water?"

Po's eyes grew wide in fear as he shook his head vigorously.

Dr. Hill took note of that in her file. "Perhaps, Ms. Lee, you might consider having Po talk to a child therapist. I can recommend one."

"Thank you, but I think we'll be fine."

Kai stood by listening, floored. Why wouldn't Jun even consider having Po talk to a therapist? Of course, on some level, he understood. Hadn't *he* avoided his own trip to a leather couch in the past year? Hadn't he brushed off suggestions from his physical therapist six months ago to go see a sports psychologist?

But he was a grown man and should be able to deal with trauma. Po was just a little boy.

"I'll give you a number for one," the doctor said. "Although I think she's probably booked. There were a lot of kids affected by the tsunami. Po isn't the only one. They lost parents or siblings, or they had injuries. Since the Red Cross has moved out, it's been harder for us to shoulder the load. And beyond the psychological toll, some kids still don't even have a good place to live."

Kai piped up. "What about the fund-raisers, to help the victims?"

"That money is long gone. All used up," Dr. Hill said.

"What if we had another fund-raiser?" Kai

offered. "I could use the surfing competition to raise money."

Dr. Hill glanced at Kai, eyes widening. "So many kids could benefit," she said. "Po is definitely not alone."

"Po doesn't need charity." Jun pressed her lips in a thin line. Kai blinked at her, surprised by the vehemence.

"Well, other kids do. And in the meantime, Po could still see a therapist..."

"No." Jun shook her head. "Po doesn't need a therapist. We'll get through it *on our own*."

"But if Po talked to someone..." Kai began, not quite believing that he was trying to convince her to give psychology a chance. He was aware of the little boy listening to every word. Kai pulled her away from Po's bedside and lowered his voice. "It could help him, Jun."

"I said *no*." Jun's eyes burned hot. Kai knew he was overstepping his bounds, but he couldn't help it. Not when she was making such a boneheaded decision, and not when she wouldn't even talk about it. The woman was so infuriating. Completely vulnerable one minute and then an absolute granite fortress the next. "He doesn't need help."

"He clearly *does*," Kai said, exasperated. "He's not sleeping. He won't go near the water. It's been *a year*."

"Don't tell me how to raise my son," Jun growled,

her temper flaring up like a tiki torch. Kai realized too late he'd gone too far, stepped into quicksand before he'd even known he was in danger. Why was she so angry? *Like a mama bear defending her cub. Ferocious.*

"I'm not telling you anything, I'm just…" *Telling her how to raise her son. Because she's being pigheaded and not listening to reason!*

"Is Po free to go?" Jun asked the doctor, who had been watching the escalating fight with concern.

"I can discharge him, but I really think you ought to consider…"

"Come on, Po. We're going," Jun said, her mouth set in a stubborn line. Kai wondered if she'd figure out now or later that she had no car or means of getting home. He'd offer to drive, but in this mood, she might insist on taking a cab.

*Maybe I ought to let her*, he thought as he trudged after the stubborn woman pulling Po along behind her.

THAT NIGHT, JUN still seethed about Kai's presumption as she angrily scrubbed dishes. She'd put Po to bed, and still, she stewed. Kai was not Po's father. His father was a professional football player who'd not bothered to check up on the boy since he was born. Yes, Kai had saved his life, but that didn't give him the right to tell him how he ought to live it.

*She* was Po's mother, and she'd decide what was best for him. And the idea of some stranger helping him when she couldn't... Well, her tiger mom would be rolling in her grave. *People who don't do for themselves are lazy or stupid*, her mom had once said.

Granted, Jun knew her mother was prone to extremes and wasn't always right. But then, wasn't there a grain of truth in nearly everything she said, even if she always went the harshest route? She'd disowned her for her teen pregnancy, and yet hadn't that forced her to become strong? Wasn't that what a good mother did?

Jun felt torn, her insides a jumble of emotions, and Kai seemed like the best target for them. His life was a mess, yet he was going to give *her* advice?

She knew it sounded irrational, but the fact was, no one in her family had ever had counseling. Not that anybody would ever admit to needing it. She'd find a way to help Po with his nightmares and his fear of water. *She'd* be the one to solve his problem, not a stranger with a degree on the wall who probably just wanted to give him some unhealthy prescription. She tried boiling some calming lavender herbs at bedtime. If Po weren't so silly about yoga, she'd make him do more of that, but the little boy was just too small to take it seriously. He thought it was more of an excuse to wrestle than a way to calm himself. Jun couldn't do Downward-Facing Dog without Po taking it as an invitation to launch himself on her back.

Still, she'd find something. Jun had a healthy skepticism of traditional medicine, and all the chemicals it prescribed, a philosophy passed on to her by her mother. She had been grateful that the doctor at the ER had checked out Po and found him healthy, but she wasn't about to seriously consider a child psychologist. Po was just four. He could barely write his name. What could a psychologist possibly do?

*Even though you've all but run out of options?* Jun thought to herself. Maybe Kai was right. Maybe that's why she was so angry.

She'd tried all kinds of things to help Po get better, to help him be less afraid, to help him stop biting, and yet, what did she have to show for it? A trip to the ER, getting kicked out of day care, and nightmares that never stopped. Some days, she felt like the worst mother in the world. And *that* feeling made her feel even less inclined to ask for help. It was those moments in her life, the ones where she felt at her worst, that her mother's hard lessons kicked in, that, instinctively, she turned inward. *The only person I can rely on is myself, even when I'm messing up.*

*Am I messing up?* she asked herself, as she did every day she woke up and made decisions about Po. And now there was Kai. The man she'd told he absolutely couldn't have sex before his competition and then she'd let him kiss the life out of her? What was she doing?

She thought about Kai kissing her on the beach, his body on hers, and the way she liked how it felt, even though every fiber of her body knew she was just a convenient distraction, just one more excuse Kai would use not to face his own issues. She'd be an empty vessel for him, a warm body, just like the countless other women he'd used the same way. It scared her that she'd been so close to letting passion rule her life once more.

*Just like with Po's father.* The last time she'd let herself be carried away in the moment, she'd gotten pregnant at nineteen. She thought about the brief fling that took her virginity and felt the old shame, saw her mother's sharp disapproval and felt the sting of her slap. She wouldn't be that helpless person again, that dumb, naive girl, who trusted that everything would work out. Po's father and her own mother had taught her to never take anything for granted. *And never trust anyone but yourself.*

"Mommy?" Po's sleepy voice caught her and she realized she'd been standing at the kitchen sink, absently rubbing the same dishes in the now-murky water. She'd been too distracted to finish the dinner dishes. She jumped at the sound of his voice, wondering if everything was all right. She'd put him to bed nearly half an hour ago.

"Is everything okay?" Jun turned, glancing at her little boy in his Spider-Man pj's, fearful that he'd had another nightmare.

"I can't sleep," he told her, and for once, she was happy to have a regular toddler problem. "Can I sleep in your bed?"

Jun opened her mouth with her usual curt refusal but stopped short. She'd been walking the boy back to his bed every night for weeks, and the only place it had gotten either of them was little sleep and now, for Po, night terrors. The doctor said they could be caused by lack of sleep. Was her insistence that Po sleep in his own bed causing him to wake up in the night screaming? She couldn't shake that persistent fear that somehow, as his mother, this was all her fault.

Her head spun with the repercussions of it all. Her mother had always been so confident, so *sure* her way was the right way, and yet Jun was plagued with doubts daily, second-guessing herself at every turn. Babies were supposed to sleep in their own beds, weren't they? She'd done all that hard work when he was a baby of letting him cry it out in his crib, and now here he was at four, begging to sleep in her bed. She felt, as she had so many times before, parenting was like trying to take a casual stroll in quicksand—she was up to her neck before she knew what hit her.

She fought with herself, wishing, for a fleeting moment, she did have someone, a grown-up, in her house she could ask for help. Someone to tell her she was doing the right thing—whatever that thing was. Or someone to at least talk it all out, reason through it and come to a decision. She envied her sister her loyal husband, who, as far as she could tell, was always the voice of gentle reason. She wished she had one of those. The doctor said Po needed more sleep. Maybe he'd sleep better in her room.

She looked at her toddler with his adorable face tilted to one side, and she caved.

"Okay," she told Po. "Go on and sleep in my room. But just for tonight."

## CHAPTER FIFTEEN

JUN STOOD ON Kai's porch the next morning, wishing she'd called ahead and told him she couldn't make the training session. Po bounced beside her, full of energy. He'd slept soundly the entire night, but Jun hadn't. Po sprawled and kicked while he slept, spreading out like some kind of helicopter playing Twister. She could almost still feel the tiny imprints of his little feet in her back as he rolled around in the bed. In the morning, his head had been where his feet ought to have been, but he'd bounded awake at 6:00 a.m., bright eyed and rested, while Jun felt as though she'd spent the night trying to sleep comfortably next to a Mack truck.

She'd been this close to calling in sick but had decided to come at the last minute. She dragged herself to work even with the worst cold, and she wasn't about to let a single sleepless night derail her. Not, of course, that it was a single sleepless night. In fact, she couldn't remember the last time she'd gotten four straight, uninterrupted hours. Kai opened the door cautiously.

"I wasn't sure you'd show today," he said, glancing at Po.

"Why wouldn't I show?" Jun was ready for a fight if Kai wanted one, and if he was going to question her work ethic, he was going to get one.

"Well, with Po at the ER and everything... How you doing, kiddo?" Kai held up a closed fist and Po eagerly bumped it with his own.

"Fist bump!" he yelled, then made an exploding sound. "I'm fine, Kai! Where's Auntie? I want to show her the rock I found outside. Auntie!" Po was already tearing through the house, looking for Aunt Kaimana.

Jun sniffed the air and smelled the pungent aroma of Kona coffee.

"Is that coffee?" she cried, feeling almost as if she were being led into Kai's beach house by her nose.

"Yes, I just brewed a pot of Dallas's special blend," Kai said. "It's for Kaimana. Not me. I'm not breaking any of your rules."

Jun's felt as if the only thing holding her eyes open at this point was the promise of pure caffeine.

"Do you want some?" Kai studied her, a blatant challenge in his eyes.

On a normal day, she'd have told him what he could do with that gloating face. But this was not a normal day. She feared she might face-plant in his foyer any second. "Yes, please."

She followed him into the kitchen, where he poured her a delicious-smelling brew.

She inhaled and took a delicious sip. Kona coffee, the finest in the world, and only grown in the lava-rich soil of Hawaii.

She examined the Hula Coffee mug she held in her hands. She recognized the logo from the local coffee shop in downtown Kona. "I suppose you know the owner of this coffee shop, too."

Kai laughed and rubbed the back of his neck, looking sheepish. "Uh, yeah. I own it. With Jesse."

Jun nearly choked on the coffee. "How much money do you have?"

Kai barked a laugh and Jun realized she was being too direct. Just like her mother. "Sorry. I mean, that's rude."

"Nah, it's just honest. Most people think it but don't say it. I like that you said it." Kai smiled at her and the soft expression in his eyes made it hard for Jun to stay mad at him or even keep him at a distance. She'd been wanting to. After the kiss on the beach and then his butting into Po's life, she wanted to be cold and unfriendly, but with his broad shoulders and lean athletic body so close to her, she had trouble staying icy. Or even remembering why she wanted to in the first place.

"I talked to my manager about setting up a

charity for kids of the tsunami and he said we could do it. Even maybe call it Big Island Kids."

Jun stared at him, waiting. "That's good," she said, trying to keep her voice neutral. She regretted biting his head off yesterday about the charity. Some kids *could* use it, she had no doubt. She just wasn't going to take a handout.

"Listen, Jun, I'm sorry about yesterday," he said. "I mean, not sorry that I said something, but...Po is your son, and I don't have a right to butt in. I just... I wanted to help."

Jun nodded. The apology went a long way toward smoothing her ruffled feathers. Po was not a responsibility she'd ever considered sharing with anyone, and yet, even as Kai stood there, she wondered what it would be like to have a partner or to have Po's father in the picture. Probably, like yesterday, it would be a huge pain in the butt. If her partner disagreed with her, then it would just lead to one argument after another. The thought exhausted her. She knew what was right for Po, didn't she? She didn't need any help.

"It's okay." It wasn't, exactly, but Jun liked the apology. She sipped some more of her coffee.

"I don't know if you've thought about it any more, but maybe the doctor was right..."

Jun's hand tightened on her coffee mug. She didn't want to go over this again. Po wasn't crazy. He didn't need to go see a psychologist.

He just needed to heal in his own time. "Did you just apologize for something you're going to do again?" Her chest grew tight, as if she was about to enter into another round of fighting. If she had to, she would.

Kai opened his mouth and then quickly shut it. He shook his head and held up his hands in surrender. "Right, not my place," he conceded. "Sorry."

He took a step closer and Jun felt suddenly as if she were being pulled into his orbit. The man had more magnetism than ought to be allowed in one person. His dark hair flopped forward across his tanned forehead. She wanted to reach up and put her hands in the thick mop and was curious whether it would be as soft as it looked.

Jun could hear Po's laughter from the other room. Would she allow Kai to kiss her, right here in his kitchen, mere feet from her boy and his aunt? Yet his lips were all she could think of, how soft and enticing they were the first time they covered hers. Was she really fantasizing about making out with the man who'd made her so angry?

"What's on tap today?" Kai asked, rubbing his hands together. "I'm ready to get to work. My manager, Kirk, he wants to get photos of me surfing and…"

"And you're worried." Jun remembered his performance, or lack thereof, on the board.

"Yeah." Kai met her gaze. "You saw me out there. How can I shoot videos for a surfboard when I can't even surf? And how am I possibly going to *compete*?"

"Okay. Let's talk about the knee. Are you ready to be honest with me about it?"

Kai shrugged. She noticed how much he wanted to shut down anytime the subject of his knee came up. It was beyond a sore spot. Jun recognized an Achilles' heel when she saw one.

"What do the doctors say?" she asked him.

"They say I'm recovered. That I'm 97 percent for strength and flexibility." Now Kai avoided her eyes. "They say I'm healed."

"But you don't think so."

Kai shook his head. "The knee feels…different. It's hard to explain. Like a rubber band, I guess, an overstretched one. One that's going to snap at any moment. I don't think the doctors are right. I keep telling them, but they say there's nothing they can do."

"No more surgeries?"

"Nope. I asked them if they could just cut it out of me and replace it with a robotic one, but they just laughed. I guess I can't go bionic yet."

Kai looked so dejected that Jun wanted to comfort him somehow. She took a step closer and touched his arm.

"Hey, Western medicine doesn't have all the

answers," she said. "Sometimes doctors miss the obvious things."

"They do?"

"Yeah. That's why I am such a fan of alternative medicines. Why I want to open my own clinic one day. Eastern medicine treats the *whole* person, not just an injury." Jun realized she'd been touching Kai a little too long. His arm felt warm beneath her hand. She withdrew quickly, her face flushing a little with heat. Could she not even casually touch the man without having a reaction?

"So when does the knee feel weak? Like when you're walking?" Jun looked down at Kai's knee. It looked identical to the other one, except that it had the scar from surgery, still too white against his bronzed skin. Kai tested his weight on the knee, bouncing on it.

"No, not really."

"Okay." Jun took a sip of coffee, thinking through the problem. "So, show me your surfing stance."

"Here? In the kitchen?"

Jun nodded. Kai glanced around, but the two of them were alone. He shrugged, bent his knees and put his arms out as if he were surfing. Jun studied the curve of his once-injured knee. To her eyes, he seemed strong. There was nothing about the motion he was doing now that indicated a problem. And yet she'd seen the knee buckle twice before.

"No pain?"

Kai shook his head. Then he bounced from one squat to another, as he might if he had to shift weight on his board. "No, it's fine here. On land."

Jun put down her mug as she studied the problem in front of her. She took a step back so she could see Kai's whole body and not just the knee. Her alternative-medicine courses taught her to look at the whole patient, not just the source of the injury. Human bodies were elaborate systems, each element dependent on the others.

"What's different about the water?"

"What isn't?" Kai shook his head. He stomped one foot on his solid wooden floor. "This has a constant support, but in water, of course, your entire body is engaged in just trying to stay ahead of that freight train barreling down on you. And the water pushes and pulls, and it's a constant battle to stay balanced. Well, you know." Kai nodded at her. Jun did know. It was why surfing was such good exercise: every muscle family was engaged.

"The knee just gives," Jun said. "Under that pressure."

"Yeah, right when I think I'm going to make it, the knee just...folds."

Jun shook her head as an idea came to her. "You know what? I don't think the knee is the problem at all."

"Then what is it?"

Jun leaned forward and stood on tiptoe. Then she tapped Kai's temple. "It's up here. We're going to do some meditation *and* visualization today."

"Why do I think I'll have to burn incense and chant?" Kai grinned.

"You just might, if you don't watch it."

"HAVE YOU DONE this before?" Kai asked as they sat in his personal gym. Kai had designed every bit of the room with his likes in mind; the gleaming wooden floor, mirrored wall and artfully arranged bamboo garden in the corner made it a place he didn't mind working out. He sat crosslegged, waiting for Jun to join him on the mat across from his. He had some doubts this plan was going to work.

"I once helped a woman who was terrified of flying to get on a plane. I took a class on using alternative medicines to alter behavior. Visualization can help you overcome your fear." Jun lit some sandalwood candles near them and plugged her smartphone into the speaker system. Soothing reed music floated into the room.

"I'm not scared of flying," Kai said, unable to keep the sarcasm out of his voice.

"Aren't you, though?" Jun said, the corner of her mouth lifting in a teasing smile. "Sometimes the brain can overthink situations. After all, our brains were engineered to survive being hunted on the open plain and in the jungle. Fear is an excellent survival tool, but for us modern people, who don't have to worry about being eaten by saber-toothed tigers, fear can be crippling, and it can get in the way."

"I'm not afraid," Kai lied. He was afraid, of the water, of the massive power of it, of finding himself being tossed like a rag doll at its whim. Before the tsunami, he'd loved surfing: the bigger the waves, the better.

"Okay, well, if you aren't, if your mind is *not* tripping you up, then you should be able to do this exercise without any trouble," Jun said, sitting in front of him, crossing her legs. "We're going to start out like we do with meditation, taking a deep breath in and letting that breath out. So close your eyes and be guided by my voice."

Kai let his eyelids fall closed but wasn't sure he believed this would do any good. Meditating might make him feel less stressed while he was doing it, but none of that helped when he was out in it, the surf threatening to take him down and drag him under.

"All right, now breathe in…and out." Kai listened to the smooth sound of Jun's voice. He tried not to think about how sexy it was. Was there nothing about the woman that was unattractive? He let out a breath and felt his chest loosen a bit.

"Now I want you to visualize the water. Can you imagine yourself paddling out?"

Kai nodded. He thought about the rolling blue Pacific all around.

"Now I want you to head to the wave. It's a perfect wave. Are you going to catch it?"

Kai nodded once more.

"Breathe in and out. Relaxing, soothing breaths. You're going to catch the wave, but it's not going to be hard. It's going to be an easy paddle. Your arms want to take you there."

Kai tried to keep in the moment, but he couldn't help thinking that somehow he'd landed in a hypnotist's office. He cracked an eye open and saw Jun focused on him intently. "Are you sure this is going to work?"

"Close your eyes," she commanded. He did so. "You're in the ocean. The ocean is working *with* you, not against you. You've got nothing to fear from the ocean."

Kai wasn't so sure. He saw a flash of memory behind his closed eyelids. The roar of the tsunami bursting through concrete and glass, shattering them like a huge vengeful fist of water.

"Kai, I see you're breathing fast. Slow your breathing. Control it. Control that heart rate. You are *not* in danger. Nothing bad is going to happen. You are in control of your body and the ocean is helping you."

Kai tried to steady his pulse as his blood thudded in his ears. He forced himself to take in a deep breath and release it. Just doing that helped calm him a little. But he was still frazzled and a bit panicky. His skin suddenly went clammy. He wasn't anywhere near the water, and he felt like this? The thought struck him as dismal, and the more hopeless it seemed, the higher his blood pressure went.

"Kai. Listen to my voice. Calm down," Jun said. The sound of her voice cut through the muck. He took in a breath and released it.

"You're paddling and the surf is helping you. The ocean is helping you. The wind is helping you. Your arms are helping you. Your legs are helping you. Do you feel how strong they are?"

Kai nodded. *Strong. Be strong.*

"Breathe in and out. In and out. That's it. Now it's time for you to surf that wave. It's coming. Everything is perfect. The way it should be. There's nothing to be scared of. You're safe. Go on. Try that wave."

Kai's heart rate spiked, even though he was sitting in his own gym with his eyes closed. "Kai, remember your breathing. Focus on your limbs. On the ocean. On the wind."

Kai tried, and then he thought of surfing with Jun, of his knee buckling beneath him. He couldn't put weight on it. The knee would give way. He knew it would.

As much as he wanted to, he couldn't calm himself. He squeezed his eyes shut tighter. And suddenly, he heard rustling. Jun had gotten up. He felt her hands on his shoulders. "Kai. I'm here. You're safe. Deep breaths."

He felt calm again as his eyes fluttered open. Kai realized cold sweat dripped down the middle of his back. He was exhausted, as if he had actually gone surfing. He was even winded.

"I'm not sure that helped," Kai said.

"I think it helped more than you know," Jun said. "We're going to do a little bit of this every day until you can do the whole scene in your mind without feeling anxious. Until it becomes as natural as breathing."

"I don't know."

"Do you know about the power of visualization? Many athletes use it. The more you *believe* you can do something, the more you can. There's nothing more powerful than the mind." Jun squeezed his shoulder. He liked the sensation of her touching him. He wanted her to do it more.

"It seems like hocus-pocus stuff."

"It's not. Even Western medicine agrees. Visualization is a powerful tool. If you don't think it works, why are you sweating? Why so anxious?"

Kai wiped his brow and looked at his wet fingers with surprise.

"Your body believed it was out there. And that was your mind's doing."

Kai realized she had him there. His shirt was damp with sweat. There wasn't another way to explain that.

"A lot of this is in your mind," Jun said. "You have to learn to face the fear before you can trust your body once more. Your mind is in your way."

Kai shook his head. "If I do this every day, then it goes away?"

"It will get better. You have to face your fear safely, *in here*," she said, tapping her own head. "Then you can face it out there, in the ocean, where things can go wrong." Jun moved so she was kneeling next to him, her face close to his. "I saw you when your knee gave out on the wave. It was only when you *realized* you were surfing, when your mind engaged, that you lost your balance. That's the truth. It's also true at the gym. As long as you weren't *thinking* about your knee being weak, then you were fine. It was only when you realized you were using the weak knee that it gave way."

Kai studied Jun's face. Could she be right? "You really think I'm sabotaging myself?"

"I think fear is making you do a lot of things.

We can't know for sure if it's all fear, but I know a lot of it is."

Jun was leaning in so close that Kai could smell the coconut scent of the lotion she liked to use. His mind abruptly shifted gears as he laid a finger in the crook of her arm. She jumped a little, surprised by the contact. He was surprised, too. Every time he touched Jun, he felt a little jolt. That wasn't something he was used to. Not with any of the women he'd dated. He'd never wanted to kiss one of them so badly as he wanted to kiss Jun right in this moment. Her eyes told him she wanted that, too, but her body leaned away from him.

"I'm not the only one who's scared," Kai said. "You are, too."

"I'm not."

"So come closer."

"No." She shook her head. "I'm not going to help you sabotage yourself. If you flirt with me, you don't have to think about all the work you have to do."

That stopped Kai cold. Was she right? Was his attraction to her nothing but his mind playing games with him? Was it all avoidance?

"But the knee buckling. That's real."

"Is it? Or is it your mind worried about trusting the knee again? Is it your mind that's giving up *before* your knee?"

Kai rubbed his chin, thinking about it. He honestly didn't know. But he was willing to try anything. He felt a flicker of hope. "You really think this will work?"

"I think it's worth a try," Jun said.

# CHAPTER SIXTEEN

FOR THE NEXT few months, Jun and Kai worked tirelessly on meditation and visualization exercises almost every day, as well as a staggering regimen of weights, cardio, yoga and Tai Chi. Jun could see the progress and could see Kai growing calmer and calmer with each session. She could see the treatment working, and that thrilled her. She couldn't believe how dedicated Kai became, and as he showed improvement, he threw himself into her system, eating well and not even complaining about her list of rules. She watched him grow lighter, witnessed the worry starting to lift from his shoulders as hope swooped in, displacing dread.

He even stopped trying to kiss her. Or touch her. Or flirt. She didn't want to be right about the fact that he'd used her as a distraction when all this was really about was surfing.

Part of her celebrated his seriousness, while part of her mourned the fact that he'd abandoned trying to get her into bed. She knew she ought to be glad, but the stronger Kai's self-control became, the weaker hers seemed to get. Jun felt painfully aware of Kai's body, wherever he was in the room and whatever he was doing. Each day her feelings grew stronger. She was beginning to wish she'd never come up with her stupid no-sex rule. Not that she'd ever sleep with her boss, but sometimes, lying in bed at night, all she could think about was what Kai's hands would feel like on her body. She'd gone nearly two years without a man, and now it seemed as though two years' worth of pent-up desire came raging to the surface. Jun struggled for self-control.

"Jun?" Kai's voice interrupted her thoughts, and she blinked, hoping she hadn't blanked out too long. Kai was sitting cross-legged on the mat on the patio outside. They'd been midsession, visualizing a wave when Jun had faded out, her mind straying away from the ocean and straight to Kai's bed.

"Oh...I'm sorry." Jun shook her head, her face flushed. "I lost my train of thought."

Kai smiled, and she felt the warmth in her stomach.

"It's no problem. I think we were nearly done. I could imagine myself going right up to the beach."

"You look calm." And he did: no profuse sweating, no pounding pulse. Jun leaned over and touched her finger to the inside of his warm wrist. Instantly, her own pulse ticked up as she made skin contact with him, her body now so close to his that all she had to do was tilt her head up to kiss him. But she didn't.

*Snap out of it, Jun.*

Yet she couldn't concentrate enough to actually take his pulse. She withdrew her hand quickly. "Your pulse is normal," she said, hoping it was true. Hers wasn't. She felt certain Kai knew it, too, that he could see her pulse thudding in her neck. She took a shaky breath in.

"You're ready to surf, I think."

"I am?" Kai looked alarmed. Right at that moment, Po trotted through the open patio door.

"We've got to test this sometime," Jun said.

"Test what?" Po asked as he picked up the Spider-Man figure he'd left on the patio. Aunt Kaimana came shuffling out after him.

"Po! Don't bother your mama while she's working."

"It's okay, Auntie," Kai said. He looked at Po. "Your mom is trying to get me to go out there and surf."

"Like this!" Po made a surfing stance again, the bright Hawaiian sunshine beating down on him as he bent his knees and stretched out his arms, his Spider-Man toy making a moving shadow against the patio.

"That's right."

"Why don't you wanna go?"

"Po, that's a personal question," Jun warned, but Kai waved her off.

"I'm afraid of the water," Kai said.

"You *are*?" Po's eyes grew wide. "But you're a surfer!"

"I know. I'm afraid of the water and of…my knee." Jun couldn't believe he'd admitted it, and to a little boy. She stood very still, listening. "Remember I hurt it last year?" Po nodded solemnly. "So, your mom is trying to help me with that. With getting better so I can surf again."

Po seemed to think about this.

"Can I help?" he asked.

"No, Po. It's…" Jun began. She didn't want her son to be in the way. Not when Kai was working so hard.

"I think you can help," Kai said, brightening. He glanced at Jun, but she couldn't read his expression. He got up and dusted himself off. "Would you walk with me to the water's edge? Just the edge. You don't have to go in if you don't want to, but maybe if we walked in a little together, then I wouldn't be so scared?"

"Kai…" Jun's voice held a warning. "You don't have to do this, Po, if you don't want to. Really. Kai is a grown-up and he's getting grown-up help and he doesn't—"

"Do I have to go in?" Po asked him.

Kai shook his head. "Only if you want to."

Po nodded and then glanced at Jun. She wanted to scoop him up and stop whatever little experiment Kai had planned. Jun's stomach pricked with nerves.

"Okay, I'll do it." Po grabbed Kai's hand and together they marched down to the waves sliding in up the sandy beach. Kai stood there for a minute, with Jun hovering uneasily behind them. She wanted to stop them, but she also didn't know if she should. She didn't want Po to see her freaking out over his being close to water. She wasn't a psychiatrist, but she knew that probably wasn't the right path forward. She surveyed the beach. It was midafternoon and the tourists lay in thick patches across the sand, which was dotted with brightly colored beach umbrellas.

"It's big and scary, isn't it?" Kai asked Po.

Po tightened his grip on Kai's hand and nodded vigorously.

"You scared?" Po asked Kai, craning his little neck to look up at Kai.

"Sure am," Kai said, and Po looked astonished.

"How are you going to win a trophy if you're scared?" the little boy asked him.

Kai shrugged and stared out over the water. "I don't know," Kai said. "I might not."

"But you're the best!" Po exclaimed. "You can't be afraid of the water."

Kai knelt down and met Po's gaze. "You and

I went through a lot. You were way braver than me. I'm scared."

Jun's stomach tightened. Anytime she tried to imagine what Po and Kai had gone through, her mind went black and her skin turned cold. She hated that Po had experienced such trauma and she hadn't been there to protect him. She'd go to her grave thinking she'd disappointed him in the worst way possible. She should've been there. Instead, Kai—a stranger—had given him comfort. Protected him when she should've.

Po tugged on Kai's arm. "You have to go in a little," Po said, pulling him to the water's edge.

"I'll go if you go." Kai nodded at the water.

Po eyed the water, biting his lip. He seemed to be making a decision. Jun hovered as if she might reach out and grab him, but Kai held up a hand. Po shook his head. "I'm scared," he conceded.

"You know what? Fear is a good thing—do you know that?"

"It is?" Po seemed skeptical. "That's not what my teacher at my old school said."

"Well, your teacher was wrong. Fear tells us all kinds of things we need to listen to, like if our house in on fire, we should get out. Nobody makes fun of anybody for being afraid of fire, do they?"

Po shook his head.

"Right, because fear is your body's way of telling you something is wrong. But *too* much fear, when you *know* it's not dangerous, that's just a little too much of a good thing." Po stared at Kai, the little boy trying to process the thought. Kai put his hand on the boy's shoulder. "Everybody has to decide *when* to listen to fear because it's the right thing to do and when fear is just getting in the way of having a nice swim at the beach."

Po grinned and nodded. He seemed to get it.

"But me, see, I'm *too afraid* these days to surf right. That's my problem. I forgot how to listen to fear that makes sense and fear that's just in the way."

"So if I go up to my knees in the water, will you go up to your knees?" Po asked.

"I don't know." Kai shook his head. "Up to my knees might be too much."

"*I* can do my knees." Po took a deep breath and then took his first shaky step into the surf. The wave came in, sloshing across the top of his foot. Jun expected shouting and screams, but none came. He flinched a little, and Jun almost leaped forward and whisked him out of the sea.

She gasped and covered her mouth. Kai held up a hand, his meaning clear: *It's okay.* Po pulled on Kai's arm. "Come on, Kai," he insisted. Reluctantly, Kai followed, clearly pretending to be scared for the little boy's sake. She didn't know whether to hug Kai or punch him as opposing feelings battled in her chest. She was glad he was helping Po, and yet she hated that he was doing it *without her*.

Kai stepped into the surf, up to his ankles. Po squeezed his hand.

"Let's go deeper," Po said.

"I don't know." Kai grimaced, acting fearful. Whatever he was doing seemed to be working, better than Jun had ever thought possible.

She watched Po take another step, leading Kai deeper, without screaming and without biting or crying. Seeing her son *helping* Kai even though Jun knew it cost him a lot to do it, she felt tears sting her eyes. Tears of pride. That was her brave little boy, her sweet little boy.

"Okay, my turn, right?" Kai said, and took another step after the boy. Before she knew it, they were to their knees, a wave splashing the scar on Kai's leg, soaking the skin. Po took another step out and he was up to his waist. Jun couldn't believe it and neither could Kai, if the surprised look that crossed his face was any indication. He quickly hid his surprise as he followed Po deeper.

"Do you think you can surf now?" Po asked Kai, gazing up at the man, blinking back against the sun.

"Since you came all the way out here, then, yes, I'll try."

Po's face broke into a huge grin. "Good!" He

splashed up to the shore and then ran back to Kai's patio, bouncing with each step he took.

Jun felt a riot of emotions in her chest. Foremost of all was crushing relief that maybe Po would finally be okay, that maybe he'd finally be the happy boy she knew before the tsunami. She met Kai's eyes and saw the same glee there, too.

But along with the swirl of hope and relief, she also felt the sour sting of jealousy. She wasn't proud of it, but she felt it nonetheless. Jun was jealous. Jealous that Kai had managed to connect with Po in a profound way she hadn't. For the briefest of minutes, she felt a little bit of a crack in her foundation. It had always been Po and her against the world, and she'd never thought he'd need anyone else but her, and now, faced with this stark new reality, she fought it with all her might. Was she not enough for Po? Had she been wrong all these years? The thought terrified her so much she didn't want to consider it for a second. Like a hot pan, she dropped it.

"Wasn't that amazing?" Kai asked her, eyes brimming with excitement. Part of her agreed, wanted to hug him, but this other part, the darker part, kept her from doing it.

"Next time you want to try something like that, talk to me first, okay?" Jun didn't like her tone, knew she was overreacting, that she was putting her fear and anger in the wrong place, but she couldn't help it. Confusion swept Kai's face, and she knew he didn't deserve her coldness. "I mean...just next time..."

Kai held up a frustrated hand. "Get your permission. Okay." Kai shook his head and stalked up the beach.

"Kai..." Jun called after him. Kai stopped and half turned. She wanted to apologize, to tell him she was sorry, but she felt that wall her mother had helped her build go up inside her. "You don't have to surf today if you don't want to."

Kai's eyes narrowed. "I told Po I would. So I will."

No AMOUNT OF visualization or practice could have prepared Kai for the wind that kicked up just as he was paddling out past the break. His toes dipped in the cold water as he swept his arms into the current, lying flat on top of his board. Sea spray hit his face. He shivered as clouds crowded the blue sky above him, suddenly covering the bright sun. Another island shower was coming, which explained the wind kicking whitecaps over the water and the sudden drop in temperature.

He tried to calm his mind and focus, the way he did in meditation, but he kept coming back to how cold Jun had been on the beach. Po had had a major breakthrough and yet Jun didn't seem excited about it. He just didn't understand that woman sometimes. First she didn't want to get a therapist for Po, and now she seemed angry with him for trying to help. It would have been different if he'd failed, but he'd *succeeded*. That, he didn't get. He paddled furiously against the water, which under the cloudy sky had quickly turned dark and murky.

The waves churned, and suddenly the small tourist waves gave way to bigger ones out in the deep. It was one thing to stand with Po in a foot of water, but now, as the waves batted his board, sending him lurching side to side, he questioned whether he was really going to be able to surf, as he'd promised. He glanced behind him and saw the tiny dots of three distant figures—Jun, Aunt Kaimana and Po—and he knew they had their eyes fixed on him, too.

If he'd been alone, he would've packed it in, paddled straight back, called it a day, but he'd promised Po, and the boy was watching him. He had to do it. At least Po had had a good day today, he thought. He held on to that thought, bright and shining as he searched the waves rolling in for the one he'd try. He saw a slow one move in and thought that would be it. He turned his board around, preparing to hit it, and as it came upon him, he popped up, just as he had a thousand times in his head during the months visualizing just this scene with Jun. The wave came at him more forcefully than he'd expected. It had looked slow, but now Kai realized his mistake: it had only been gaining momentum the whole time, like a freight train coming over a hill with faulty brakes.

He wobbled on the board, his toes gripping hard as he fought for balance. *Po*, he thought. *I can't disappoint Po.* That little boy had done his part, so Kai had to do his. Even if that meant just staying on his board five minutes. He'd have to go long enough for the boy to see him.

This was the time panic usually welled up in him, but he'd practiced defusing the feeling during meditation. He'd concentrated on his breathing with Jun, and he did that again now, calming himself, emptying his mind of fear. It was easier when he was sitting cross-legged on a mat in his gym, and much, much harder with an angry wave welling up beneath him, hissing mad and doing everything it could to drag him under. But he didn't go into the drink. He stayed steady, arms out, and, miraculously, his knee held.

*Got to do this for Po. That little boy needs me to do this.*

Thinking about Po, he found he didn't have time to worry about his knee, about whether he was going to hurt it again, about whether the rubber band would snap. He just…surfed. The wave, which had seemed so scary and out of control, suddenly backed down, losing whatever monstrous momentum it had had when he'd first stood up on it. It felt a little bit like the old days. *Throw whatever you have at me, ocean. I can handle it.*

He carved his board into the wave as he whipped wet, cold hair off his forehead. The cloud cover and wind chilled him, but he didn't care. He was doing it. He was surfing. He was standing up and making the ocean bend to his will. For the first time since the tsunami, his knee held. His chest burst with excitement, with dangerous hope. He felt the way he had when he saw Po wading into the ocean up to his knees. *Maybe we're going to be all right.*

The wave drove him close to shore, cruising him almost to twenty feet from Po, Jun and Aunt Kaimana. Po was jumping up and down and cheering, and Jun was clapping, her eyes bright. Aunt Kaimana's expression was carefully neutral. Maybe she didn't want to encourage him too much.

"You did it!" Po shouted, still bouncing as Kai jogged through the shallow water to the shore.

"You helped me, little man," Kai said. "I couldn't have done it without you."

Po hugged Kai, even though he was wet. Kai glanced up and saw Jun watching them, smiling, and Kai felt right then that there couldn't be bigger joy in the world. Such a small accomplishment, if he stopped to really think about it, and yet it meant so much to Po and Jun. For the first time in a very long time, Kai felt proud. Then the skies above them opened up and the warm tropical rain beat down on their heads and they all ran for Kai's house, the rain plunking wetly on the sand as they went.

LATER THAT EVENING, the rain still beat hard on the roof, and water rushed into the drainage ditches down the small street leading to Kai's house. This was a torrential downpour and no small tropical storm, and it looked as though the clouds had moved in to settle there for the night. Jun, mostly soaking wet, had run to her ancient hatchback, hoping to pull it up to the front door so Po could get in, but with a quick turn of the ignition, she had found her engine was dead. She wasn't sure if it was the battery or the alternator. The car was so old and banged up that most of the time, she was shocked when it did run. She wanted to get a new one, but she wouldn't until she knew she could count on her extra income.

Kai had offered to help, but he couldn't get her car running, either, and now both she and Po were in Kai's Jeep, being chauffeured back to their apartment.

"You didn't have to do this," Jun said for the hundredth time as they moved slowly down the rain-slicked roads, the windshield wipers working hard.

"I know I didn't have to, but I wanted to," Kai said. "I can't have you stranded. And you turned down my offer to stay. Auntie is happily tucked away in a guest bedroom for the night, but I have three more! You could've taken one."

Jun felt goose bumps rise on her arms. The idea of spending a night under Kai's roof… It made her think things she shouldn't. She was already struggling with how much he'd helped Po that day. Her jealousy had subsided, and now all she felt was grateful and sorry for biting Kai's head off. The combination might push her to the edge, she thought. Might make her say things—or, more likely, do things—she regretted. Even now, sitting so close to Kai in the front seat, she sensed every little movement he made. She was so aware of him: his lean legs in his cargo shorts; his muscled, tanned forearms as he gripped the steering wheel. Behind them, Po sat happily in his booster seat, his head lolling forward. The poor kid was tired. It was nearly seven thirty, practically his bedtime. The sky grew darker, and Jun couldn't tell if it was the storm or the setting sun.

Once they pulled up to her apartment, Jun thought that would be it: she'd be able to dash out, away from the close quarters of the car, where it seemed as if she could almost hear Kai's heartbeat. But Po had fallen asleep, his head against the window. She hesitated, dreading waking him, wondering if he'd ever get back to sleep once they were inside if she roused him now. Even a ten-minute nap could wreak havoc on a toddler's sleep patterns. She knew that firsthand.

"Can I help?" Kai asked, brown eyes studying her cautiously. She didn't miss the fact that he'd asked first, just as she'd requested. "I could carry him in."

Jun could've tried but Po's recent growth spurts meant he was big and lanky in her arms. Jun fought with not wanting to accept Kai's help on the one hand and then worry about waking Po on the other.

"Okay," she said reluctantly. Kai nodded swiftly and ducked out into the rain, holding an umbrella as he swung around to the passenger side. Jun got out, too, and took the umbrella, positioning it high over her head and his as he leaned into the back-seat, gently undoing Po's seat belt. Watching him, Jun thought it was as if he were a pro at extracting sleeping toddlers from car seats. He easily picked the boy up into his arms, and Po hardly even shifted. The rain thumped hard on the umbrella, but Kai held him steadily until they reached the apartment building's awning. Kai followed Jun up the outside staircase, and she walked to her apart-ment, unlocked the dark wooden door and pushed it open. She felt relieved that she'd tidied up that morning before they'd headed over to Kai's. Normally, there'd have been a discarded juice box on the coffee table or a pile of Po's toys. She'd tucked everything away, though as she looked at her simple living room, she knew it was below the standard Kai was used to. She didn't have expensive modern furniture or an ocean view. Her windows opened out to the apartment parking lot.

Kai still carried Po, and Jun led him down the hall and to the left. With tender care, he laid the boy down on the bed. Jun held her breath, ready for her son to wake up and start crying, but he didn't open his eyes once. Jun slipped off his sandals and tucked the covers up over his tired little body. He sighed, shivered and rolled over. Jun and Kai tiptoed out, and Jun snugly shut the door. A bright flash of lightning shot across her window, followed shortly by a huge crack of thunder that rattled the ceiling, making Jun jump. Before she could make it to the front door, the lights flickered and went out.

"This is some storm," Kai said. "Do you have a flashlight?"

Jun racked her brain. "Drawer in the kitchen, I think." In the dark room, Jun could barely make out even the outlines of her furniture in the mess of black-and-gray blobs. She moved to the kitchen and Kai followed, and somewhere in the middle of the living room, they collided. Kai's strong arms went around her, steadying her, as her eyes adjusted to the pitch.

"Whoa," he said, but Jun just froze there, realizing that since Po was sleeping soundly in the next room, this was the very moment she'd dreaded. Being so close to Kai, she could practically feel his body heat radiating outward. She had to crane her neck to look up at his face, but in the dark, she couldn't read his expression. They stood there, hardly breathing, for what seemed like forever. Jun's heart sped up.

"I'll get it," she managed, unable to stand the silence anymore. She wiggled by him, brushing against him as she went. His hard body sent shivers down her spine and she suddenly felt disappointed she'd escaped. She dug around in her junk drawer until she found a flashlight. She clicked it on but found the beam weak and hardly worth much, the batteries running low.

"Do you have a fuse box?" Kai asked, and Jun nodded, pointing the flashlight to the gray panel at the back of the kitchen. She hadn't even thought of the fuse box. Usually, when the power went out, she just waited for it to come back on. It happened now and again with the big storms. "May I?" he asked, gesturing. He was being so careful to ask permission for every little thing that Jun wished she'd never made an issue of it. He opened the panel and clicked a few switches.

"Looks like it's not the box," he said. "Must be the main."

Somehow, having him there looking at her fuses made her feel…taken care of. She realized she didn't want him to go.

"Can I get you something? A drink?"

Kai hesitated, and right then Jun felt like a fool. He was probably in a hurry to get back to his enormous beach house. Why would he want to stay in her cramped apartment?

"You're not offering me alcohol, are you?" he teased. "That would be breaking rule number one."

Jun remembered a beat too late. "Right. No. I mean, I've got some tea."

"Tea would be good," Kai said.

Jun fumbled for glasses and the pitcher from her dark and powerless fridge. She poured them both iced green pomegranate tea and then she hurried into the living room with hers and took a seat on the couch. Kai followed, sitting on the other end. In the dark, it was hard to tell, but she had another chair in the far corner of the room. Now Jun regretted her seat choice. Her couch was tiny and Kai's knees nearly touched hers.

They drank tea in silence for a second or two. Then Jun felt as if she needed to say something.

"Kai, I'm sorry about earlier. About…not appreciating what you did with Po." Kai remained silent, and unable to see his expression, Jun couldn't gauge his reaction. "I'm used to doing things on my own, and I'm not used to relying on anyone…and, well, I get defensive where I shouldn't. I know that. I'm glad you helped Po today. You did more for him in an afternoon than I've been able to do all year."

"It was nothing." Kai's voice was so casual, so completely self-effacing.

"It *was* something. I mean, it's just that. This job, helping Po…all on top of saving his life. I don't think I'm ever going to be able to repay you."

"You need to stop thanking me." Kai sighed in frustration. "I didn't *do* anything to save Po. It was all just luck. I was there, and he was there. I mean, that's pretty much it."

"No." Jun shook her head. "The preschool teacher told me. She told me that she left on the bus with the other kids. That Po wandered off. That you had come to check on…your cousin? And *you* volunteered to stay behind and look for him. She left, but you stayed."

"It was only dumb luck that I found him, Jun. And even then, the water hit, and I only barely got him back inside the day care. And even *then* it was a bad choice. The water washed us out of the building, straight out the second floor. It was just a miracle he didn't drown. It was only because he swam so hard and hung on to me so tightly that we stayed together through all that." Kai made all his effort sound like so little.

"But you were there for him…when…" Jun heard her voice crack with the heaviness of the guilt she'd been carrying for over a year. "When I wasn't."

"Hey." Kai set his glass down on the table. He pulled Jun into his arms and she let him, tears stinging her eyes. As much as she tried to get over the past year, she couldn't shake the feeling that she'd failed her boy in a fundamental way.

"On the day when he was the most scared, when he needed me the most, I wasn't there," Jun admitted to Kai's chest. "What kind of mom does that make me?"

"You were at work, trying to provide for him, Jun. You were being a good mom. You can't be everywhere."

Jun realized then how she'd longed for someone to tell her that. How she'd been desperate for absolution, for someone to tell her it wasn't her fault. She hadn't known the heaviness of the guilt she'd been carrying until that very moment.

"Jun, I've never seen anyone else love a child the way you do. You work so hard to give him everything he needs. You're more like Wonder Woman."

Lightning flashed outside the window, illuminating the room for a split second. Jun tilted her head up, realizing that she was barely an inch from Kai's lips. Gratitude poured out of her, a warmth welling up within, and before she knew what she'd planned, she stretched up and kissed him.

# CHAPTER SEVENTEEN

THE KISS STARTED SLOWLY, a warm dance of her lips on his, but it didn't take long in the shadowy dark of her living room for it to grow into something more. Jun's carefully crafted restraint, the willpower she'd used to deny her body this little pleasure, suddenly exploded into tiny shards, and what was left was a desire so powerful it shocked her. She pushed Kai further, and he responded. Hungrily, she devoured his mouth, and in seconds, Kai's hands roamed up her back. Before she realized it, they were horizontal on the couch, her on top of him, her body pressed to his, feeling the hard length of him pushing against her thigh. What was she doing? Her mind screamed, but her body didn't care. Nothing mattered but tasting Kai, feeling his tongue in her mouth and his hands on her body.

This time wasn't anything like the beach, when Kai had been the aggressor. Now it was her turn. Passion she'd thought long dead rose up in her, and her body felt hot and cold all at once, Kai's hands like fire on her hips as he held her tightly.

She felt herself grind against him, her body taking over, her mind long gone as instinct and animal lust drove her. She'd always thought her abstention from sex proved she didn't need it, but in this moment, she realized just how much she did.

Kai's hands slipped into the waistband of her yoga pants, sliding downward across her bare bottom, and he groaned in her mouth as he kneaded her well-formed muscles. She arched her back, pushing herself into his hands, not wanting them to stop. Her body felt like a river of fire, and despite the fact she could run three miles and not break a sweat, right here, with Kai, she couldn't catch her breath. It came ragged as she broke free of Kai's mouth. He trailed kisses down her neck, each one a tingling blaze of passion, and she groaned, the heat growing between her legs. It had been so long, so long since she'd felt this that it all seemed new and yet hauntingly familiar.

In the dark, she could pretend it was all okay. That there'd be no consequences. For once, she didn't want to think about tomorrow. Didn't want to think about anything but releasing this tension inside her. She wanted Kai. Wanted this. Her mind reverted to a toddler's: all id and no ego.

"Jun…" Kai growled in her ear. "So damn beautiful…"

His words felt like honey across her skin, doubling her desire. She found his mouth again, and

she nearly came right then, her body all welled up
and ready. She felt as though if he simply touched
her *there*, she'd explode. His hands tugged at her
pants, and she helped him push them down. She
didn't think about how she was on her couch out
in the living room, Po just in the next room. She
didn't want to think about anything but the feel
of his skin beneath her hands.

"Wait," Kai said, panting.

"What's wrong?" Jun asked, suddenly worried
this all would stop.

"The rules," Kai said, a touch of humor in his
voice.

"Screw the rules," Jun said, and grabbed him
by the back of the neck, pulling him to her for
another kiss.

Kai picked her up then. She wore just her shirt
and underwear as he carried her to her bedroom,
bouncing into a wall or two on the way.

"Ow," Jun protested.

"Sorry," he murmured into her mouth as he
ducked into her bedroom and laid her gently on
the bed. Lightning flashed again, illuminating the
room, and Jun saw Kai taking off his shirt, saw
his amazing chest, the chiseled muscles smooth
and taut and hard. She shrugged out of her own
shirt. Her body ached for this, for Kai.

Her hands were at his waistband. She wanted

him as much as he wanted her, and the dark, the storm, somehow made it all okay.

She thought about Po's father. About him clutching at her in his dim hotel room, about him telling her it would be okay if they didn't use protection. He'd just pull out. He'd never gotten anyone pregnant before. She'd believed him. She'd trusted him. And look what had happened.

Kai released her mouth long enough to run kisses down her throat.

"I... I...I'm not on the pill." Why would she be? Jun never planned on having sex, and that was forty dollars a month she could use for something else, like groceries or toys for Po.

Kai pulled a foil packet from his pocket. She tried not to think about what it meant that he carried condoms with him, deciding not to dwell on it. Her whole body was on fire. She heard the rip of the package as she fumbled for him in the dark. Lightning again slashed through the darkness as Kai pressed down on top of her, his weight delicious as his tongue found hers. She arched her back, pressing her bare stomach against his, yearning for what only he had as he slipped between her legs. Suddenly, she felt him, amazing, thick and full, filling her in a way she hadn't known she needed.

"Oh," she moaned as he found a steady rhythm. It felt so good, so wonderfully good. Why had she avoided this for so long? In that moment, she couldn't remember. And then Kai moved, flipping her over, and suddenly she was on top.

"Kai," she protested, but his hands were already on her hips, guiding her on top of him, and it felt so delicious and so good that she soon took over, finding her own perfect spot. She let the moment take her, and she lost herself a little as she rode him, as his hands roamed her chest. Normally, she never took the lead, never ever, always being the passive partner in sex, but with Kai she felt strangely liberated, amazingly free. She ground her hips against his, and a minute later, she toppled over the edge as waves of pleasure hit her, one after another, until she thought she'd pass out from sheer goodness. Kai pulled her down to him, smothering her shrieks of pleasure with his kisses.

She thought she couldn't take any more, but Kai nudged her back, still rock hard and wanting more. Soon he found her soft center again and she moaned with pleasure and exquisite soreness. He reached around, grazing her most sensitive spot, teasing her. Suddenly, she opened up for him, letting him take her from behind as the tension in her built. She'd never had more than one orgasm before, and here she was about to have her second. In a few moments, beneath the magic of his gentle fingers, she was right there on the edge. He nibbled her neck, pushing deep inside her, his arm wrapped around her, his hand between her legs. She hit another even more incredible high, waves of pure white pleasure exploding in her mind. Behind her, she heard him find his release, letting out a guttural grunt, his body tense with the power of it before he relaxed into her with a satisfied sigh.

"You took all my Chi," he murmured in her ear, and she had to laugh. She had. She could almost imagine it, the power of his essence.

Reluctantly, she rolled away from him and Kai let out a whine of protest. He disposed of the condom and then grabbed her before she could escape. "Come here, Chi stealer," he demanded, spooning against her.

She laughed again. Kai pulled Jun closer against his chest. She hadn't felt this good in years. Her knees felt like Silly Putty, and she didn't care. The rain pelted her window and all she could think was *I feel amazing*.

"Tell me about Po's father," Kai whispered in her ear.

In the dark, it seemed easier somehow.

"He was a Pro Bowler, and after the game he stayed on the Big Island for three weeks as an extended vacation. I…I met him the first day and it all happened so fast. I mean, I never even had a boyfriend before that. My mom was…very strict. My dad died when I was little, so she had to be even more strict, I guess."

"I see where you get it, then," Kai said, and rolled her over so they faced each other. He hugged her tightly to his chest. As the urgent need to kiss him faded, she began to feel safe in his arms. She liked this. This closeness. Sharing her life. Was this what it was like when you let someone in?

"He was my first. He told me... I was so dumb. I mean, I believed everything he said. That he wanted to marry me. That he wanted to be with me." Jun felt the bitterness return, like bile in her throat. "But he had a fiancée on the mainland. He was never going to marry me. When...when I found out I was pregnant, he shouted at me on the phone, told me it couldn't be his, told me anybody who would do what I did probably did it with everyone."

Jun had never admitted this to anyone. The sting of it hurt too much.

Kai held her close. "Sounds like a real asshole," he murmured into her hair. "You better hope I never meet this guy."

Jun liked the idea of Kai standing up for her, but she doubted it would work. "Dante is like six-three and two hundred pounds."

Kai shrugged. "I bet I could still take him. I'm fast and scrappy."

Jun laughed against his chest.

"What did you do? I mean, after? Did you take him to court?"

"No," Jun admitted. "I didn't have the money to take him to court. And even if I did, I didn't want anything from him."

"I don't blame you," Kai said. "My own father left my mom, too. He was a deadbeat." The resentment in Kai's voice reverberated through the room. "Then my mom remarried. He was a good guy, a stand-up guy. But then they both died in a helicopter crash, so that left Jesse and me orphans."

"That must've been hard."

"Aunt Kaimana raised us."

Jun's heart broke for him. Just when he got a stable family, that family was whisked away. She thought about her own situation, about how she'd learned the hard way you couldn't rely on the people closest to you. Kai had learned the same lesson but in a different way.

"Did you ever see your biological father? Did you ever want to?" Kai was more like Po than she'd known. She'd often wondered if Po would want to see his dad. So far, the subject hadn't come up too much, but she feared he would eventually.

"I saw him at my mom's funeral. He came to bring me back to the mainland. But I didn't want to go. I went to visit him in Chicago when I was in high school. He'd remarried and…he was this great dad *to them*. I just… I never got over that. He left me, but it seemed like he did it so he could start a new family somewhere else. Like my mom and I weren't good enough for him. That he wanted something else. I didn't want to live with him. To be reminded of that. I haven't talked to him since, and he hasn't reached out, either."

Jun snuggled into Kai's chest, wishing she could take away that hurt for him.

"Really, if I hadn't had surfing, I probably would've ended up some kind of delinquent," Kai said. "I channeled all my stuff into that. You can't be thinking about how your dad did you wrong if you're trying to survive a seventy-foot wave."

Jun nodded. "It's hard when people close to you disappoint. My mom…she…she never approved of Po. She died when he was a baby, and she never saw him. Not one time."

"Not one time? Never?"

She told Kai about her mother shunning her, refusing to have anything to do with her pregnancy. About how she'd cut her out, told her she had to be on her own. That she wouldn't help.

"She didn't even want to *see* the baby?" Kai sounded incredulous. "I don't understand."

"She was trying to make me strong," Jun said, although even to her own ears the excuse sounded flimsy. How many years had she been making excuses for her hardheaded mother?

"No," Kai said. "No, she was being stubborn, and so she died not even meeting her own grandson. She turned her back on you when you needed her most. That's not *'ohana*. That's…something else."

Jun tried to push herself up away from Kai, but he held her tightly. He hugged her against his chest, and eventually she stopped fighting. His embrace felt warm and good and safe, and she realized he was right: her mother might have tried to make her strong, but she'd done it by turning her back when her daughter needed her most.

"And if she'd lived, would she have ignored Po? Think of how that would've hurt him."

Hot tears pressed the backs of Jun's eyes. Kai was right. She knew he was, and yet she didn't know how to live with it.

"My mom never made mistakes," Jun protested.

"Yes, she did, Jun. She made a mistake with you and with Po. I can see that clear as day."

Jun had always thought her mother had been perfect. She couldn't reconcile what she'd done with a mistake, but at the same time, part of her believed Kai. But admitting her mother had made a mistake would mean that she'd been fallible, that she'd made a poor choice, that she hadn't had all the answers, as Jun had once thought. It made her feel both sad and relieved simultaneously. Maybe her mother had just been doing the best she could, just as Jun did with Po. Maybe she hadn't been this perfect person who always had all the answers. Could her mother have been just as scared as she was?

Kai silently stroked Jun's hair, and Jun leaned into him. For so long, she'd relied on Po for all her hugs and her connection to another person, and yet here, now, she realized how much she'd missed a genuine connection with an adult, someone who'd understand her. The storm rumbled on outside, and in the circle of Kai's warm arms, she found herself growing sleepy. With Po's night terrors, she'd not been getting a lot of sleep. Before she knew it, her heavy eyelids closed, and she fell asleep against Kai's chest.

# CHAPTER EIGHTEEN

KAI LAY VERY STILL, listening to Jun breathe. He felt closer to her than he ever had before, and his blood still seethed when he thought about that no-good man who'd left her when she was pregnant. *And* about her mother, who'd simply left her all alone and just as scared. He'd never be that man. If it was *his 'ohana*, he'd not turn his back. He was determined not to be like his own father, discarding the family that wasn't convenient, only to go start another. Or Jun's mother! He couldn't imagine Aunt Kaimana doing the same thing. Prodding him and trying to get him to do things her way? Yes. Being a pain in the butt? Sure. Turning her back on him? Never.

Kai badly wanted to be the safety net Jun had never had. He found himself wanting to take care of her. She needed him, and Po did, too. He only wished he could help her see that.

Just as the thought entered his head, he found himself surprised. Was he falling for Jun? Really falling for her? It had been so long since he'd actually fallen in love with a woman that he wasn't sure. All of his relationships in the past year had come with their own expiration dates. But not this one. For the first time in a long time, he wondered what it would be like to really be in a relationship. To fall in love.

Kai closed his eyes and fell asleep.

He didn't intend to sleep through the night, but sleep he did.

The next thing he heard was a soft knock on the door. "Mama?" came a little voice. Jun shot up in bed next to him, naked, frantically searching for her clothes.

"What's wrong?" Kai murmured.

"Shh!" she hushed him as she grabbed a robe from a hook in her closet. In another second, she'd thrown his clothes at him and pantomimed getting dressed.

"Just a minute, sweetie," Jun called through the door, her back against it, her hand trying to keep the knob still as she flicked the small button lock. Kai started pulling on his clothes, figuring Jun didn't want to scare the boy by opening the door when he was naked. He got that. He tugged on his shorts and shirt. Jun stood on her nightstand and pushed open a window, which led to the walkway outside the front door. He stood sleepily, blinking at the open window. Was she kicking him *out*?

Furiously, she gestured to the window. She was! She was kicking him out. He couldn't believe she wanted him to sneak out the window like…like someone sleeping with his friend's wife. He shook his head. *No way.*

She frowned at him, her face growing flush. She gestured again, and this time she threw his flip-flops straight out the gaping window. He couldn't believe it. The woman had thrown his shoes *out the window*. Then, she tossed his wallet. *His wallet.* She was about to toss his brand-new smartphone, but he grabbed it and angrily climbed over the windowsill to fetch his shoes and wallet. *The nerve of this woman!*

After he was free of the window, she promptly shut it *and locked it*. Then she pulled the blinds closed. He was now officially locked out. He picked up his wallet and slipped into his flip-flops and glanced around, seeing the shocked expression of an old woman with a tiny little poodle on a leash sidestepping him. She shook her head at him and minced by, her wide hips covered by a billowing pastel sundress.

The dog snarled at him as he went by.

This was beyond embarrassing now.

He ran a hand through his messy hair and thought about knocking on her front door but hesitated. She probably wouldn't open it, and there wasn't any need to freak Po out. Kai had done his share of sneaking out of bedrooms, but usually it was on his own terms. He'd never had a woman *kick him out* before.

He shook his head, amazed, as he followed the path to the stairs and his waiting Jeep.

JUN RUSHED PO through breakfast, still unnerved by the close call that morning. Po had almost seen Kai...*in her bed!* Thank goodness she'd gotten to the door in time. She felt like the worst mother on earth. She'd vowed never to have this happen, to never be the type of mom whose bedroom had a revolving door. She just didn't think it was...seemly. Jun believed she already spent too much time fighting stereotypes of being a single mom, and she didn't need to worry about what her neighbors would think when she kicked Kai out at six thirty that morning.

She could still feel the ice-cold sweat on the back of her neck as she sat bolt upright in bed, shocked to find Kai's naked body beside her and Po nearly at the door. Her heart still leaped to her throat when she thought about what it would mean to explain a naked man in her bed to her little boy. What had she been thinking?

She couldn't stop berating herself.

Granted, sex with Kai had been mind-blowingly amazing, but she still couldn't believe her own recklessness. She'd had sex with him when Po was sleeping down the hall! She'd let him sleep over when Po could've found them together, especially since he'd been wandering into her room late at night after his nightmares.

She shook her head, shame burning her neck. She couldn't believe how dumb she'd been. But then again, as she replayed the night in her head, she realized it probably couldn't have gone any other way. She'd had a moment of weakness, and Kai had been there, and, well, she'd made a mistake. No sense in wallowing in it, as her mother would say. Time to pick herself up and move on.

She was so grateful Po hadn't caught Kai in her bed, hadn't started to ask all those uncomfortable questions he'd probably have, like if Kai would be his daddy now. Po had asked *that* one back when Jun had briefly dated when the boy was just two. That little question had sent her boyfriend at the time running for the door. She'd introduced Po to that man after just one month of dating, and he'd been gone by month three. She most certainly wasn't going to make that mistake again.

*But you nearly did*, a voice in her head said. *How could you let him sleep over?*

There was only one thing to do now: she had to nip this whole thing in the bud. Po was so innocent, so trusting, and she was the gatekeeper, the one who kept him safe. And that was why Jun couldn't date Kai. It was already too complicated:

he was her boss, and he was Po's hero. The stakes were just too high.

By the time Po finished up the last of his cereal, Jun had made a decision: she'd tell Kai she was sorry about the night before, that it had been a rash mistake, that they should get back to their lives *before* sex, that her rules for training should still stand. Given how quickly women slid in and out of Kai's life, Jun figured Kai would probably be relieved, even grateful, for the out. The more Jun thought about it, the simpler it seemed. She tried not to recall how outraged he'd looked when she'd pushed him out her bedroom window.

While she thought about that, her phone lit up with an incoming call.

"Ms. Lee? It's Julie Ryan from Kona Day Care. We've had an opening come up and you are at the top of our waiting list."

Jun had almost forgotten—she'd been taking advantage of Aunt Kaimana's babysitting these past few months. "Yes, that's right."

"We can take your son this morning, if you'd like. All you need to do is come by, fill out some forms and, of course, leave a deposit, and—"

"I'll be there," Jun said, almost too eagerly.

She needed to talk to Kai, and she needed to do it without Po hearing, and while Kai's aunt had been lovely in taking care of him, it was high time Jun took back a measure of control, especially when it came to Po. She was beginning to feel too tangled up in Kai's generosity, and she was almost certain her feelings of obligation had probably led to bad decision making last night.

Having Po in day care would at least provide some separation. *And stop him from getting any closer to Kai.* She had to protect Po. *But what about yourself? Can you protect yourself?* she wondered.

Jun called Aunt Kaimana directly on her cell that morning to let her know she didn't have to watch Po. The woman sounded disappointed, and so did Po, who stubbornly claimed he *didn't* want to go to a new "school," no matter what kind of playground they had or which blocks or toys they'd offer. Eventually, Jun had to put her foot down, and even worse, she left Po at his new day care in the middle of a full-on tantrum, his cries haunting her as she walked out the door.

*I'm doing the right thing.* But then she instantly doubted herself. Was she? Aunt Kaimana couldn't watch Po forever, and Jun had been too complacent these past few months, letting Kai take care of everything. In the long run, it would have hurt Po worse if he'd stayed longer at Kai's house. Besides, the boy needed structured preschool again and classmates, and the babysitting arrangement wouldn't have taught him what he needed to know, no matter how great Kaimana was.

*I'm doing what's right for Po.* Then she sucked in a deep breath and headed to her car, his cries still ringing in her ears.

KAI DID NOT take the news as well as Jun had hoped.

"I can't believe you didn't talk to me first." Kai paced in front of her in his gym, running agitated fingers through his thick dark hair. He was angry and sullen. "You just put him in day care? And tell my aunt she's done sitting? You couldn't *talk* to me first?"

"There's nothing to talk about." If Jun had felt uncertainty before, then defensiveness now, in this moment, wiped it clean. She found herself hardening her position. "Po is *my* son. I thought he needed to be in a more structured environment." She hadn't for a second thought Kai would be upset. She knew he looked forward to seeing the boy, but how many times during the day, despite Kaimana's best efforts, did Po manage to interrupt them? He was just four, and keeping him away from his mother when he knew she was in the same house was an all but impossible task.

"I thought Po was happy here."

"He is. Was. But he needs preschool. Lessons your aunt can't provide. He needs kids his own age." *He needs some space from you*, she wanted to add but didn't. *I need some space, too.*

"Is this…is this about last night?" Kai somehow managed to get right at the truth of the matter, taking Jun completely off guard.

"N-no," she stuttered, but didn't meet his eye.

"It is. It's about last night." Kai blew out a frustrated breath. "That doesn't have anything to do with Po."

"He almost found…almost found *you* in my…" Jun's face burned. "I can't have that."

"So you ship him off to day care? I just don't get it. Aunt Kaimana loves Po and he loves her." Kai was taking this far more personally than Jun had ever thought he would.

"What does it matter to you? I'm here to help you train. Po's not part of the training."

Kai glared at her and shook his head, as if she was missing something obvious.

"Po's not your responsibility."

"You've made that clear." Kai let out a frustrated sigh. "You know you won't ever be able to have a relationship with anyone if you keep pushing people away. If you keep making decisions *for* everyone else and not *with* them."

"Who said I want a relationship?" That stopped Kai cold. He looked at her, brown eyes wide in surprise.

"Is this about you doing everything by yourself again? Just like you decided Po doesn't need to see a therapist."

Jun folded her arms protectively across her chest. "He doesn't."

"He *does*," Kai said, emphatic. He softened his voice and he rubbed Jun's shoulders. The touch sent an electric shock down her back. "You can't do everything by yourself—no one can. You can't fix Po, but you can get him help. Let me *help* you with Po. I can do that."

Jun wasn't ready for this. The men she'd dated before always seemed jealous of Po, always seemed to be fighting for her attention. She hadn't expected an offer of help.

She looked down at Kai's hands on her arms and thought of what they'd felt like on her body the night before. She just…couldn't think when he was around. She felt as if her world were upside down. It was how she'd gotten pregnant with Po in the first place, by not thinking. By letting her hormones make her decisions for her.

Jun pulled her hands away from his. Her mother had taught her the hard way that the only one she could count on was herself.

"We're fine. *I'm* fine on my own."

"After last night, I thought maybe you'd be open to…"

"You thought wrong." Did he really think sleeping with her one time meant he could step in and be Po's father? That he could tell her what to do?

That somehow he had *sway* over her? That wasn't how this was going to work.

"Po needs help. He does. I can give it to him. Last night should've shown you that there's something here."

Jun realized then with a shock that maybe last night hadn't been what she'd thought at all. Was this all about him getting close to Po? She felt as though she'd been hit with a bucket of cold water. Had he used sex to manipulate her? So she'd do what he wanted about Po? Had seducing her just been a means of trying to keep a close relationship to the boy?

Inwardly, she almost scoffed at the thought, and yet the way he kept insisting he wanted to help Po gave her doubt. Suddenly, her suspicions flared. After all, he could have any woman on the island. Why her? And why his obsession with her child? That was what it was, wasn't it? What was his angle? Her mind darted to the darkest corners of human nature and she realized she didn't want to find out. But she was going to protect Po. Even if Kai meant well, he wasn't the boy's father.

"About last night," she said. "I realize…it was a mistake."

"A…mistake?" Hurt flickered in Kai's eyes for a millisecond before it disappeared behind anger. Jun found she couldn't look him in the face, so she studied the laces of his sneakers instead.

"I'm sorry for… It was unprofessional. I think we should just go back to…back to the rules."

"The rules." Kai snorted and crossed his arms across his muscled chest, which was covered in a faded T-shirt. She could feel him boring a hole into her head with his glare. She glanced up briefly and away again.

"Yes, the rules. No drinking. No junk food…"

"No sex." Kai eyed her somberly.

She met his gaze and nodded. He stared for a long minute as if she were a puzzle he was trying to figure out. He pushed away from the wall and she took a step backward, worried that if he got closer, her resolve would melt away along with all her clothes. Even in that moment, he managed to look deliciously sexy, fire blazing in his eyes, his mouth a rigid line. How could she possibly think clearly when he was in the same room? How could she make a decision and stick to it when he was right there, daring her to change her mind?

There was such a fine line between anger and passion that she almost wanted to jump on him right there, wrap her legs around his waist and kiss the life out of him. She remembered the feel of his warm lips on her neck. She desperately wanted that feeling again. *Which is why you can't do this. Not with Kai. Not now.*

Last night had been a one-time slipup. It wasn't going to happen again. But Kai was so close, so touchable. She backed up and hit a stack of weights. They clanked together as she put her hands out to steady them. Kai loomed over her, putting one hand against the wall by her head. A half smile played at the corner of his lips as if he could read her thoughts, as if he knew exactly what she was imagining right at that moment. Suddenly, the balance of power tipped to his side, and she felt strangely, wildly vulnerable.

"You're sure?"

She shifted uncomfortably beneath his gaze, wanting to look away but unable to do so.

"I…" She wasn't sure. Ten seconds ago, she'd been adamant, but now, this close to Kai, his lips millimeters from hers, she was anything but certain.

"This is what you want?"

Jun's mouth went dry. Was he asking if she wanted sex? Or if she didn't want it? She'd lost all trains of logical thought, and all she could do was stare at his mouth.

Jun didn't trust herself to speak, so she just nodded her head once, not sure what she was agreeing to and not caring as long as it meant she could taste him once more.

Kai leaned in, kissing her roughly. Her whole body responded, as if primed just for this, made expressly for this purpose. Any hesitation she had melted as she tasted him, that perfect, warm sweetness that brought all the memories of her bed the night before tumbling back into her brain. Before she could come to her senses, she'd already wrapped her hands into his hair at the nape of his neck, already hungrily answered his kiss with a want she hadn't known she had. She pressed her body into his, her lower belly on fire with need, and she realized then that if he pulled off her clothes, she would let him take her again, right there on the floor. His hands roamed down her waist, clutching her hips in a way that made her groan. He pulled her close to him, and she felt his hard body against hers, and all she could imagine was the perfect way they had fit together last night.

But just as suddenly as the kiss started, Kai pulled away and cool air hit her lips. She opened her eyes, confused, and she saw Kai, flushed and panting.

"Just so we're clear, *no more of that*," he said, and wiped his mouth before taking another step back. He shook his head slowly. "You know what you should be asking yourself? Do you really think *I* need those rules? Or do *you*?"

He turned and left her, out of breath and dazed, staring after his stiff retreat, her body aching and unsatisfied.

## CHAPTER NINETEEN

TRAINING WAS SHOT for the day. Kai couldn't even look at Jun, much less concentrate on exercising. He'd stalked straight out of the house, without even thinking about what she'd do there. Sit and have a cup of tea? Scribble some more ridiculous *rules* on her whiteboard? He didn't care. He couldn't believe that woman. She was so... stubborn. Pigheadedly independent.

He took a deep breath as his feet sank into the pristine dry sand, already dotted with the umbrellas of tourists out to get their daily dose of tropical sun. The air was thick with the smell of coconut sunscreen as he maneuvered around the bikini-clad bodies. He could see a high-rise hotel in the distance, and he already planned to stop in the bar.

*No alcohol*, he could hear Jun say to him. Well, so what? She'd said no sex, too, and then she'd all but jumped him the second he'd gotten close enough to touch.

Not that he minded the sex. The sex had been... amazing. Absolutely amazing. He'd never been with a woman so...voracious before. It was exactly as he'd thought: once she'd loosened her tight coil of control, she'd been nearly insatiable.

But apparently, all she wanted was a quickie, nothing more. He'd recognized that look when she'd sputtered on about him being a mistake. It was the same one he probably used when he tried to gently push a tourist out of his house the morning after, when the mai tais had worn off.

If Jesse were here, she'd laugh her ass off and tell him it was what he deserved. But he'd never been anything but honest with the women he'd slept with. He'd always said it was just for fun, that he wasn't looking for commitment, and so far, that had been great for everyone. No tourist fell into his bed looking for forever. Everyone wanted the same thing; it was simple, just the way he liked it.

Since when did he ever like complicated?

Since…Po. He wasn't ready to walk away from that boy. He didn't want him to be afraid of water for the rest of his life, and he *knew* in his gut he could help him. That maybe, even, they could help each other. He remembered how well he'd surfed when he knew Po was watching. Yes, he thought he could help the boy, but perhaps at the heart of it, he thought Po could save him right back. Even now he felt as if he was so close to really recovering, to getting his surfing legs back. He'd never considered himself a family man, hadn't even given much thought to having kids, and yet now that Po was in his life, he felt different. He realized that ever since they'd survived the floodwaters, Kai had felt responsible for the boy. He'd fought it for a year, but with Jun and Po in his life, he couldn't deny it any longer. And he wasn't like his own father. He took his responsibilities seriously.

He'd reached the hotel high-rise, and the aquamarine pool glistened in the sunlight. Tanned bodies lay on reclining chairs, soaking up sun, as soft ukulele music tinkled out across the open patio. The bar, open-air and near the pool, beckoned him with empty stools at the ready. A brunette in a white gauzy cover-up, mostly transparent and unbuttoned to her navel, showing off a flattering string bikini, sat sipping a piña colada. She reminded him of Jun, which was dangerous. She removed a big chunk of fresh pineapple from the rim of the glass and proceeded to nibble at it as she scrolled through her smartphone.

His own phone rang, and he saw it was his manager, Kirk, calling. He'd been bugging him about the ad video for the new surfboard. He couldn't put him off forever.

"Hey, Kirk," Kai said, answering the call as he moved away from the woman with the piña colada.

"Kai! You're a hard man to reach. We've been putting together that charity you asked for—Big

Island Kids—and the site goes live tomorrow. People can 'sponsor' you for the surf competition and then every point you earn, the kids get some dough."

"That's great news."

"You know how I feel about charities, man."

"You mean the only thing you think they are good for is a tax write-off," Kai said.

"That's *right*. So you know that I'm really doing this Big Island Kids thing for you. I mean, who's a swell manager?"

"You are."

"Yeah, so since *I've* done *you* this big money-draining favor, here's what you need to do. I have to have those advertising shots, bro. We need to unveil the new surfboard next month."

"Right… About that…"

"I was thinking you could do some shots—still *and* video—at Jaws. You know, since that's where the competition's going to be."

Kai glanced around him at the bar, wishing he had a stiff drink.

"I've got a camera crew coming out there this weekend."

"I don't know about a commercial right now, Kirk." Kai saw out of the corner of his eye that the woman in the bikini seemed to be interested in his conversation. "The competition is soon. I can't shoot that now. I've got training and…" Kai desperately wished for a better excuse.

"What better way to train, bro, then *on* the break where the competition is? I would've thought you'd be camped out there already!"

Kirk was right. Kai knew it, too. He glanced at the back of the bartender, who was busy taking an order across the bar. He definitely needed a drink. The woman with the piña colada leaned in and took a big sip from her straw.

"Fine. You're right. Okay."

"Great. Oh, how's the new trainer working out? What's her name? April? August?"

"Jun," Kai corrected. "Uh…" Kai imagined Jun stark-naked beneath him, smooth and pale. "She's…fine." And about as complicated as a person got. It still didn't stop him from wishing she were here with him. The woman at the bar only resembled her. She wasn't Jun.

"Uh-huh. Keeping things professional?" Kirk asked.

"Sort of."

"Kai! This is your career we're talking about, bro. Do not kill the cash cow, man."

"Believe me, I know it," he said. "I'll be fine. Send me the details on the photo shoot, okay?"

He clicked off and saw the woman at the bar was openly staring at him.

Now that he was closer, he saw there were

fewer similarities to Jun than he'd thought. He ran a hand through his thick hair. The only reason he was even considering taking that empty seat next to this woman was that vaguely, and at the right angle, she reminded him of Jun. He realized then that he had it bad.

He almost laughed out loud. The one woman who made it clear she *didn't* want a relationship with him, and he'd fallen for her. He'd fallen for her *and* her little boy. At a time when he wasn't supposed to get distracted, he'd fallen in love.

He'd fought it since the day she'd stood on his porch with that little gift bag, but now there was no use in fighting it anymore.

Then he did laugh. He couldn't help it.

"What's so funny?" the woman who only slightly looked like Jun asked him from the bar.

"Love," Kai said, and shook his head ruefully.

"That bad, huh?" she asked him.

"Worse." Kai grinned.

"Hey, you look familiar. You're that surfer guy. Kai Brady!"

Reluctantly, Kai nodded. "That's me."

"Famous surfer in the house! Can I buy you a drink?" she asked, and Kai knew what that meant. It was an invitation that went deeper than a round of fruity cocktails.

On any other day, he would have said yes. He wouldn't have hesitated. But when he looked up at the woman, all he saw was Jun's stubborn face. He was doomed. In love with a woman who didn't love him back.

"Thanks, but no," he said.

Disappointment shadowed her face, but then she rallied. "How about a picture, then? Just one?"

"Okay," Kai said, and let her snap a selfie with him.

"I HATE SCHOOL," whined Po from the backseat the next morning. "I don't want to go." He'd groaned nonstop since she'd picked him up the day before, and it had been a constant refrain since. He didn't like the other kids, didn't like the teacher, didn't like that they failed to teach him how to count in Hawaiian like Kaimana did. "I miss Auntie K.," Po added as he kicked his Spider-Man sneakers into the back of the passenger seat.

"No kicking," Jun said absently, feeling worn down and beaten up. Why was figuring out the right thing for her son so hard? Why couldn't *one day* be easy? She shook her head.

She felt as if she'd failed at everything this week. Normally, she didn't entertain thoughts of self-pity, but today she wished she could go back to bed and throw the covers over her head. She fought so hard to prove her mother wrong, and yet, on days like this, it seemed as though she was proving her exactly right. Maybe she *was* too young to be a mom. Maybe she was too in-experienced. Maybe she didn't know what she was doing.

Maybe she was a girl without morals, after all. Just as her mother had said. Just like what her mother had called her before she slapped her across the face.

The insult burned in her memory like red neon.

She thought about what she'd done with Kai the night before and instantly felt as if she'd been toppled by a salty ocean wave. She'd done the right thing pushing him away, she knew she had, yet why didn't it feel like the right thing? Po was miserable and so was she. Maybe Kai had been right. Maybe the rules weren't for him at all—they *were* for her. Why couldn't she control herself better? Why did he get under her skin...and under her sheets?

Jun pulled up to the day care, fully expecting Po to not want to get out of the car, but miraculously, he did. She walked him to the door anticipating waterworks but instead got just a long look of disapproval from his sad face. That look was worse than a full-on tantrum. She left him at the day care and got back into her car, dreading the drive to Kai's. She sat there a moment, and her phone lit up with an incoming message. It was from Tim.

Have a minute to stop by the gym? Just for a second?

Tim hadn't given up asking Jun to take her old job back. She'd been avoiding him while still trying to be nice for the past few months. But he simply wasn't getting the message. Jun hadn't wanted to be blunt with him, because she always worried the job with Kai might fall through at any moment and because she knew if she needed a job, Tim would take her back.

She thought about the lovesick look in his eyes the day she'd left the gym and shuddered. She didn't want to flat-out tell him he had no chance with her, and yet he kept nudging, kept pushing her.

Tell your boss you'll be five minutes late! I've got an opportunity I think you'll like. Please? Business!

Jun sighed. She'd put him off every day for the past week, and she knew he'd just keep texting.

It's time sensitive. Got to have a decision by the weekend. Just let me pitch you the idea, okay? I've been asking for a whole week! Five minutes.

Jun gave in. Five minutes. What could it hurt? Plus, he said it was business related. He was always coming up with new ideas for healthy drinks or some new fitness gizmo. He'd probably just ask her to taste some new protein shake and then she'd be on her way. It seemed a harmless detour. Still, the drive would take her off her route. She texted Kai. Told him she had to run by Island Fit before heading to his house for their training session but wouldn't be more than ten minutes late.

Why don't we just train there for the morning? Will Tim be okay with that?

Tim would definitely not think that was a good idea, she was pretty sure.

Jun pulled into a parking space in front of the fitness center and took a deep breath before she headed to the entrance. When she saw Tim's beaming face as she walked in, her shoulders sagged. He looked so darn…hopeful. Immediately, he crossed the gym and enveloped her in an unwanted hug. He smelled strongly of too much cologne and she did *not* want to be touching him. He kept his hand too long on the center of her back and she squirmed away. She was all too aware how much she'd rather Kai be touching her right then.

"I've missed you, Jun," Tim said. "You look great. Really great." His eyes swept over her and she was beginning to wish she hadn't come.

Maybe this had been a mistake. Tim rubbed her arm and she pulled it back, slightly uncomfortable.

"I can't stay long. You said something about a business idea?"

Disappointment flickered across Tim's features, but he quickly hid it. "Uh, yeah, sure… Well, I'm opening a second location of Island Fit. On the other side of the island."

"Really? That's great, Tim. Good for you." Jun was happy for him. He'd always want to franchise his gym across the islands, and it sounded as though he was on the verge of doing just that.

"I need someone to run it when it opens in six months." Tim stared at her, his blue eyes steady. "I want that person to be you."

"Me?" Jun was completely taken aback. She'd never considered running her own gym before or thought that anyone, even Tim, would hand her the keys to one.

"You." Tim nodded. He took a step forward. Still reeling from the offer, she almost missed the determined, almost steely, look in his eyes. "I think you know how I feel about you."

Now Jun felt as though she'd been whipped back into the present, and she was suddenly very aware that Tim was touching her arm, running his finger up her biceps. This wasn't good.

"Tim, look, I…"

"We could make a great team, Jun. Professionally…and personally."

*No, we definitely couldn't.* All she could think about were Kai's warm brown eyes and chiseled good looks. Tim had a flat nose and a hard curve to his lip. She hadn't noticed it before, but Tim looked a little like the ugly guy on the football team, mean and muscled.

"Tim, look, I'm really flattered, but…"

"Jun. Come on. Give us a chance." Without warning, Tim grabbed her arms. She tried to pull away from him, but he had at least sixty pounds of muscle on her. He bench-pressed twice her weight.

"Tim… I don't feel that way about you."

But then he was kissing her. It was sloppy and wet and awkward, and nothing at all like Kai. Jun managed to shove Tim away. "Tim, stop."

Tim's face fell, his hope crumpling, and she knew she was breaking his heart, but she had to draw the line.

"Tim, we're not going to be a couple. I don't like you like that."

"Why won't you even give us a chance? Is it that surfer? Brady? He's no good." Tim grabbed his phone from his pocket. "I mean, he was clubbing *just yesterday.*"

"What do you mean?" Now Jun had a laser-like focus on his phone. Tim pulled up a picture of Kai with a dark-haired beauty at the bar of the

Four Seasons. She had her face pressed close to his, the picture revealing the plunging neckline of her barely there bikini. It was time stamped the day before.

Jun felt jealousy blaze in her chest. Had he gone to the bar yesterday? Had he picked up a girl? Had he blatantly disregarded her rules? Of course, she realized her reaction had nothing to do with his training. That wasn't why she was upset. Not in the least.

The bell on the front door dinged then, and Kai walked right in, eyes flashing. "Am I interrupting?"

Jun jumped away from Tim, as if she'd been caught doing something wrong, when she wasn't.

"No," Jun said, shaking her head, and moving farther from Tim, who looked exceptionally pissed to have had his moment ruined. Jun vowed he wouldn't get another one. She was immensely relieved to see Kai. "I was just going."

Jun turned to leave.

"Will you think about it?" Tim called after her. "I mean…the gym?"

"No. Tim, I won't. I'm not interested."

"But…"

"Tim… I said no."

Tim looked crestfallen, but there wasn't any way around it.

Kai said nothing, just opened the door for her as she walked through.

He followed her outside.

"What did that greaseball ask you to think about?"

Jun stopped by her car. "He wants me to manage his second gym. He's opening one soon. But I don't want to do it."

Jun pulled her door handle.

"Let's take mine," Kai said, steering Jun away to his car.

"But…"

"Or, we can have this conversation in full view of Tim."

Jun glanced over at Tim, who was practically pressed against the front glass.

"Let's take your car," she said, realizing the last thing she wanted was a scene in the parking lot. Once inside his car, he quickly pulled out of the parking lot.

"So, are you going to tell me what you were doing kissing him?" The muscle in his jaw twitched.

"He kissed me. I didn't kiss him."

"Oh."

Jun realized with a start that Kai was jealous. He'd seen Tim with his sloppy come-on and was actually jealous. Well, good. Served him right.

He took a left turn down the road that would take them to his beach house.

"Why do you care? You were the one out yesterday picking up tourists. I saw the picture at the Four Seasons. With the brunette at the bar."

Understanding dawned on his face. "Stalking me online?"

"No. Tim showed me." Jun glared out the window as Kai angrily turned the steering wheel. He pulled up in the drive and shut off his engine.

"Tim only wants to get in your pants."

"It's not going to happen."

"You seemed fine letting him kiss you."

"I wasn't fine, for the record. He kissed like a wet fish."

A grin broke out across Kai's face.

"But that's none of your business." Jun opened the door and hopped out of the car. Kai followed her.

"It *is* my business." Kai rounded the Jeep and stood in front of her. Jun blinked up at him, taking in his body, lean but strong. His blue linen button-down shirt looked new and made his dark eyes even darker. She felt a hot roiling of emotion, like a kettle about to boil. "And why do you care so much if I sleep with another tourist or not?"

"I don't," Jun lied. "It's just the rules."

"So, then, just so we're clear, you're not going to sleep with me, but I can't sleep with anyone else, either?" Kai's voice sent reverberations down her spine.

"That's the rule," she said, stubbornly raising her chin. "No sex until after the competition."

"Oh, I see." Kai rubbed his chin, the sarcasm clear in his voice. "So, you wouldn't care, then, if *after* our training and *after* the competition, I took someone to bed? *That* would be okay with you?"

"No! I—" Jun realized she'd been about to blurt out the terrible secret she'd been holding inside. She *did* care who he slept with and when. She *didn't* think sleeping with Kai was a mistake in the sense of wishing she hadn't done it. She was *very* glad she'd done it. Too glad. *That* was what made it a mistake.

"Well, just for the record, I *am* attracted to that tourist from yesterday. I think she's pretty."

Jun felt herself stiffen. The girl was pretty. She was dark haired and tanned, petite and delicate. She looked as if she had a runner's body, lean and in shape.

"But do you know why I think she's pretty?"

Jun shook her head, not trusting herself to speak.

"Because she reminds me of you. She's not nearly as pretty as you, not nearly as...amazing. But, in some small way, she reminds me of you. I think she's pretty. But I think you're damn near beautiful."

Jun was frozen to the spot. No one had called her beautiful before. Pretty, sometimes. Cute, even, but beautiful? Never.

Kai took another step closer. Jun didn't know if she wanted to run away or kiss the man. "I know you don't want this. Want *us*. But trust me when I tell you that *this*—" he gestured to her breast and then his own "—doesn't come around every day."

Kai brushed hair from Jun's face as she stood immobilized.

"But… I…"

"Don't tell me you're not interested, because I know that's a lie," Kai said, so close to her she could feel his body heat.

Jun's mouth went dry.

"Do you think I can't read you?" Kai put his hands on her shoulders. "Do you think I don't know that if I kiss you right now, you'll kiss me back?"

Jun's knees went weak as she instinctively leaned toward him. What was it about him that made resistance so futile? He was right. More than right. If he leaned down right at that moment, she would kiss him. And more. She'd lose herself. Completely.

Jun swallowed, hard. She couldn't speak. She didn't know what words might slip out of her mouth.

"You're going to tell me that this is a distraction from my training. And you're damn straight it is." Kai squeezed her arms. "So, I'm not going to kiss you. I want to. Oh, damn, do I, but I won't even touch you."

Disappointment rushed through Jun. She should've been relieved, but instead, all she felt was loss.

"You were right. You've always been right. Sex and…this…are distracting me from the job I have to do right now." Kai sighed with frustration. Jun had never thought being told she was right could feel so wrong. "I've got to surf Jaws, and if I'm thinking about you, I'm liable to die trying."

Jun opened her mouth to protest, but he shook his head.

"So, I'm going to abide by your rules. No kissing. No hugging. No sex. Nothing." Kai took a step back, hands in the air. Jun suddenly wanted to jump on him, to test his resolve, and hers. Yet the look on his face told her he was dead serious. Why did that news bring with it a stab of bitterness?

"But I'm giving you fair warning right now, Jun Lee." Determination flashed in his dark eyes. "After this competition, I *will* come for you. You won't be able to hide from me, so you'd better be ready."

# CHAPTER TWENTY

OVER THE NEXT couple of days, Kai was indeed a perfect gentleman.

It should've brought Jun relief, but instead, his careful businesslike persona drove her wild with frustration. He'd become little more than an automaton spouting pleasantries, and he vigilantly avoided touching her. But she hadn't forgotten his words. Some days she wondered if he'd even said them at all, but she'd never forget the look on his face when he had.

*I* will *come for you.*

What did that mean? Was he going to ravish her on the beach near the announcer's stand right after his surfing stint? The fact was, she didn't know, but she couldn't help but enjoy a delicious sort of anticipation. She should've been feeling dread, but she wasn't. Not at all. In her imagination, the possibilities got more and more elaborate, more passionate, and absolutely more...naughty.

What was wrong with her? She had time to breathe, to switch back to her no-sex mode, and yet, even working alongside all-business Kai, all she could think about was sex.

She tried to muster up some indignation. After all, she wasn't a surfboard he could buy and then ride whenever he wanted.

Come for her. She wasn't property that he could claim. She was a person. With a will of her own and a mind she intended to use.

She wasn't living in prehistoric times: a man couldn't hit a woman over the head and drag her back to her cave, for goodness' sake.

Yet, as time ticked down to the competition and she grasped that she had less than a week to get her libido and her willpower back under control, she questioned whether she could do it. Kai's deliberate ultraprofessional demeanor still irked. She wasn't sure if it was because she wanted to kiss him or because she wanted to tell him what he could do with his random declarations of war.

She retaliated by making him lift heavier weights and run farther and take meditation sessions to a whole new level. Still, the fact that he spent more time on the water was a good thing. His knee was stronger, and for that she felt a certain level of pride, but even more, she was glad to have a break from his relentlessly polite, diabolically detached behavior. She didn't like the no-funny-business Kai. She didn't like him one bit.

She was thinking about this when she showed

up on his doorstep on a Friday morning to discover an empty house. No one answered his doorbell, and when she called his cell, it went straight to voice mail.

That was when a message popped up on her phone.

No training today. Envelope for you in my mailbox.

Odd, Jun thought as she went to his mailbox and pulled out a letter that had her name scrawled on the front. She opened the envelope and a check for more than $30,000 spilled out along with a note.

Dear Jun,

I had to fly to Maui to shoot ads on Jaws and prep for the competition this weekend. Should've left before now but realize the move won't work for you and Po, so I'm giving you a bonus check. I'm further along than I ever thought possible, but now I have to finish training on my own. Jaws is dangerous, as you know, and I'll need my full concentration here.

I want to thank you for the tools you gave me. I had doubts about ever getting on a board again, but you and Po made it possible for me to try.

In the meantime, I know you probably won't accept this bonus check without another assignment, so I'm asking that you take on the role of director of my charity, Big Island Kids. In this envelope you'll find contact information for some local contacts, including Dr. Jean Ann, a pediatrician who has been helping volunteer efforts and is a very good contact. Please touch base with them to get up to speed.

I am writing you this letter because I think it will be harder for you to argue with this paper.

Yours,
Kai

She read and reread the letter, and then she stared at the check in her hand. That was it? He was going to head to the finish line without her? She couldn't believe that he'd just decided on his own, without even talking with her! She could've told him that she still had something to offer, that she knew she could help him take the visualization further, that she had a whole notebook of calming techniques she'd still planned to try, along with acupuncture and a hot-stone massage. She had a *plan*, but he'd decided it all for himself. Without consulting her.

He was infuriating! He complained about *her* making unilateral decisions, but he was just as guilty. She reread the letter again. What did she know about managing a charity? Nothing! She was a personal trainer. She flipped the letter over and realized there was more to his message.

PS: We'll have more to talk about after the competition. I haven't forgotten what I promised.

Oh, he hadn't, had he? Again, he assumed she'd just welcome him back with open arms? Completely ludicrous.

And this check? She glared at it, anger thrumming in her temples. A bonus check? It felt more like a "shut up and leave me alone" check, and she didn't want to take it.

She thought about tearing it up but then hesitated. What if he never even *noticed* she hadn't cashed it?

She needed to give it to him in person. *And* she wasn't about to let him go surf Jaws without her.

Not when they'd worked so hard. She was going to fly to Maui and see him herself.

She grabbed her phone and dialed her sister.

"Kiki," she said. "Can you watch Po for a couple of days?"

# CHAPTER TWENTY-ONE

KAI SAT ON the warm sand on the north shore of Maui, watching the waves roll at Jaws. They were churning up there today, bigger than forty feet, yet the monsters didn't keep surfers away, especially with the competition in just a few days. An army of Jet Skis hit the waves, with surfers trailing behind like water skiers, trying to get the timing just right, taking their lives in their hands to get the ultimate rush.

"Whoa, that is some *crazy shit* out there, man," cried one of the camera crew. They were milling about the beach, trying to get their stuff together. "The surf reports weren't kidding."

"Yep," Kai said. "We call that pure Hawaiian juice."

"You're crazy, man. You are. All of you are." The camera guy shook his head as he watched a surfer let go of the towline, balancing on his surfboard, and crest the fifty-foot wave. He rode as though his life depended on it, because it did.

Falling at Jaws felt like falling off a five-story building—or having one fall on top of you. Kai had once hit the surf going at least fifty miles an hour, and the force of impact was so strong it had ripped his life jacket straight in half.

*That* was Jaws.

The huge waves broke into foam, churning the water white for about a hundred yards in all directions. The surf came ashore onto a rocky lava beach, where broken Jet Skis lay scattered like metal corpses. Rising up from the craggy beach was a tall cliff, where spectators parked their cars and sat on the hoods, watching the surfers crazy enough to try tow surfing. Kai glanced out at the powerful waves crashing into the jagged black shore and almost felt the bone-jarring crunch of them pounding his own head.

Nerves swam in his stomach. He tried to close his eyes and meditate, but the roar of the ocean invaded his every thought. It was loud; too loud.

He hadn't been back since the last time Bret had towed him.

Kai hadn't been ready; his knee had given way after he'd ridden a little while. He'd crashed, hard, dragging his board behind him. It had been a hard fall, but Bret had powered in to save him on the Jet Ski. He'd had seconds between crushing waves. With sixty pounds of weight in every cubic foot of water, a forty-foot wave could break bones. Mere seconds, and he'd managed to time it just right and dragged Kai to safety on the back of the towline of the Jet Ski.

Bret had asked him to quit surfing then. Not for good, just for the day. He'd asked him, and Kai had said no.

Kai had asked to go again. It had been stupid, he knew, but it was like riding a bike and falling off. He wanted to make sure he wasn't traumatized, that despite that he'd bit it on his first big wave since the injury, he could still do this. It was about ego, too, wanting to go out on a good wave. Bret had argued with him and Kai had yelled in his face. How a real friend would man up and do this. Kai wasn't proud of what he'd said, of the bile that he'd unleashed on his longtime friend. But Kai had been scared, and he'd had something to prove, and the only way he knew how to do that was to throw himself at the mercy of that monstrous wave.

"You have a death wish, you know that?" Bret had screamed at him at the time.

And maybe Kai did. If he'd died that day, at least the world wouldn't have discovered he was a fake. He would've gone out as a kick-ass extreme surfer, not some guy with a bum leg, someone to be pitied.

On Kai's second ride that day, he'd fallen almost as soon as he crested over the wave. He plummeted down the face of what was almost Niagara

Falls, with such force in the bowl below that it broke his board in two and pummeled him once, twice, three times. He was held down beneath that engine of water for a full minute. *I'm going to become a fish*, he thought. This was it.

Bret got him out of the worst of it, but the Jet Ski, stuck in the foam, unable to push water through its engine, had stalled. Then the two of them were sitting ducks for the next wave. It swept the Jet Ski out from under them. The wave crashed into Kai's head, knocking him senseless. Bret, arm broken, nearly drowned but still somehow managed to get to Kai. The Jet Ski was smashed on the rocks, yet they got to shore. Bret was carried out on a stretcher. Kai walked on his own. He insisted on taking Bret to the hospital.

But the real tragedy happened later.

When Bret's wife found out what had happened, she rushed to the hospital in a panic. She sped through a red light and was hit by a delivery truck. She'd survived, but she'd lost her baby.

Bret blamed Kai for it all. And so did Kai. If he'd listened to Bret, if he hadn't gone out that second time, none of that would've happened. Kai understood Bret's anger. He got it. He deserved it. He'd apologized countless times, but Kai knew that some things, you just couldn't be forgiven for.

Ever since that day, Kai had a fear he'd never had before. He'd lost his edge. His ego had cost him his best friend. And now here he was again, about to die. This time without Bret to save him.

*What am I doing here? The competition's in a matter of days, and I'm not ready. I'm miles from ready.*

A wiry twig of a boy bounced into his view. "Hey, Kai Brady, right? I'm Henley James. Gonna tow you today."

"You?" Kai didn't bother hiding his surprise. The boy was half his age. Barely looked old enough to drive a car and even had a smattering of acne on his forehead. How could this kid maneuver a tiny Jet Ski through and around hundred-foot waves?

"Been doing it for two years."

"Since you were ten?" Kai asked.

"Hey, man. I'm eighteen," he said, sounding offended. Kai shook his head. Maybe Jesse was right and he was getting too old for this sport. Henley, however, recovered quickly. He was likely too excited to stay mad. "You probably don't remember this, but you saved my brother, man."

"I did?" Kai scratched his head, drawing a blank.

"Two years ago. Hamilton James? We call him Hammy. He was out riding Jaws and probably shouldn't have been. Scrappy blond kid? He went down hard and was knocked out. You pulled him out."

Kai vaguely remembered a kid who'd had a spectacular wipeout there, before the tsunami. Kai nodded. Probably one of many he'd dragged out of the drink only to yell at them for being out in a place they had no business being.

"Yeah, I remember."

"Hammy never surfed big waves after that. Said he learned his lesson."

"Good." Kai nodded. Big surf wasn't for everyone. *Might not be for me anymore, either.* But anytime Kai really thought about quitting, he wondered, *What else am I going to do with my life?* He knew of plenty of retired surfers who made surfboards or put their names on shirts, and he could do all that, *was* doing all that, but what did it matter if he couldn't do the one thing he thought he was born to do? What then?

Not to mention, he had sponsors, endorsements, and some of that money was going to Big Island Kids. If he didn't surf, the charity didn't get that money. He thought about Po and about all the other kids he could help. He had to finish the competition.

"I'm still your biggest fan," the boy said. "I hate to ask this, bro, but could you sign this for me?" He produced an old surf magazine featuring Kai at the base of a seventy-foot wave crashing at Jaws, the crystal-blue water towering up above his head. He looked like an ant. He remembered that wave and that cover. The photographer had shot it from a helicopter that hovered near the top of the break and hardly anyone had seen anything like it before. That cover had been groundbreaking, and it had put big-wave tow surfing on the map.

The boy pulled out a pen and Kai scribbled his name on the white foam of the wave in the upper corner.

"*Thanks*, man."

"Sure." Kai stared at his younger self, the one in the photo, the one who took on any challenge without blinking. What had happened to *that* Kai?

*The tsunami happened to him, that's what.*

The camera crew worked hard to attach cameras to the drones they'd power down over the waves.

"You guys know how to fly those?" Kai asked, wondering how the little drones would fare against a wall of water. Probably not so good.

"We've done this before."

"Uh-huh." He wanted to tell them to get a close-up of his knee when it gave out. He shook his head and shut his eyes, trying to use Jun's advice to visualize himself successfully surfing Jaws. Of course, he knew visualization was worthless at Jaws. The break felt different every time you rode it, and you could never predict how any of it would feel. There was always a surprise. Usually a nasty one.

Dark clouds sat on the horizon and he watched them closely. Was a storm coming? Jaws was powerful enough under normal conditions. Storm swells would make it ten times worse.

Henley slapped Kai on the back. "I think it's go time, man. You ready for this?"

JUN RUSHED OUT of the airport and got into the first cab she saw. She figured Kai would be at Jaws and decided to head there. Her blood boiled. How could he just leave her like that? Why on earth did he think she'd be content to let him finish out the competition without her? She got angrier the more she thought about it.

The cabdriver poked along the coastal highway and Jun leaned over the front seat. "Can you go a little faster?" she asked, knowing he probably wouldn't. Unlike cabbies in big cities, cabbies in the island chain took their sweet time.

She took out her phone and dialed Kai's number again, but her call went straight to voice mail. After what seemed like an eternity, the cab finally pulled up near the cliff lookout a hundred feet above Jaws. Trucks and cars crowded the small inlet, and spectators sat on car hoods and roofs, watching the dozens of surfers and Jet Skiers below trying to navigate the massive blue swells. The sky above grew overcast, and on the horizon, Jun saw a dark storm approaching. But worse were the choppy waves below. Even from this height, she could tell they were monsters— thirty feet and higher. She knew Kai took risks, and the picture of him in Po's room showed him testing his mettle on a twenty-footer, but somehow she'd had no idea the conditions were *this* extreme, *this* perilous. She felt silly, suddenly. She'd been training him for *exactly this*, and yet she hadn't really considered how dangerous it could be until now.

She asked the driver to wait and then jumped out of the cab and hurried to the edge to look out at the surfers. They were being whipped around by the surf, and even as she watched, one wiped out in amazing fashion, flying headfirst into a crushing wave. Frantically, she looked from board to board, trying to see if she recognized Kai's. Beside her, two women sat on the hood of an open-top Jeep with a pair of binoculars next to them on the towel they'd thrown over the grill.

"Could I borrow those?" Jun asked, and one of the girls nodded, handing them over. Quickly, she scanned the surf, examining every dark-haired surfer out there. Finally, she found Kai. He was being towed out by a Jet Ski, balancing on his board, and above him, two drones floated, no doubt with cameras attached. She saw his lean form clad in a formfitting wet suit and a life jacket as he held on to the towline.

She couldn't talk to him now. He was already headed out to an enormous wave. Panicked, she glanced ahead of Kai and saw the wall of water he was heading toward, an intimidating swell.

She felt suddenly scared for him, her stomach one giant knot of muscle. She watched, fingers clutching the binoculars, as the Jet Ski led him straight to the crest of the wave. Then he let go of the line and he was free, cascading down the face of a wave that was six times his size. He looked like a tiny fleck next to the massive stretch of blue cresting above his head. Jun held her breath. The drones with the cameras buzzed around him, getting his ride from all angles.

She could see his face through the binoculars, his steady concentration. If he was afraid, he didn't show it, his square jaw firmly clenched as he focused, every ounce of his body about balancing on that board, every muscle engaged as he tried to outrun the mountain of water behind him. For a second, she felt elated: he was doing it. He was surfing. His knee was holding. Thank God. She looked again at the towering wave behind him and thought…he was amazing. How could he do that? It seemed to defy all laws of physics, and yet there he was, riding that enormous wave, cresting atop one of nature's most powerful forces and standing tall.

Pride bloomed in her chest. She'd helped him get back to this.

As she watched him, she saw his leg twitch. Her heart dropped into her stomach.

*No. Not the knee. Not now.*

He had a wall of water behind him traveling faster than a car, a wall of water that weighed more than a ton, ready to crash down on him. His leg twitched again. She could see Kai struggle to hold on, to keep his form and balance. She saw the will on his face to keep his knee from giving. Yet she saw the uphill battle, knew in her gut that the knee wasn't going to hold. A second later, it buckled, and down Kai went in a spectacular whirling fall. He hit the wave hard, and it threw him back up, thirty feet or higher in the air, his board snapping free of its tether and shooting out in the opposite direction. Kai, pinwheeling, plummeted into the churning water, taking out one drone as he fell. The other popped up, spinning high above the water.

The crowd near her gasped at the horrific wipeout. Concerned murmurs rose in a hum around her, but all she could do was stay mutely rooted to the spot. She searched the white foam of the frothing water, but Kai didn't come up for air.

# CHAPTER TWENTY-TWO

A WALL OF WATER hit Kai on the head so hard it felt like a baseball bat ramming his skull at full force, batting him down so deep beneath the surface of the water that the sunlight faded almost entirely and when he looked up, he saw the churning surface far, far above him, seventy feet at least. He kicked futilely, trying to move to the surface, his life jacket on him with just one buckle, the force of the fall having snapped the other two clean in two. He felt disoriented and fuzzy, his ears ringing with the impact and his vision blurred.

He kicked hard, but just when he got to the surface, another wave pounded him back down, sending him even deeper this time. He rose to the surface once more, caught a wet breath and then was pummeled back down into darker, blacker depths.

The water wasn't letting him up; the ocean had decided that today he wasn't getting a second chance. Somehow he knew that. He'd pressed his luck, used up all his lives, and now, finally, the ocean would take what belonged to it. His ego.

He'd been stupid, he realized, so stupid. Bret had been right. He should've retired. Should've given up this folly of chasing the biggest, baddest waves on the planet.

He thought about his father, about how silly it seemed, Kai, a grown man now, using surfing to battle such old demons. Who cared if his father had another family on the mainland? He was a man now. He shouldn't care what his father did or didn't do, what his father had done or not done.

Father. Now he'd never be one, and he'd thought, he'd really thought, he could've been a good dad to Po. He realized now, being held down by a wall of water, that playing a meaningful role in that boy's life wasn't scary. Drowning, now, that was scary. Being a dad was…an opportunity to do something that mattered. That wasn't about ego or thumbing his nose at gravity or about fame or money. That was what had been missing in his life: things that mattered.

He saw Jun's face in his mind. He'd never get a chance to convince her they were right for one another. In that moment, staring straight at what he thought would become his watery grave, he didn't even think about the surf competition. Or the endorsements. Or selling surfboards. All he thought about was Jun and the things he'd wanted to say to her but hadn't.

*I'm not ready to go yet. I'm not ready.*

The ocean didn't care. The ocean would show him no mercy.

His lungs burned and stars clouded his vision. This was it. Seconds more and he'd have to breathe in, breathe in the water that would kill him. With one last great effort, he kicked upward, his life jacket propelling him, and miraculously, he popped up to the surface once more, inhaling a huge breath. In the roaring surf, he saw a shadow and heard a sputter: a Jet Ski.

"Grab on!" Henley called, turning around in his seat, and Kai grasped the floating barge attached to the back of the ski and held on for all he was worth. He'd never been so glad to see a pimple-faced teenager before in his life. Henley gunned the engine and whisked him away from the next approaching wave. Kai looked at the fierce blue water. *That wave would've killed me.* No doubt in his mind whatsoever. He watched it as it crashed monstrously against the black rocks, shooting up a wall of white foam in all directions as he coughed up brine.

He made it to the rocky shore and just lay there, breathing in deep gulps of air.

"You saved me," Kai told Henley. "Thanks, man. Sorry I doubted you."

"No trouble," the boy said. "Just paying you back for Hammy. Glad to do it."

The two men from the ad agency who'd been

operating the drone cameras came clambering up then. "You okay, man?" one asked.

"That was the most heinous wipeout I've ever seen!"

"It felt even worse than it looked," Kai said, staring up at them both.

"Anything broken? I thought for sure you'd split yourself in half, bro!" Henley was all agitated adrenaline.

Kai did a quick assessment of his body but found nothing but his head hurt. His life jacket was mostly wrecked, two of the three buckles split clean in half. It was a miracle it had stayed on. "I don't think I broke anything." Kai was amazed he'd gotten out in one piece. "I thought I was going to die out there."

"Looked like you were, too," Henley said, nodding in agreement.

"Kai!" a voice shouted from the distant rocks. Kai looked up to see Jun headed for him, slowly and awkwardly picking her way down the lava-rock beach. He blinked, wondering if it was hallucination, an effect from having a five-ton wave bash him on the head a few times. He quickly realized what he was seeing, however, was real. She was here, in the flesh, wearing a white sundress and impractical sandals that weren't giving her any traction on the rocks, but that made her muscled legs look amazing.

"Jun?" he asked, sitting up, his head feeling as if it were in a vise as he swiped wet hair from his forehead.

"Kai! Are you okay? I saw…you fall. I saw…" Emotion overcame her then and she lost her ability to speak. She made it to him and collapsed on her knees beside him. "Are you okay?"

"I'm bruised and battered but fine."

She threw herself on him, ignoring that he was wet and seawater would soak through her dress. She squeezed him tight, and he nearly fell over. He wrapped his arm around her and hugged her back. He felt a sob ripple through her chest.

"Hey…don't cry. I'm fine."

Henley and the others busied themselves with packing up gear, trying to give the two a moment.

"You scared me," Jun sniffed as she pulled back from him, wiping at her eyes. "I saw you go down. I didn't see you come up. I thought you were going to drown out there."

"So did I," Kai admitted.

Jun shook her head, as if wanting to deny all of it. "It's too dangerous. I just… I didn't understand what I was training you for. I should have, but I didn't. I had no idea it was like…this." She swung out her bare arm toward the roaring waves still coming in about a hundred yards out.

"Jun. This is big-wave surfing. This is what I do. Thankfully, I was in good hands." He glanced over at Henley, insanely grateful the young kid had a solid head on his shoulders. If he'd panicked or hesitated, Kai would've been at the bottom of the ocean right now. Kai held Jun's face. "I'm okay, all right? I'm okay." He didn't like to see her so upset. He didn't like knowing *he* was the cause of the upset, either. "Where's Po? How did you get here?"

Jun sniffed and sat back on her heels. "Never mind that. What are you doing? Just leaving me a note and coming out here to surf one of the craziest breaks without me? Are you crazy?"

Henley, who'd been giving them space, now intruded. "Hey, bro, you think you're going to call it quits today? Or are we going to try again?" Henley asked.

"He's not going again," Jun said. "I'm his trainer, and...*he's not going again today.*"

Henley eyed her, surprise on his boyish face.

Kai thought about fighting her, but even he knew he didn't have it in him. "She's the boss," he told Henley. "Looks like I'm done for the day."

Henley nodded. "Hey, I don't want to step on your toes, but do you mind if I go out there once? I've got a buddy who can tow me. I mean, if you're okay with it."

"Are you better than Hammy?" Kai asked, half joking, half serious.

"Way better, dude."

Kai nodded. "Sure, man. Go ahead."

Kai watched the kid get geared up and then another baby-faced teenager took the controls of the Jet Ski. Miraculously, Henley managed to catch a killer wave and tame it. He crushed an eighty-footer as though it were a walk in the park. Amazing. Kai had to admit, the kid had talent. Reminded him of himself when he was ten years younger. Back when he had no fear and a knee that worked. As much as he wanted to believe the injury was all in his head, he knew it might not be.

Kai looked at the sea of surfers out there behind Henley, all risking their lives to ride Jaws. Half of them had no business being there. And now he had to face facts: maybe he didn't have any business out there, either.

"YOU WERE LUCKY," said the ER doctor at Maui Memorial Hospital as he crossed his arms across his white jacket. Kai sat dutifully on a gurney in a curtained exam room, Jun standing anxiously beside him. She'd insisted he come, and so he was here, but he could've told the doctors there was nothing wrong with him.

"The CT scan came back clean. No brain bleeds, and amazingly, not even a concussion." The doctor frowned. "Like I said, you were lucky. You know, I see more and more surfers dying out there." He shook his head. "Don't know why you guys think you've got to do the impossible."

Kai wanted to tell him that there was nothing like challenging Mother Nature on her own terms, that you never felt more alive than when you could lose your life. But he stayed silent. There wasn't any point in arguing. Jun worried her lower lip and fidgeted beside him anxiously. He hadn't thought it would affect her so much—but he had to admit, he liked that she cared.

"If you care about him, Ms. Lee, you'll make sure he stays off those waves for a while," the doctor said as he scribbled his name on a discharge sheet and handed it to Kai. "You're free to go, but I'd suggest you stay on land for a while."

"I've got a competition to win," Kai said, shaking his head.

"How many surfboards do you think you'll sell if you kill yourself on one?" Jun barked, which took both Kai and the doctor by surprise. Kai fell silent as the doctor and Jun exchanged a glance, both clearly on the same page, and then the doctor nodded at Kai and left the exam room. Kai's head still hurt, a headache that pounded just behind his temples. He felt as though he'd been chewed up by a garbage disposal and then washed down the drain. He had nicks and cuts from the pummeling of the waves and the fragments of shells and coral in the foam. He felt a bruise forming around his ankle where the surfboard had been tethered, and his ears still rang a little from the impact.

His throbbing knee seemed to be the least of his worries at the moment. All he wanted to do was crawl into bed and sleep for a month.

"You ready to go?" Jun asked him, dark eyes wide with concern.

"Yeah, I'm ready." Kai stood up. Jun rushed to help him, but he shooed her away. He wasn't an invalid. He could get around.

*I just can't surf.*

A wave of bitterness washed over him then because he knew it was true.

They drove to his Napili Point condo mostly in silence. Kai had insisted on taking the wheel. He needed something to do. Jun had fought him on it, but he won with the argument that the doctor had cleared him. His brain wasn't rattled. He was fine.

As they were pulling up to his two-bedroom condo, Jun's phone rang, and she fumbled in her purse for it. "Hi, Jesse."

Kai sent Jun a sharp glance. Since when did his sister have Jun on speed dial?

"Kai's fine," she continued, worriedly glancing at him. "But how…YouTube? This fast." Jun's eyes grew wide in surprise. "I don't know who posted it…"

Kai did. Henley, probably, or one of the crew guys. "Great," he muttered. "Just great." He tugged his own phone out of his glove compartment, where he'd stored it for safekeeping that morning. He'd had dozens of calls and messages, including one from Dallas.

You okay, man? That was awful. Text me and let me know you're alive.

Kai sent off a quick message. No sense in letting Dallas worry.

And Dallas wasn't the only one who'd been worrying. Kai also realized he now had a dozen new voice mails and twice as many missed calls. The YouTube video must've gone viral, because it seemed everyone he knew had called him. Kai flipped through Twitter on his phone. He was actually trending.

Jesse had left two voice mails, and there'd also been calls from Gretchen, Allie, his cousin and some others, and three from Kirk. It was nice to know people cared. Even if Kirk was most likely concerned about his bottom line. Kai scrolled through the missed calls and stopped when he saw Bret's number. He blinked. Bret hadn't called... since the last time he'd towed him to Jaws. He hadn't left a message, but Kai could guess Bret was furious he'd surfed Jaws once more. Bret had warned him off it.

"I know it looks bad, Jesse," Jun said, still talking on her phone to his sister. "But Kai's fine. Really. We just came from the hospital and the doctors say he was lucky." Jun paused, listening. "I will…I know…I will…He's right here. Let me see if he'll come on the phone."

Kai shook his head furiously, but Jun handed him the phone anyway, thrusting it nearly into his lap. Reluctantly, he picked up. "Hi, Jesse."

"Kai! What the *hell*! Are you trying to die out there?"

"I know it looks like it, but…"

"You've got to quit this. You realize that? You've *got* to quit. My heart can't take it."

"Jesse, I…" Kai had nothing meaningful to say. Part of him knew she was right. He just wasn't ready to admit it out loud.

"Kai, you've got to stop this…okay?" Jesse's voice broke and Kai felt the reverberation in his chest. He didn't want to make his sister cry or worry or any of those things. He hated upsetting her.

"I'm sorry, Jesse. Listen, let me call you back later, all right? I'm okay. I'm fine and we can talk later."

Jesse let out a long sigh. "Okay," she finally said. "I'm still mad at you, though."

"I know." Kai knew he deserved it. He hung up and handed Jun her phone back. He looked at the missed call from Bret.

*You have no business being out there*, he'd said the last time they'd ever worked as a team. *You need to face facts*. Kai wasn't ready to face Bret or anyone else. He trudged to his condo's front door and went inside, feeling fatigue heavy in his bones. Jun followed him, anxiously shadowing his every move, as if worried he might suddenly faint. Kai switched on the lights. Jun watched him as he gingerly walked to the kitchen to grab a bottle of water. The wall of windows behind him overlooked a peaceful little cove where he often found sea turtles swimming. Above his head loomed the open-air balcony of the loft master-bedroom suite, complete with Jacuzzi tub and multispray showerhead. The condo was the least luxurious of all his properties, yet Kai felt at home here. He was also acutely aware, given his modest upbringing with his Aunt Kaimana, that most people wouldn't find anything "common" about the split-level condo with the seaside views.

He watched Jun appraise the property, gazing at the modern stainless-steel kitchen and the hardly lived-in living room. She twisted her hands together.

"I came here, angry…" she began.

"Because of the check," Kai said, remembering the note he left.

She nodded.

"But now…" she hesitated, and in that moment,

she looked so beautiful. He moved closer, and he wobbled a little. Jun was there, rushing to his elbow, helping to steady him.

"I'm not made of glass," Kai snapped, annoyed.

"Just because you keep saying that, doesn't make it true," Jun said, her arm entwined in his. "I almost lost you out there."

Kai realized tears had sprung to her eyes. "Are you *crying*?" Kai hadn't expected that. The shock of seeing how much she cared about him floored him.

The pain in her eyes was real, as was the fear in her voice. Kai suddenly understood that all the pushing away she'd been doing was just a ruse: she cared for him. She cared for him more deeply than she'd ever let on. The knowledge felt like lightning in his blood.

He felt a surge of emotion inside his chest then—the frustration of the day, the fact he'd nearly died and the stubbornness of Jun, who loved him but wouldn't admit it. He wasn't a weakling; he was a survivor. And in that moment, all he wanted to do was prove to her he was still a man.

He reached out and pulled her to him, his mouth covering hers even as she gave a squeak of surprise. It didn't take her long to respond, ferociously matching his passion, and he could almost taste her own relief. She'd been worried about him, too, and now that they had a quiet moment together, he wasn't about to waste it. He knew, on some level, he was doing what he always did: postponing hard questions for the morning after, distracting himself with the body of a beautiful woman.

And yet part of him knew this felt *different* somehow. As he kissed her, pushing her up onto the counter and furiously pulling up the hem of her thin sundress so he could feel her smooth thighs, he knew this wasn't just a way of losing himself. As he leaned back to look at her beautiful face, he realized this time he desperately wanted to find himself. He wasn't running away from something. For the first time in his life, he was running *to* something. To Jun.

"Kai…I…" Jun gasped. "I…"

"You want me to stop?" Kai's heart was thudding, his whole body on fire. He wanted her in a way that frightened him, in a way he hadn't wanted anyone for a long while.

"No," Jun said, voice ragged. "I don't want you to stop." She pulled him in closer for another kiss, sending Kai's head spinning. Seconds later, he was the one who broke free. He didn't want this to be rushed on the kitchen counter. He wanted to explore every nook and crevice of her body, to catalog every freckle, every mole. He wanted to savor her and take his time. Kai wanted to show her exactly how this was different from casual. He wanted to show her just how serious he could be. Kai tugged her down from the counter and led her by the hand up the open staircase to the master suite above, his huge king-size bed carved out of coffee-colored wood taking up half of the immense room. Jun barely took it in before she tangled her hands in his hair, pushing him backward on the bed. Now she became the aggressor, yanking at his shirt and his shorts, eager to get them off. Naked, he stood before her, his desire obvious as he grabbed her arms and twisted her body to his. They collapsed on the bed, Kai on top because he had every intention of slowing this down. He planned to enjoy it. He also planned to torture her with pleasure, from the tops of her ears to the tips of her toes. He gently, teasingly, pulled up her sundress, lifting it off her body and over her head. He caressed her inner thigh, enjoying the soft smoothness. She sighed, a high-pitched whine as he slipped his fingers into the elastic of her delicate lace underwear. He found her moist and swollen and ready.

"Kai," she murmured, eyes dilated and round as she arched her back up to meet his touch.

Kai barely heard, and he barely cared. He tenderly laid a trail of kisses along her stomach until he got to her front-closing bra. In seconds, he'd unhooked the clasp and freed her, her breasts spilling out, nipples hard. He licked one and then the other, and she arched her back again, moaning.

Just when he thought he was firmly in control, she reached down and wrapped her fingers around him, squeezing him, making him lose all sense of time and place. She stared at him, and desire took control of him as she methodically worked him.

He let out a groan, unable to help himself, the pressure building inside him too much, the want for her taking over, crippling his willpower and blinding him, bleaching out coherent thought. He just wanted to take her, to possess her in the most primal of ways, to make her *his*. She wouldn't be able to deny any longer that he cared for her and she for him.

Kai observed, distantly, that he ought to get a condom. He ought to stop what he was doing and be responsible, but right then he didn't want to be responsible. He wanted to have Jun, in every way possible. He wanted to make her see they belonged together. He wanted her to realize just how much he needed her, wanted her, to be his. He understood suddenly that part of him wanted her to have his baby, that all he wanted was to claim what he thought was his.

He pushed inside her, unable to keep himself away any longer, and delving into her warm wetness, he nearly lost his mind. The sensation of pleasure made him cry out as she wrapped her legs around him, pulling him in deeper, her arms holding on to his neck, her breath coming in short gasps. She came almost instantly, her gasps loud and long as he felt her squeeze the life out of him, work him deep inside her body with the rhythm of her pleasure. He felt her nails on his back as she gripped him, the orgasm shaking her very core and his. He wanted to hold off his own climax, to make her come once more, but he couldn't rein it in. It had gone past his control, and there was no turning back. He came in a rush of heat and a low shout, pleasure buzzing through his brain as he collapsed, satiated, on top of her, their sweat-slicked bodies sliding together on his immense bed.

"Oh, God. What did we do?" Jun rolled off Kai and grabbed a sheet, which she pulled up to her neck. Outside, the sun had just dipped below the horizon, and it bathed the room in a dusky, warm glow, but the atmosphere was evidently lost on Jun. There was no mistaking the fear in her voice. "I was so careful for *years*, and now...this."

Kai propped himself up on one elbow and studied her.

"I don't care. Whatever happens, I'll...support you. I wouldn't have...done that if I hadn't been willing to accept the consequences." As the words left his mouth, he realized he *meant* them. It wasn't just something he was saying to be polite or to ward off his own inner panic. Incredibly, he *had* no panic inside over the thought of an unplanned pregnancy.

Did part of him even *want* a pregnancy? The idea exploded in his mind. Could he imagine himself as a father? Actually, after spending time with Po over the past few months, he knew he could.

"I can't have a baby. I've got Po, and…"

"You're not pregnant yet," Kai reminded her.

Jun covered her face with her hands. "I'm doomed. It only takes one time with me. *One time.* My body is superfertile. I'm surprised I don't get pregnant just walking by underwear billboards."

Kai barked a laugh. "That sounds like the worst superhero ever invented." He grinned. "Superfertile Woman."

Jun laughed. "I'm serious!" she exclaimed. "I am!" She buried her face in her hands again.

Kai's lips quirked up in a playful smile. "Do you fight evil with maternity wear and wet wipes?"

"Yes, and morning sickness and swollen ankles. You won't think it's so funny in nine months."

"I love you, Jun Lee."

That shut her up but quick.

"You…what?" Jun pulled the sheets down and blinked at him.

For once, Kai didn't feel like backpedaling or making excuses. For once in his life, he was telling a woman the truth about how he felt.

"I *love* you."

"You do?" Jun looked baffled.

"Now's the time you're supposed to say 'I love you, too.'"

Jun's mouth opened and closed like a fish's, and no sound came out. Kai laughed some more. "You don't have to say it right away," Kai said. "I'll give you...at least twenty-four hours."

"Hey!"

Jun grabbed a throw pillow and batted Kai over the head with it. He deflected the blow easily with his arm.

"I give you a day at most until I start love-shaming you."

"Love-shaming?"

"I keep saying 'I love you' loudly and often in public until you answer me *properly*."

"That's blackmail." Jun's eyes gleamed as she thwacked him in the head with the pillow again.

"That's it, missy." He whipped the pillow out of her hands and tossed it across the room as he pounced on top of her and pinned her arms above her head. She struggled, but she laughed at the same time. He kissed Jun until she stopped fighting him. He knew she cared for him. He was going to be patient and wait her out. If *she* hadn't figured out she loved him yet, then he'd wait until she did.

# CHAPTER TWENTY-THREE

JUN STILL FELT as if she'd been the most irresponsible woman on the face of the earth. She couldn't believe she'd just gone with the moment, not thinking of the repercussions. She hadn't done that since her brief fling with Po's dad, and it had ended with her being a single mom, disowned by her own mother.

Did she never learn?

The hot water from the shower cascaded over her head as she rinsed away what was left of their little tryst, knowing that the soap and water would do nothing to derail whatever was happening inside her body.

*It's probably already too late.* In a panic, she tried to quickly calculate her cycle in her head.

Kai took it so nonchalantly, so *easily*.

*Then again, he's not the one who has to have a baby, if it comes to that.* Jun remembered the indifferent voice on the other end of the long-distance call to Po's father, the one where he outright denied it could be his, said she must've slept with someone else in the six weeks since they'd been together. She'd only ever slept with one person. It couldn't have been anyone else's. Dante had taken advantage of her innocence back then. Told her he'd pull out in time. Told her not to worry—he did this all the time.

And maybe he did. Maybe he knocked up women in every city he visited. Jun imagined a legion of Po's half brothers and sisters living across the country. The man had challenged her to prove Po was his, which meant she'd have had to go to court and force him to take a paternity test. Jun hadn't had that kind of money then. Besides, she'd wanted to make it on her own. She was never going to beg anyone for help.

*Now here you are again.* The hot water fogged up the bathroom mirror and the smoky glass door, and sent up steam from the five rotating shower nozzles. The gleaming marble tile intersecting with the small glass rectangles seemed like something belonging in a movie, as did the enormous Jacuzzi tub in the corner of the massive bathroom. Jun inspected the expensive sweet-smelling shampoo in the stainless-steel rack and sighed. She could get used to this: fluffy new towels, sparkling bathrooms, fancy shampoo.

Kai said he loved her. Did he? Or was that something he said to every woman he undressed in his bedroom?

She thought he was different from Po's father, yet she wasn't sure.

Jun closed her eyes and imagined for a moment what it would be like *not* to worry about money for once. She'd scraped by her whole life, fighting for every cent she earned. What would happen if suddenly, overnight, she was rich? She'd never even considered it a possibility before, but now, in Kai's posh condo, she knew she could get used to that kind of luxury. The question was, should she?

But his money and his fancy houses weren't why she'd let Kai come in her, and she knew that. She'd wanted him to as much as he had, and that thought scared her to her core.

"Knock, knock." Kai opened the bathroom door and entered, letting a rush of cool air in. "Finished my phone call. It was my manager."

"Oh," Jun said. "Everything okay?"

"Just more fallout from YouTube."

Jun heard the resignation in his voice. Sometime soon she needed to talk to him about how he had paid her too much, about how she wasn't going to take money for a job she didn't do.

And she realized with shock that she wanted to tell him to quit.

When she saw him take that tumble into the mouth of a foamy wave monster, bleak emotion had taken over. She'd been terrified. She had really thought she'd lost him. And now she knew she never wanted to see him risk his life like that again. Not on a hope and prayer that everything would be okay. Now, she realized, it wasn't about *him* being strong enough, it was all about *her* not being ready to lose him. The fact that she was so emotionally invested frightened her most. If Po's father had taught her anything, it was that caring got your heart broken.

Kai shrugged out of his shorts. "Mind if I join you?"

"It's your shower," Jun said, rinsing her hair. Water flowed down her front, and Kai looked on appreciatively. Jun didn't see the point in being modest. Not after what they'd just done. "Plus, I think there's room." The shower was big enough to fit four people comfortably and had a little marble bench against one wall, in case one of them got tired. "You could have a party in here," Jun said, then stopped, recalling with excruciating clarity the hot-tub photos. "Wait, you haven't, have you? Had a naked party in here?"

Kai slipped in and wrapped his arm protectively around her waist. "Wouldn't you like to know?"

"No, actually, I don't think I would." Jun felt a prick of jealousy.

"Here, let me do that," Kai said, taking the soap from her and gently lathering, rubbing the suds along her curves. His touch brought her body alive again, even when she thought she'd been completely satiated. Kai pulled her in for a kiss that quickly turned hungry. Jun felt herself forgetting why she was jealous. In fact, she forgot nearly everything except the taste of Kai's mouth. Then she managed to regain her senses for a second and pull away.

"Didn't we already do this?" she asked, a little breathless.

"Are you tired of me already?" Kai studied her with amused dark eyes.

"No," Jun said, wondering if every time she was with Kai, she'd let hormones and not sense rule her decisions. "But if we keep at this, we'll be here all night."

"What's wrong with that?"

"Dinner?"

Kai swept a line of suds off her chest. "I *guess* I'll let you eat. But first maybe you should tell me you love me." He held her waist tightly, and for an instant, Jun considered saying just that. *Did* she love Kai Brady? The thought thrilled and scared her at the same time. She wasn't ready to say it. She wasn't even sure it was true.

Jun flung a wet loofah at his chest, and it landed with a splat. He let her go, laughing, and then she jumped out of the shower and into one of his fluffy monogrammed towels. She swiped at the condensation on the mirror as she tucked the towel around her. She looked at her face, her mother's eyes. What would her mother say about her now? Would she still call her a woman with no morals?

Memories of her mother seemed to conjure her ghost, setting a chill to the room. She left the steamy bathroom and hurriedly got dressed. Her stomach rumbling, she tugged on her sundress. Outside, the sun had long set and the sky above the ocean had turned a dark almost black. A nearly full moon hung just above the waves, shedding a silvery light across the water. Her phone rang, and she dug in her bag to get it. Seeing her sister's photo on the screen, she answered, feeling a hard pit in her stomach.

"Everything all right?" Jun didn't bother with a hello. Kiki wouldn't be calling at eight thirty, past Po's bedtime, unless something was wrong.

"Everything is okay now, but..."

Jun held her breath. It was the night terrors again. Jun knew it before her sister said another word.

"But he had a pretty bad nightmare, Jun. He was screaming about the water. I mean, it kind of scared me. He wouldn't wake up."

"Dammit." Jun sank down on the bed. They'd gone weeks without one, but it appeared they were back. Kai wandered out of the bathroom then, shirtless, a towel tied around his waist. He went to his overnight bag, pulled out a shirt and tugged it over his head.

"I thought you told me he was better," Kiki said.
"He was."

Kai met Jun's gaze. "Po?" he mouthed and Jun nodded.

"He's sleeping now, but do you think he'll wake up? Will this happen again?" Kiki was asking.

"I don't know, but just keep him calm if he does. Don't try to wake him. Just speak calmly and tell him to get back in bed. Eventually, he goes." Jun rubbed her eyes, feeling suddenly tired. She heard as she spoke how useless her advice sounded, because it was. When Po was in the middle of a night terror, there really wasn't anything *to* do. The doctor had said if he got more sleep, he'd have fewer of them, but she'd also suggested a psychiatrist.

Kai put on shorts and then sat down on the bed next to her, rubbing her shoulders. She felt so glad to have the little comfort.

"I'm coming home tomorrow," Jun said. "Call me if anything else happens tonight."

"I will," Kiki said, and then ended the call.

"More night terrors?" Kai asked, big brown eyes full of sympathy. Jun nodded. Kai took her hand in his and squeezed it. "He'll be okay."

"Will he?" Jun wasn't so sure. "Maybe I should go home. Get him."

Kai put his arm around her shoulders. "There's probably only one flight left out tonight, and even if you managed to get on it, you wouldn't get to your sister's house before eleven. You won't do Po or yourself any good dragging him out of bed. If he's sleeping now, he might sleep through the night."

"You're right." Jun leaned into Kai's strong shoulder, feeling protected and warm, glad that he'd talked her off the ledge. She could be over-protective—she knew that.

"I know... I mean, it's not my business, but—" Kai squeezed her tighter "—have you thought more about the psychiatrist?"

Jun sighed. "No," she said, defeated. She didn't have the strength to fight him then, although she wanted to. She might have shared her body, but she wasn't yet ready to share Po with Kai. She wasn't ready to give over her tight rein on his care. She didn't know if she'd ever be open to sharing that. Raising Po was in no way a democracy. It was her responsibility and hers alone. "I just don't see what a psychologist could do that I can't."

"Maybe something, maybe nothing," Kai said. "You don't know until you try. And when we get home, I'll talk to him. Spend some time with him. Maybe that will help."

"Kai... I know you mean well, but..."

"It's not my fight, is it?" Kai shook his head as Jun nodded slowly. Not the words she would've used, but appropriate nonetheless.

"Okay." He sighed. "How about I feed you dinner? Will you let me do that?"

KAI TOOK JUN to a modern new five-star fresh-seafood restaurant on Maui's coast where, normally, she wouldn't have been able to afford a single appetizer. While everything on the islands was casual, Jun felt a little underdressed in her white sundress. She had packed but one change of clothes, and those were shorts and tennis shoes for her return trip tomorrow. The restaurant was all open to the sea, a giant patio bathed in moonlight and firelight from the twinkling candles on tabletops. A few patrons recognized Kai. Some even whispered as they came in. Jun noticed more than a few of the women follow Kai's fine form to their table and wondered what it would be like to be on Kai's arm all the time. Would she get tired of the attention? She thought she might. As she settled down at the table, she saw someone near them snapping a picture. How quickly would that make the social media rounds? Probably instantly. Everything about Kai seemed to go viral.

"Given the day we've had, *and* the fact we've broken rule three already today, what do you say to loosening up the alcohol rule?"

Jun didn't see any harm. What was the point of sticking to the rules? Any of them? "I guess that's okay."

"Good. Do you like white or red?"

"Either." Jun didn't really know much about wine. What she'd had to drink, she liked, but she didn't drink very often.

"Red it is, then. I know just the bottle." He proceeded to order a $200 bottle of wine. Jun almost choked on her water.

"That's too much!"

"It isn't." The waiter quickly brought the bottle and poured two glasses. Jun took a sip and thought she'd died and gone to wine heaven. No wonder the bottle cost $200. Every sip brought her taste buds alive.

After they'd devoured delicate appetizers, the waiter delivered her mahimahi and Kai's swordfish. Jun thought she'd never tasted anything so good in her life.

"You're spoiling me. Why?"

"You might be eating for two," Kai joked, and Jun nearly spit out her wine.

"That's not even funny."

"Why are you smiling, then?" Kai reached over and took her hand. She let him. Being with Kai made her feel lighter, happier. Made her think of herself in some way other than as Po's mom, a label she'd buried herself under for the past four years. Yet in her heart, she knew it could be only temporary. For all she knew, Kai declared love to every woman he ever slept with, and besides, Jun wouldn't ask him to take on Po as a responsibility. They owed him enough as it was. If things got serious and they moved in, then what? She couldn't stand having that kind of debt.

Kai let go of Jun's hand.

"Bret," he breathed. Jun turned and saw a tall but stout man headed their way, his face all storm clouds and disapproval.

Bret stalked right up to their table. He was a looming wall of a man, his bleached-blond curls doing nothing to soften the anger in his stark blue eyes. He wore a cheerfully bright Hawaiian-print shirt that seemed to clash directly with his stormy mood.

"How'd you find me?" Kai asked.

"Just followed the stink on Twitter," Bret said, jaw twitching. "Get up," he told Kai, his hands balled into fists. Jun felt her heartbeat tick up. This man wanted to harm Kai—that much was evident in the stiffness of his jaw. This man was *not* a well-wisher.

"Bret, man, let's talk, okay?"

Jun thought for a split second he might be the husband or boyfriend of one of Kai's conquests and then immediately felt terrible for assuming that. Still, why was the man so angry?

Bret shook his head once, slowly.

"I warned you not to surf Jaws. I'm here to show you that I was serious. Come on. Get up."

Bret's determination to cause trouble had quickly been noticed by everyone in the restaurant, including their anxious waiter.

"Is everything all right, sir?" The waiter hurried to their table, eyes worriedly on Bret.

"Not here," Kai said. Bret glanced around them, and his blue eyes lingered on Jun for just a second. Then he seemed to reconsider.

"The beach. Five minutes." And with that, Bret turned around and stalked out of the restaurant. Jun watched him go, a little stunned.

"What was that about?"

"That's Bret, my old tow partner." Kai's gaze followed him, dark eyes narrowing.

"What does he want?" Jun asked, balling up her linen napkin in her lap and twisting it between her fingers.

Kai let out a defeated-sounding sigh. "Wasn't it obvious?" he said, shaking his head as he stood, dropping his napkin near his empty plate. "Bret wants to kick my ass."

# CHAPTER TWENTY-FOUR

KAI WALKED OUT of the restaurant, Jun on his heels peppering him with anxious questions, but his focus lay elsewhere. He could think only of Bret's angry face. He was partly relieved that at least they'd be working on what had happened between them, even if Bret would be doing most of the working with his fists on Kai's face. Bret wouldn't talk with him, wouldn't accept his apology, but maybe after he got out some of his frustration, maybe then, the man would listen to reason. Outside the restaurant's main doors, Jun threw herself in front of Kai, desperate for his attention.

"Are you even listening to me? You can't go *fight* that guy! Call the police!"

"Can't do it," Kai said, and tried to duck around Jun, but she stood her ground.

"I mean it, Kai. This isn't the school playground. You just got your head beaten in by Jaws, and now you're going to let some musclehead—"

"His name is Bret."

"Okay, *Bret*, who is built like a linebacker, bash your skull in?" Jun's face was contorted in worry as she clawed at his shirtfront. Kai would've found the concern sweet if she weren't preventing him from going to get his due.

"I won't let him do that. But he does get to hit me. At least once. Maybe twice."

"Kai!" Jun protested. Kai firmly but gently pushed her out of the way. She trotted after him down the narrow stone path leading to the moonlit beach. In the distance, Bret was waiting for him, all beefy muscle as he paced furiously across the wet sand.

"You can't do this!" Jun pleaded with Kai.

"Stop." Kai grabbed her hands and held them. "You need to stay here. Go inside the restaurant and wait for me. I'll be fine."

"You've got an audience already." Jun flung an arm up, and Kai saw then that all the patrons of the restaurant had shifted to the edge of the balcony to get a better look. *Great.* His ass-whooping would be on YouTube by midnight. Kai shook his head and glanced down at Bret, who was still stalking back and forth like an angry bull. He had to go. He had to face Bret. Bret had told him never to surf Jaws again. That there'd be consequences. He assumed these were those consequences.

"Jun. Let me go."

"Kai. I'm not going to let you go down there."

"You *have* to stay here." Kai couldn't make this any plainer to the woman. "You could get hurt.

Bret is mad, and he has a right to be, and you have to trust me that I know what I'm doing. This is *my* fight. Not yours." The words stopped her cold, just as he meant them to. Now she'd get it. Po was her fight. Bret was his. Kai marched past her and closed the gap between him and his oldest friend on earth.

It wouldn't be the first time Bret had clobbered him. After all, they'd been just eight when they'd tried to figure out who hit the hardest. Bret had won because he'd reared back and knocked out one of Kai's baby teeth. He'd had a deadly right hook even then. Kai wasn't looking forward to feeling how much power he'd gained in twenty-five years.

Jun stood still, halfway up the rocky path to the beach, and Kai powered on, finally meeting his once-best friend on the damp shore. He stopped about twenty feet away. Bret had already taken off his shoes, which lay tossed haphazardly nearby. Kai kicked off his own sandals, slowly and methodically, his eyes never leaving Bret.

"I warned you, man," Bret said as he cracked his knuckles and shook his shoulders loose. "I told you to stay off that break."

"Competition is in two days."

"You will *not* surf in that competition!" Bret spit into the sand, taking three steps forward. "You gonna keep on trying until you kill someone? Like that kid you were with? You could've killed him."

"I know, but the ocean is my life. What am I supposed to do without it?"

"Find another hobby. I don't care. You've got no business out there anymore, and you *know* it."

Bret paced, rubbing his hands together, like a man trying to decide what to hit first. Kai understood. He knew Bret was angry about Jaws, but it was more than that. This was all about his wife and the baby and how Bret still blamed him for it. Kai blamed himself, too. Maybe they'd both feel better if Bret broke his nose.

"Listen, Bret. We need to talk. About your wife. About the—"

That pushed Bret over the edge, and with an animal grunt, he charged, swinging wildly. Instinctively, Kai ducked the first blow, but he was too slow to miss the second, a forceful punch straight to Kai's cheek, and for an instant, he saw only stars as he wheeled backward. Bret's right hook had only gotten more fierce with age. Damn. Kai shook off the blow and tried to orient himself because he knew another one was coming. Jun shrieked in panic somewhere behind him.

Kai had meant to just let Bret have a go at him and not fight back, but survival instincts took over, and he regained his balance, his fists up.

"Come on, hit me, you son of a bitch," Bret spat, swinging again. Kai bobbed out of the way.

"I don't want to fight you, Bret."

"Well, then I'll do all the hitting." Bret went after Kai, but he kept dancing out of the way. "Stay still!" Bret roared. As much as Kai knew he deserved to get hit, he couldn't quite manage to tell his body to lie down and take it.

"Bret. I am sorry, man. You've got to believe me. I never meant for any of that to happen. I am sorry!"

"If you were really sorry, you'd quit." Bret swung once more, and Kai dodged him. Then Bret lowered his shoulder and plowed it into Kai's midsection, sending both men tumbling to the sand near the surf. A wave rushed in and soaked Kai's shoulder. Bret held him there, the water rushing over his chest. For a split second, Kai looked up at Bret's rage-filled face and wondered if his oldest friend in the world planned to drown him. The water was only an inch deep here, the end of the wave soaking the back of his head.

"You should've quit!" Bret was shouting at him now, holding him as the water leaked into his shirt.

Kai fought to unpin himself, not liking Bret's full weight on top of him. Kai struggled, even as Bret cocked his fist back. Kai dodged at the last second and Bret hit sand. Kai strained, trying not to hit his friend but not get hit in the process. He managed to kick out hard, and Bret went sprawling on the sand. Bret swung his leg out, making contact with Kai's bad knee. Painful fireworks exploded in his brain. His *knee*. His damn knee. Kai folded instantly, falling to the ground as Bret scrambled back to his feet.

"Kai!" screamed Jun. Dazed, Kai could just make out Jun running toward him, white dress flouncing in the moonlight. Her scream distracted Bret, too, whose head whipped in her direction. It was just enough of a window. Kai hadn't intended to fight Bret, but his throbbing knee demolished the last of his self-control. He reared up and punched Bret square in the jaw. Bret flailed backward, landing on his back, half in the surf. The punch seemed to knock some of the anger out of him, and he lay there coughing. Jun ran to Kai, trying to help him up. Once on his feet, he held out a hand to Bret, who refused it.

"Bret. I'm sorry. I wish your wife never lost that baby. I wish my knee wasn't destroyed. I wish… I wish there was some way for me to make it up to you. I do. You're my best friend, Bret. I never wanted any of this to happen. You've got to believe that."

Jun stood stock-still, frozen as her head swiveled from man to man, her arms twitching anxiously at her side.

Bret glared at Kai as he shakily rose to his feet, swiping blood from his mouth. For a second, Kai thought his friend would accept his apology. Bret shook his head ruefully as he stepped forward. Kai expected him to offer his hand for a shake.

Instead Bret wheeled back and punched Kai hard, straight in the belly. Kai bent over, wheezing, the breath knocked out of him as he stumbled, nearly falling to his knees. Jun gasped behind him.

Bret leaned in then to Kai's ear.

"Stay off Jaws, Kai," he grumbled. "For your sake and everyone else's."

Bret straightened, and Kai struggled to breathe. He nodded once at Jun, and then he stalked back up the beach.

Jun grabbed Kai's elbow, trying to help him. Breath came slowly as his stomach muscles contracted.

"I'm going to call the police," Jun cried, glaring at Bret's retreating back.

"No..." Kai panted. "Don't."

"He needs to be arrested... He..."

"No." Kai waved her off as he took in a shaky breath. Every muscle in his abdomen protested the act. Bret had gotten him good. "Let him go." He tried to straighten up but a sharp pain rippled through his side. He grimaced, holding his belly. "Let's just go home."

BACK AT HIS CONDO, Kai lay sprawled on his squared modern sectional, his feet propped up on his expensive koa-wood coffee table. He had a bag of frozen corn over half his face. Jun handed him a cold beer from the fridge. She felt a mix of emotions that made her jittery. Most disturbing of all was the fact that Kai wasn't explaining anything.

"You want to tell me what the hell all that was about?" Jun asked when she couldn't take it anymore.

Kai cracked open his good eye and looked at her. He was bruised and battered, but even so, Jun had to fight the urge to go to him and wrap her arms around his neck.

"Bret and I, well, we were among the first to surf Jaws. He's been my best friend my whole life. He was the one who first told me I should surf." Kai swallowed.

Jun nodded, keeping silent as she listened intently.

"We used to do everything together, you know? We practically invented big-wave surfing. We were out there just flying by the seat of our pants for years, trying this new thing that only a handful of surfers—like Laird Hamilton—ever even dreamed of doing. The only reason we came to Jaws was because Bret lived here. He'd moved here to work at some bar, but he thought Jaws was *it*. He was the one to convince me I had to try surfing it."

Kai shook his head, as if he was suddenly flooded with memories. Jun took a seat near him. She didn't say a word, and Kai continued.

"There was no way to practice this stuff, because there were no rules. We made them up as we went. That was back when no surfers ever even dreamed of surfing Jaws or any of the other big waves. Jet Ski towing was a completely new concept."

Jun tried to imagine it. The first people to surf waves that big. The rush must've been immense.

"After the tsunami, it took me some time to recover. But about six months ago, I tried to surf Jaws." Kai swallowed, and Jun could see the intensity of the memory. "It was as if the wave was personally out to get me. Teach me a lesson." Kai shook his head. "Bret told me right then I should quit. I didn't want to listen to him. I couldn't." She heard the words catch in Kai's throat. She could tell he still didn't like to think about quitting. He still didn't want to let that possibility in. "I told him I was going back out there, with or without him. And then I went down, and he came after me, and he nearly died doing it."

Jun sucked in a breath. "Oh, Kai." She crossed her arms and hugged herself.

"He went to the hospital. Bret's wife was pregnant at the time and when she heard, she jumped in her car in a panic." Kai loosened his grip on the bag of frozen corn, letting it fall to his lap. He ground his teeth. "She ran a red light trying to get to the hospital. She was in a car accident and miscarried."

Kai looked at the bag of veggies in his hand, as if not wanting to meet Jun's eyes.

"So, is Bret going to beat you up *every* time you go surfing?"

"Every time I surf Jaws," Kai said, gently laying the corn on his eye once more.

"He really thinks you should retire." Jun felt the same way. And now she needed to tell him.

Jun took a deep breath. "I think Bret is right."

Kai's face hardened. "What do you mean?"

"I mean…I don't think you should surf. You need to pull out of the competition."

"*You* think I should quit?" Anger flared in his voice as he jumped up and began to pace the living room. "You said all I had to do was meditate." Kai frowned. "*You* said the problem was all in my head."

"I know. But, Kai, some things are out of our grasp. Sometimes it's better not to fight the universe when it's trying to send us a clear message."

"And that message is I'm washed up?" Resentment pinched his face. "You think I'm a loser like everyone else?"

"I don't think that, Kai."

"Then why don't you want me to surf?"

"Because it's too dangerous…" *Because I love you and I don't want you to die. Because Po and I need you, and you can't be there for us if you drown.* The words she wanted to say clogged up in her throat, bunched together and wouldn't come out.

"You think I'm too weak. You think I'll never surf? Is this what you're telling me, after everything we've been through? You're giving up on *me*?" She saw hurt flash in his eyes as his voice rose.

"No, Kai, I'm not giving up on you. I—I love you. I need you." She thought about Po and all the wonderful ways Kai had helped her boy become stronger and better. "Po needs you." *And we won't have you if you go kill yourself.*

"Why would you need a weak cripple?" Thunder raged in Kai's face. "That's what you think of me, isn't it?"

"No, Kai. I'm very proud of you for how hard you've worked. We tried our best. We really did, but sometimes you have to admit when a problem is too big."

A sour laugh escaped Kai's throat. "Just like you do? You, who refuses to accept help for Po because you're so determined to do it all on your own? *You* never admit when a problem is too big, even when it's clear you're holding Po back. Maybe *you're* the reason he's not getting better."

Jun felt the barb as if he'd hit her. He thought she was a bad mom. The one time she admitted she needed a man, this was what happened. He told her she was a bad mother. Fury welled in her belly. This was why she never trusted men, because they couldn't be counted on. *This* was why she never asked for help, because when she did, she was slapped down. Her mother had done it, and now Kai was doing it, too. Maybe she was a bad mom, but she'd damn well never ask for anything else again. If Kai didn't care about her or Po enough to stay alive, then that told her all she needed to know.

"I knew this would happen. This has been a waste of time."

"*Waste* of time!" Kai's eyes grew hard. "Maybe you're right. Maybe *we* are a waste of time."

The air in the room felt too thick, too hard to breathe. Jun hadn't meant that they were a waste. She'd meant that trying to talk sense into him was a waste of time. But Kai had made it personal. He'd made it hurt.

He snatched his car keys off the kitchen countertop. "I'm going out," he said.

"But...we need to talk," Jun managed. Was he really going to leave it like this? It sounded like he was ending it.

"There's no point in talking," Kai said. "No point at all."

Jun watched helplessly as he walked out the front door and slammed it behind him.

# CHAPTER TWENTY-FIVE

AFTER THE DOOR SLAMMED, a sob escaped Jun's throat and she collapsed on the couch, crying. How had it all gone off the rails so fast? She loved Kai, and yet now it was all dark and twisted and…broken. Kai didn't understand her, not one bit.

But he was right that she'd failed Po. She'd failed Kai. She'd now failed herself. She was a terrible mother and an even worse personal trainer. She'd led Kai on, got him to believe that he could surf again when she really had no business promising that. Just as she had no business trying to cure Po. She'd been trying for more than a year, and Po was no closer to getting over his fear of water. Hell, in just a few weeks, Kai had managed to get the boy to at least stand in the water. That was more than she'd gotten him to do.

Jun let the tears run down her face. *Well, you were right, Mother. You were right to shun me. I'm worthless, moralless, just like you said I was.*

The thought made her cry harder. She swiped

furiously at the tears on her cheeks, yet they kept coming.

*Fat lot of good it did, Mom, you trying to make me tough. Look at me now! Weak. So very weak.*

Weak mother. Weak personal trainer. Weak *woman* who let Kai have his way with her. Begged him to, actually, and now he was probably out there drinking and flirting and doing his best to forget she even existed. And that was what truly hurt the most. Not that he'd insulted her mothering wisdom or her skills as a personal trainer or that he was angry she wanted him to quit surfing, but that at the very first sign of trouble, he'd bolted. She loved him and believed in him enough to know that he would be fine without big-wave surfing. Surfing didn't define him. If she could only get him to see that.

But she couldn't. He wasn't going to listen to her. He hated her now.

He'd said he loved her *that very evening*, but now, only a few hours later, he'd run off. It proved to her that he wasn't sincere, that his idea of love and hers were two very different things. In some ways, it meant he was more like Po's father than she wanted to believe.

Jun sniffled, wiping her nose, and forced herself to stop. She was going to get a cab to the airport. Even if she had to sleep in the terminal, she would, and then she'd catch the first flight home.

KAI HAD EVERY intention of going to the very first tourist bar he saw and getting so hammered that he'd probably have to spend the night in the drunk tank. But the second he'd gotten halfway down the road, he thought about turning back. He saw her face when he'd told her there was no point in talking. Did he really believe that? Or was it just a defense mechanism because she'd hit him where he was most vulnerable: surfing. He felt as though she was the last person to abandon him. Yet, wasn't it just because she cared? Bret, Jun and Jesse—they'd all been telling him what he knew all along, and just because he was too stubborn to let the truth in, didn't make it any less true.

Hadn't he known from the moment he'd careened off the top of that wave today that his career was over? Sure, he'd be able to bodysurf or maybe even paddleboard some two-foot waves, but the big kahunas, those were over for him. He knew it. In his heart of hearts, he knew it, and yet he just wasn't ready to let go.

He felt bad about what he'd said to Jun. He saw her struggle so hard to keep it together, and then he could see the hurt in her face and how deep the knife went. But she'd cut him back even deeper. *What a waste of time.*

His mind spun, and he realized he'd driven half-way around the island and passed a dozen tourists bars. He could've stopped in any one of them, but he hadn't. He didn't feel like stopping. He decided to head back home, the long way, and maybe Jun would be willing to talk again.

When he finally made his way back to the condo, he felt calmer.

The lights in his place were all turned out, and after he slipped in the front door, a quick search found the place empty. He called Jun, but her phone went straight to voice mail.

*Not good. Not good at all.*

He glanced down at the coffee table and saw her bonus check, ripped cleanly in two, sitting there.

Now there was no use hoping she'd come back. In his heart, he knew she wouldn't. Had he lost her forever?

He realized that he'd only *thought* he'd reached rock bottom when that tsunami hit. Now he knew a life without Jun was far worse than one without surfing. He tried calling her phone again but got her voice mail a second time.

Where could she have gone?

He didn't want to admit it, but he needed advice, and there was only one person he could think of who could give it to him, *if* he didn't break Kai's nose first.

KAI DROVE TO the small dive bar Bret owned on Maui—not a flashy tourist place, but a locals' joint. No neon lights, just strung-up old Christmas lights and a big open patio with mismatched chairs. Kai parked, wondering if his old friend would punch him, kick him out or call the cops.

Bret had bought the place from Pete Simpson. Pete's Paradise it was called, though the sign had long since been rusted out by the sea air and taken down. You found Pete's only if you already knew it was there, and that meant you'd spent most of your life on Maui. Bret had taken Kai here after one of their first successful missions to Jaws. Bret, who had an unusual talent for finding the most authentic hangouts wherever he went, had ended up buying this one from Pete when he retired last year.

Kai sat in the driver's side of his four-wheel-drive SUV, an antique Ford he kept on Maui because he couldn't bear to part with it just yet. It had been one of his first cars, before he'd gotten rich and famous. Now he kept it here for nostalgia, mostly. He opened the ancient creaking door and then slammed it shut, the only way the sucker would close all the way. He headed to the entrance of the bar and went in, not sure if his plan to find Bret was really all that wise. In any case, he needed a little liquid courage.

As soon as he walked into the darkened bar

with the mismatched chairs and the floor sticky with spilled drinks and crunchy with old bits of sand, he saw Bret standing behind the bar.

Kai thought about backing out, abandoning his plan, but Bret saw him, made lingering eye contact and then, without much fuss, looked away. At least he didn't storm across the room and punch him in the gut, Kai thought. That was progress.

Kai decided to take the safest spot, the stool at the other end, next to the sad older man in the faded landscaping button-down. He looked as though he'd had almost as bad a day as Kai had, with a cut on his lip from someone who must have taken issue with the way the man cut grass.

Thankfully, a second bartender asked him what he wanted. He gave his order to the frazzled woman in her forties, who chewed gum and smelled like cigarette smoke. She didn't even comment on his eye or his busted-up appearance, which meant she was more than used to seeing such injuries.

The landscaping man downed his Scotch and pushed himself away from the bar, taking Kai's cover and leaving a direct line of sight between Kai and Bret. Kai's black eye, now swollen almost completely shut, obliterated his peripheral vision on that side, so he wouldn't be able to tell if Bret decided to scoot on down and sucker punch him again. Kai angled his chair, and just as he did so,

Bret poured himself a mug of beer and moved to the empty seat next to him. Bret had a nasty bruise on his chin and his nose was swollen.

"You look like hell," Bret said.

"You gave me the makeover," Kai said.

In that moment, both men laughed, and Kai felt the tightness in his chest loosen a little bit. Maybe Bret wasn't lost to him forever.

Kai looked at Bret for a long beat. He knew he had to take the first step and he knew what that step had to be. It was time for him to stop fighting the inevitable and to stop hoping for miracles. Whether it was his knee or his mind-set or just the fact he was getting older, it didn't really even matter anymore. Big-wave surfing was too dangerous for him now. He realized that.

"I'm going to quit surfing. The competition will be my last surf. I've got this charity. I've got to do it for the kids. But after that, I'm done."

Bret shook his head. "It'll kill you, you know."

"It's my decision to make. Just the one last time. Then at least if I die, the kids have their charity. Probably more people will donate. Just have to do one last run. Then I'm done."

Bret let out a long sigh. Kai feared Bret might punch him some more. He couldn't tell what his friend was thinking, as he stayed silent a long while. He took a slow swig of his beer. Then he spoke.

"I get it," Bret said. "I think you should quit now. While you're alive. But it's your life. I get that now. I'm sorry for the...for the beach." Those words were hard for Bret to say and Kai knew it.

"Nothing to apologize for, man. I deserved it."

"You did, yes, but I know it was my stuff out there as much as yours. I was beating up on me as much as you."

"Didn't feel like it," Kai joked. Bret smiled ruefully.

"I'm serious, man. I blame myself for that day. I should've not towed you out that first time. I knew you weren't ready, but I did it anyway. I should've put my foot down that morning, after I saw you do that practice run, you know, on the tourist beach?"

Kai knew exactly what he was talking about. Bret and he had taken a few early-morning waves to warm up. Kai had thought he'd done pretty well. He'd stayed upright, at least, but clearly Bret had seen through the charade.

"You can't babysit me. I mean, I made the decision to go out there. I probably wouldn't have listened and would've gone out there on my own. Or found someone else to tow me."

"That's what I thought you'd do, so that's why I went. But I knew you didn't have any business out there, and I should've said something *before* we went out. But I didn't. So, Sarah and..." Bret got choked up a little and wasn't quite able to get out the word *baby*. "That's on me as much as you."

Kai was floored. All this time, Bret had carried the same kind of guilt about that day as Kai did, when it was obvious to Kai that Bret was blameless. Kai shook his head. He should've known his friend would take the responsibility. That was exactly the kind of man Bret was.

"No, man," Kai said. "It was *my* fault. I put you in harm's way. It wasn't your job to convince me not to go. It was my job to man up and admit I'd changed. That my damn knee was useless." Kai gave his weak knee a hard slap. Bret signaled the bartender for another round and the men sat drinking beer in silence for a few minutes.

"You know, we couldn't do it forever anyway. At some point or another, we'd both have to quit. We couldn't have been out there riding waves at seventy."

Kai laughed and Bret joined in. What a difference a few years made. When they had been in their twenties, neither one of them had even wanted to live to seventy. That had seemed like a death sentence all on its own, but now in their thirties, the idea of going down in a flame of glory on some monstrous wave just didn't seem so palatable anymore. The dangers of getting older, Kai thought. You got used to living.

"How's Sarah?" Kai asked at last. "I really want

to know. Is she...? Are you two...okay?" This was the question Kai most feared asking. He wasn't sure if he could take more guilt. What if the miscarriage had spurred on a divorce? What if Bret's whole life had unraveled after Kai's stupid mistake?

"Sarah wasn't fine for a long while, but she's back now." Bret gazed into his nearly empty beer mug, as if he could see the past in dredges. "She bosses me around. Tonight she was furious I got into a fight with you. Told me I needed to get over it. Said I needed to go cool off, and I couldn't come back until my blood was dry because she didn't want me to bleed on her new sheets."

Kai laughed. "She's a tough one." And she was. Bret wouldn't have given up extreme surfing for a pushover. Sarah knew what she wanted and usually got it.

"You have no idea, brother," he said, shaking his head. "I love that woman. God, do I love her, but she *is* a pain in my ass." Bret laughed and finished off the last bit of his beer. "Maybe you were right to stay single."

"Not single," Kai said quickly. Too quickly. "Well, I don't want to be anyway."

Bret looked as though he might fall off his stool. "You? In love? Somebody call CNN. This is newsworthy." Bret clapped his friend on the back. "Who's the lucky girl? Wait, the woman at the beach?"

Kai nodded.

"Fine woman. Fine, indeed. Athletic. Firm." Bret nodded his approval.

"Hey, *watch* it. She's my girl," Kai warned him. At least, she had been, he thought grimly.

Bret just threw his blond head back and laughed. "You *are* in deep, my friend."

"Not sure if she wants to be with me, though."

"Don't blame her," Bret teased, and Kai gave him a playful shove, feeling as if he had truly gotten back his old friend, the one who never let up on him. Never coddled him and always gave him shit. Kai realized just how much he missed it.

"I shouldn't compete, should I?"

"You know what I think." Bret looked at Kai. "But I can't stop you. No one can. Only you can do that."

"How can I let down the charity?"

"Don't surf. Donate your own money there, Mr. Clothing Line. A charity isn't worth your life."

"I don't have that much cash just lying around," Kai said. "Besides, wouldn't that be the coward's way out?"

"Dude, *nothing* about our lives has ever been the coward's way." Kai laughed at this and the two clinked their mugs together.

Kai glanced at his nearly empty glass. "If I

quit, what do I do after that, man? What do I do if I don't surf?" Kai asked, realizing that was the question he'd been asking himself for months. Bret had given up that kind of extreme surfing two years ago. Maybe he'd have a game plan. Or at least some advice. Because when Kai looked into his future without big-wave surfing, all he saw was a blank, boring slate. An *average* life, a *small* life, a life he didn't recognize and didn't want.

He stared at his old friend, his thirtysomething face weathered by sun and surf. "What do I do?"

Bret held Kai's gaze a long time. "You miss the hell out of it," he finally said. "That's what I do."

JUN STEPPED OUT of the airport on the Big Island, having taken the first flight out of Maui. She passed the open-air baggage claim, shaking her head once more about how so many buildings in Hawaii seemed to hate walls. But why put up walls when the outside temperature was a perfect seventy-five degrees? She walked out into the warm sunshine and headed to the parking lot where she'd parked her car. Jun double-checked her phone as she went, browsing through the message from her sister. Po had slept fine through the night and was now safely at day care for the day, which left Jun without anything to do for the moment.

She'd been in such a hurry to put miles between her and Kai that she hadn't thought about what would happen when she got back. In her mind, she'd cut ties, but she was learning it wouldn't be that easy. She felt the urge to call him, to see if he was okay, to find out if he was still going to go through with the competition. She didn't want to think about it.

While she was on the flight, she'd gotten several calls from numbers she didn't recognize and one from Jesse. Only Jesse had left a message. She thought about deleting it but then worried Kai's injuries might have gotten worse. She listened to Jesse's voice mail. Apparently, there was a meeting about the Big Island Kids charity later that morning at her coffee shop. Of course, after that weekend, Jun didn't know if Kai wanted her leading anything anymore. Or if she even wanted to. Could she spearhead a charity when she couldn't seem to get anything else right in her life?

Jun decided to drop by the coffee shop anyway, if only to tell Jesse she wouldn't be working for Kai anymore. It was the least she could do. But when Jun arrived, she found a huge white tent set up in the parking lot of the little shopping center with a banner for Big Island Kids, and there had to be at least fifty people milling about. Eventually, she found Jesse, handing out flyers.

"Jun! Thank goodness you're here. Can you

help me hand these out?" She offered Jun a stack of flyers.

"Where did all these people come from?" Jun asked, surprised as she glanced around at all the faces—some of them familiar and some strangers.

"Some wanted to help, but most of them really *need* our help. Dr. Jean is trying to coordinate visits, get people treated, but she only has so many charity hours she can manage, and most of these people have insurance that doesn't cover psychiatric care."

Jun blinked as she looked around at all the families and *all* the kids, so many no doubt just like Po, having trouble adjusting to life after the tsunami. "Most of these people need help?"

Jesse nodded. "I knew there was a need, but I just didn't realize how much."

"Excuse me," a woman said. She had a toddler on her hip and was tugging along a preschooler by the hand. "Is this where we sign up for an appointment with the doctor? My daughter, Em, needs some help." The preschooler hid shyly behind her mother's brightly colored skirts.

"Dr. Jean is at that table, but if you can't wait to speak with her, then you can simply sign up to be contacted later." Jesse pointed the woman in the direction of a sign-up clipboard. Jun saw there were several tables under the tent, one labeled Volunteers Needed, one Services and another Donations. Crowds of people thronged around each one.

"What happens if Kai doesn't surf the competition and he doesn't raise money for the Big Island Kids?" Jun asked Jesse.

"We'll raise money another way," she said. "Were you able to convince him?"

"Not exactly," Jun said, glancing around. "But how much money would he really raise if he went down in the first round of competition?"

"Not enough," Jesse said.

"*This* is the reason Kai is surfing, though. I know if he knew that it wouldn't much matter, if we could do it another way, then maybe he wouldn't do it."

Pretty soon Jesse and Jun found themselves inundated with requests, and they both directed people to the appropriate places as Jun handed out flyers. The crowds kept coming, and more and more families arrived, either to support the cause or to ask for help. It seemed an even split to Jun, fifty-fifty.

Several hours later, however, the crowds finally subsided. Jun helped Jesse gather up the sign-in logs and that was when she felt a tap on her shoulder.

"Jun Lee? I'm Dr. Jean. Kai told me you'd be helping organize Big Island Kids?" Jun liked her almost immediately. She had a warmth about her that Jun found comforting. She could instantly see how the woman might put her juvenile clients and their parents at ease.

Jun nodded. "Uh, actually..." But she didn't get to finish.

"Listen, I hope you don't mind, but Kai told me...a little about your son."

Right away, Jun felt her defenses come up. What had Kai said? Why had he told her problems—or Po's—to a stranger? But then, she *knew* why.

"That wasn't his place," Jun said, feeling irritated.

"It was only because he wanted to help your son," Dr. Jean said. "Believe me, he came to me for advice on what to do not because he thought you were doing anything wrong. And not because he wanted to interfere."

Jun felt her feelings shift a little. Why did she always assume she was under attack? That was something she had to learn to manage.

"Okay."

"Children who suffer traumas like these can react to them in a number of different ways. I know it can be frightening as a parent. My own daughter had a trauma when she was little—and it took a long time for her to get over it. I felt powerless for a lot of years. I was supposed to be the one to help her through it, but I couldn't."

Jun's guard went down. This was another

mother, just like her, doing the best she could with the hand she was dealt. Jun recognized herself in Dr. Jean's story and felt glad to hear another mom admit to shortcomings. It felt like a rare treat.

"If you'd like to talk more about it, here's my card. It's completely up to you."

Jun liked Dr. Jean. She wasn't at all what she'd thought a child psychiatrist might be like. She wondered if she'd imagined a woman like her mother, someone ready and eager to point out all her faults. That wasn't Dr. Jean at all.

"Thank you," she told the woman and meant it. She tucked the card in her pocket, deciding right then she *would* call her.

A few weeks earlier, Jun would've ripped up that card or wouldn't have taken it at all. But the past few days had shown her that as much as she wanted to have all the answers, she didn't. And Kai had made an impact, she realized. He had been the one to help her open her horizons a little bit. Without him, she'd still be plowing away on her own, getting nowhere. She understood, in that split second, just how much she and Po needed Kai.

And in no time at all, Kai would be surfing Jaws in the competition that would probably kill him. She had to get back to Maui.

THE NEWS TRUCKS and the ambulances that waited on the overlook of Jaws on Maui made for quite a backdrop as the annual World Big Wave Surf Championship began. Kirk tried to settle Kai's nerves with small talk, but Kai didn't want to talk about the weather or what his competition looked like or the judges, legendary surfers whom he knew well. Instead he sat cross-legged on a towel on the ground and meditated, visualizing what he planned to do when he got out there. Even though in his bones, he knew it was a lost cause. He knew exactly what he'd do when he got out there: he'd fall on his ass. Just like last time. Bret and Jesse and Jun were right: he wasn't ready for this. But he had to do it anyway. For the charity and because he'd said he would. Besides, Jun had left him, and he was beginning to think that maybe trying to convince a woman as stubborn as she was that she needed his help was hopeless. It was like trying to persuade Jaws that it needed to settle down, be a tamer wave.

Jun had made it abundantly clear that she thought he was a lost cause. It was about time Kai accepted that. Without Jun and Po anchoring him to the earth, Kai felt as if risking his life at Jaws didn't much matter. After all, who would really miss him if he died out there? Jesse and Auntie Kaimana, sure, but it wasn't as if he had a family to take care of.

"You're up next, man," Kirk said, more excited than he should have been. Kai wondered if his manager would even care if he died, or if he'd just print up in-memoriam shirts and make a mint. Somehow Kirk would find a way to make more than a few dollars from his demise. Kai tried not to take it personally as he stood and went about collecting his things.

"I need a minute, okay?"

Kirk shrugged.

"Sure. Whatever you need. You take care of him, all right, Henley?" Kirk clapped the young surfer on the shoulder. Henley flinched a little and watched Kirk go. Kai got the impression Henley wasn't impressed with his manager.

"You don't have to do this, man," Henley said. "I mean, your eye is still swollen."

"I can see out of it fine," Kai said, dismissing the concern. The swelling had gone down, and now it was just an ugly shiner.

"Are you concerned about your rep? About the cameras? I mean, screw the cameras here, dude. Even if you walk away right now, you are still a legend. You made this sport, and no one will fault you for walking away."

"You think I should?" Kai asked the kid, who blinked rapidly.

"That's your call, bro. I'm…I'm just saying you have options."

Kai realized that his judgment was clouded by self-pity. Jun might have dumped him, but it didn't mean he ought to go drown his sorrows, literally, by drowning.

"If we're going to go, then the boat's here. Ready to take us out." Kai glanced at the schooner that would take Henley, Kai and the Jet Ski past the breaks.

"Kai!" He turned and saw Jun making her way over the rock-strewn beach. She held Po's hand and the boy carefully picked his way over the rocks. Behind her, his aunt and sister stood, waving. He was surprised to see them all. He felt his heart leap for a moment. He was so glad that tears almost sprang to his eyes. He wanted a last goodbye. It only seemed right, and yet he didn't want Po to see him drown. He didn't want any of them to see him die.

Jun ran up to him and threw her arms around him, taking him by surprise. "I caught you," she breathed. "I wasn't too late." Po wrapped his tiny arms around Kai's legs, silently hugging him, too.

Henley stood back a bit. Kirk, who had wandered down the beach, turned in time to see the embrace.

Jun pulled away from Kai. "I don't want you to do this."

"Jun, we talked about this. Big Island Kids—"

"Can survive *without* you. We found some big donors to help out. You don't have to do this. You don't have to kill yourself."

"Bad boo-boos out there!" Po added, his little face solemn as he looked up at Kai.

Kai felt as if he'd been blindsided. Was that true? Could the charity go on without his doing this competition? Could he really drop out? Then Kai thought about all that would mean. He'd told Bret he'd retire after the competition, and he'd meant it at the time, but was he truly ready to walk away from the love of his life?

"Jun, I appreciate that, but…" He trailed off, not sure what to say. Without her in his life, he didn't really care what happened to him.

Jun bit her lip, and tears filled her eyes. "But you're going to surf anyway, aren't you?"

"I…" Kai wavered. He shook his head.

Jun kissed him with everything she had. Then she pulled away. He felt a little breathless.

"You can't go out there today. Po needs you. *I need you*," Jun said, and the words stopped him in his tracks. "I love you, Kai."

Kai blinked fast. "You do?"

"I do, too!" Po chanted, excited as he bounced up and down.

Jun nodded. "We need you."

Po nodded seriously.

"Really?" If this was true, if Jun wanted him, if he was going to be a father for Po, could he really do something so risky? Suddenly, he understood why Bret had given it all up. Because he had *'ohana*, a family to care for.

Now Kai knew he wouldn't be able to go out there. He felt a sharp disappointment but also a sweet relief. Jaws wasn't going to kill him. Po tugged on Kai's board shorts. Kai knelt down so he was face-to-face with Po.

"Don't do it," Po said, his eyes wide. "That wave…it's like your house is on fire. Good fear says don't go in!"

Kai couldn't help but laugh a bit, as the boy had twisted the metaphor he'd told him on the beach about fear. Still, he wasn't wrong. Jaws was about as dangerous as a house fire. Maybe more so.

Kai's heart squeezed as if the boy had wrapped his tiny hands around it. How could he deny the boy something like this?

"Okay, little guy. I won't go." Jun hugged him and squeezed, squealing. He almost couldn't breathe, she held him so tightly. Once she let him go, he swooped Po up into his arms, much to the boy's delight.

"Good call, bro," Henley said, and clapped Kai on the shoulder. He gave him a nod of respect.

"What's a good call?" Kirk had stalked back over to the launch and glanced at Kai, Jun and the big schooner bobbing in the sea. "Why aren't you set? You're up next."

"I'm not surfing today, Kirk."

Clouds gathered around Kirk's face. "What do you mean, *you're not surfing*? You've got endorsement deals. You've got obligations!"

"Yes, I do. Important ones." Kai stared at Jun and she grinned back up at him.

"You can't just quit!" Kirk always valued money above everything else. Sacrificing that, to him, was worse than risking a life.

"I'll surf for him," Henley volunteered. "By proxy."

"You don't have to do that, man," Kai said.

"I know I don't, but I want to. If it's okay with you."

Kai saw that the kid wanted to do it. And he'd seen him surf the other day. He had talent and moxie. And, Kai realized, surfing for him now, on this kind of stage, could launch his career.

"Can he do it?" Kirk asked Kai.

"He can. He'll destroy those waves out there. He'll be the next big thing."

Kirk considered this. "If he's as talented as you say, I might be able to talk to some of the corporations. See if they will be okay. I might be able to finesse this."

"You have someone to tow you?" Kai asked, and Henley nodded, pointing to a group of his friends down the beach.

"Okay, man. You go for it." Kai offered up his

hand for a shake and Henley swiped it away, preferring instead to hug his idol.

"Thanks, man. Thanks a lot!" Henley trotted back down the beach, and as he stared after him, Kai felt as if he was officially passing the torch. It felt bittersweet but right.

"I'll be up there on the cliff, watching you," Kai called after him.

Kirk was on his phone, frantically making calls and talking about the "next big thing." Kai walked with Jun, Auntie K., Po and Jesse back up the beach. They drove up to the lookout, and when they got there, they had to fight through journalists peppering him with questions and flashbulbs lighting up in his face. But the media frenzy died down just before Henley went out on a perfect fifty-foot wave. The kid killed it out there, just as Kai had thought he would. Pretty soon the journalists clued in to what they were missing and trained their cameras on the ocean.

"Do you wish that was you out there?" Jun asked Kai as she snaked an arm around his waist. Po, who clutched Kai's neck, rested his head on his shoulder.

Part of him did, but he knew he had so much more to live for. His knee wasn't the same, probably would never be, but that didn't mean he had to give up everything else about life. In that moment, Kai grasped that he *did* have a life beyond surfing, one that he very much wanted to live. One with Jun and Po in it, a family and maybe a bigger foundation for all the kids on the island who needed his help.

"I've got everything I want right here," he said, and he meant it. He kissed the top of Jun's head and squeezed Po tighter. He realized that he had everything he needed and more as Jun leaned her head against his chest.

\* \* \* \* \*

# LARGER-PRINT BOOKS!
## GET 2 FREE LARGER-PRINT NOVELS PLUS
## 2 FREE GIFTS!

**HARLEQUIN®**

*Romance*

### From the Heart, For the Heart

**YES!** Please send me 2 FREE LARGER-PRINT Harlequin® Romance novels and my 2 FREE gifts (gifts are worth about $10). After receiving them, if I don't wish to receive any more books, I can return the shipping statement marked "cancel." If I don't cancel, I will receive 4 brand-new novels every month and be billed just $5.09 per book in the U.S. or $5.49 per book in Canada. That's a savings of at least 15% off the cover price! It's quite a bargain! Shipping and handling is just 50¢ per book in the U.S. and 75¢ per book in Canada.* I understand that accepting the 2 free books and gifts places me under no obligation to buy anything. I can always return a shipment and cancel at any time. Even if I never buy another book, the two free books and gifts are mine to keep forever.

119/319 HDN GHWC

| | | |
|---|---|---|
| Name | (PLEASE PRINT) | |
| Address | | Apt. # |
| City | State/Prov. | Zip/Postal Code |

Signature (if under 18, a parent or guardian must sign)

Mail to the **Reader Service:**
**IN U.S.A.:** P.O. Box 1867, Buffalo, NY 14240-1867
**IN CANADA:** P.O. Box 609, Fort Erie, Ontario L2A 5X3
**Want to try two free books from another line?**
**Call 1-800-873-8635 or visit www.ReaderService.com.**

* Terms and prices subject to change without notice. Prices do not include applicable taxes. Sales tax applicable in N.Y. Canadian residents will be charged applicable taxes. Offer not valid in Quebec. This offer is limited to one order per household. Not valid for current subscribers to Harlequin Romance Larger-Print books. All orders subject to credit approval. Credit or debit balances in a customer's account(s) may be offset by any other outstanding balance owed by or to the customer. Please allow 4 to 6 weeks for delivery. Offer available while quantities last.

**Your Privacy**—The Reader Service is committed to protecting your privacy. Our Privacy Policy is available online at www.ReaderService.com or upon request from the Reader Service.

We make a portion of our mailing list available to reputable third parties that offer products we believe may interest you. If you prefer that we not exchange your name with third parties, or if you wish to clarify or modify your communication preferences, please visit us at www.ReaderService.com/consumerschoice or write to us at Reader Service Preference Service, P.O. Box 9062, Buffalo, NY 14240-9062. Include your complete name and address.

HRLP15

# LARGER-PRINT
# BOOKS!

**HARLEQUIN**

*Presents*®

PASSION
GUARANTEED
SEDUCTION

## GET 2 FREE LARGER-PRINT
## NOVELS PLUS 2 FREE GIFTS!

HPLP15

# REQUEST YOUR FREE BOOKS!
## 2 FREE WHOLESOME ROMANCE NOVELS
## IN LARGER PRINT
## PLUS 2
# FREE
## MYSTERY GIFTS

✶✶✶✶✶✶✶✶✶✶✶✶✶✶✶✶✶✶✶✶✶✶✶✶✶✶✶✶

# HEARTWARMING™

✶✶✶✶✶✶✶✶✶✶✶✶✶✶✶✶✶✶✶✶✶✶✶✶✶✶✶✶

*Wholesome, tender romances*

---

**YES!** Please send me 2 FREE Harlequin® Heartwarming Larger-Print novels and my 2 FREE mystery gifts (gifts worth about $10). After receiving them, if I don't wish to receive any more books, I can return the shipping statement marked "cancel." If I don't cancel, I will receive 4 brand-new larger-print novels every month and be billed just $5.24 per book in the U.S. or $5.99 per book in Canada. That's a savings of at least 19% off the cover price. It's quite a bargain! Shipping and handling is just 50¢ per book in the U.S. and 75¢ per book in Canada.* I understand that accepting the 2 free books and gifts places me under no obligation to buy anything. I can always return a shipment and cancel at any time. Even if I never buy another book, the two free books and gifts are mine to keep forever.

161/361 IDN GHX2

| | | |
|---|---|---|
| Name | (PLEASE PRINT) | |
| Address | | Apt. # |
| City | State/Prov. | Zip/Postal Code |

Signature (if under 18, a parent or guardian must sign)

### Mail to the **Reader Service:**
**IN U.S.A.:** P.O. Box 1867, Buffalo, NY 14240-1867
**IN CANADA:** P.O. Box 609, Fort Erie, Ontario L2A 5X3

\* Terms and prices subject to change without notice. Prices do not include applicable taxes. Sales tax applicable in N.Y. Canadian residents will be charged applicable taxes. Offer not valid in Quebec. This offer is limited to one order per household. Not valid for current subscribers to Harlequin Heartwarming larger-print books. All orders subject to credit approval. Credit or debit balances in a customer's account(s) may be offset by any other outstanding balance owed by or to the customer. Please allow 4 to 6 weeks for delivery. Offer available while quantities last.

**Your Privacy**—The Reader Service is committed to protecting your privacy. Our Privacy Policy is available online at www.ReaderService.com or upon request from the Reader Service.

We make a portion of our mailing list available to reputable third parties that offer products we believe may interest you. If you prefer that we not exchange your name with third parties, or if you wish to clarify or modify your communication preferences, please visit us at www.ReaderService.com/consumerschoice or write to us at Reader Service Preference Service, P.O. Box 9062, Buffalo, NY 14240-9062. Include your complete name and address.

HWI5

# LARGER-PRINT BOOKS!
## GET 2 FREE LARGER-PRINT NOVELS PLUS
## 2 FREE GIFTS!

**(H) HARLEQUIN®**
™

# INTRIGUE
## BREATHTAKING ROMANTIC SUSPENSE

**YES!** Please send me 2 FREE LARGER-PRINT Harlequin® Intrigue novels and my 2 FREE gifts (gifts are worth about $10). After receiving them, if I don't wish to receive any more books, I can return the shipping statement marked "cancel." If I don't cancel, I will receive 6 brand-new novels every month and be billed just $5.49 per book in the U.S. or $6.24 per book in Canada. That's a saving of at least 11% off the cover price! It's quite a bargain! Shipping and handling is just 50¢ per book in the U.S. and 75¢ per book in Canada.* I understand that accepting the 2 free books and gifts places me under no obligation to buy anything. I can always return a shipment and cancel at any time. Even if I never buy another book, the two free books and gifts are mine to keep forever.

199/399 HDN GHWN

| | |
|---|---|
| Name | (PLEASE PRINT) |
| Address | Apt. # |
| City | State/Prov. | Zip/Postal Code |

Signature (if under 18, a parent or guardian must sign)

### Mail to the **Reader Service:**
**IN U.S.A.:** P.O. Box 1867, Buffalo, NY  14240-1867
**IN CANADA:** P.O. Box 609, Fort Erie, Ontario  L2A 5X3

**Are you a subscriber to Harlequin® Intrigue books
and want to receive the larger-print edition?
Call 1-800-873-8635 today or visit www.ReaderService.com.**

\* Terms and prices subject to change without notice. Prices do not include applicable taxes. Sales tax applicable in N.Y. Canadian residents will be charged applicable taxes. Offer not valid in Quebec. This offer is limited to one order per household. Not valid for current subscribers to Harlequin Intrigue Larger-Print books. All orders subject to credit approval. Credit or debit balances in a customer's account(s) may be offset by any other outstanding balance owed by or to the customer. Please allow 4 to 6 weeks for delivery. Offer available while quantities last.

**Your Privacy**—The Reader Service is committed to protecting your privacy. Our Privacy Policy is available online at www.ReaderService.com or upon request from the Reader Service.

We make a portion of our mailing list available to reputable third parties that offer products we believe may interest you. If you prefer that we not exchange your name with third parties, or if you wish to clarify or modify your communication preferences, please visit us at www.ReaderService.com/consumerchoice or write to us at Reader Service Preference Service, P.O. Box 9062, Buffalo, NY 14240-9062. Include your complete name and address.

HILP15